I LOVED THAT ABOUT HER

C.R. Everett

COPYRIGHT

First Paperback Edition: April 2014

ISBN: 978-0-9882641-3-7

Discover other titles by C.R. Everett at this website:
http://www.creverett.com

PRAISE FOR C.R. EVERETT'S *LOVE, CARRY MY BAGS*

"Okay C.R., you are truly horrible to make me cry and laugh in the same breath . . ."
  —Gigi Siguenza, eBook Lovers Co-Op Admin/Owner

"A real page turner that kept me involved and offered a riveting look at love and relationships."
  —C. Beard

". . . there were times in the book when I laughed out loud and also times where I had a lump the size of a tennis ball in my throat and had to re-read a page because I couldn't stop the tears from falling . . . in some parts, I felt like I was reading about myself."
  —N. Townson

"This is a well written story that can and will tug at your heartstrings. I fell in love with the characters and had a hard time putting the book down. Highly recommend this book!"
  —Pauline Hulstein

Please turn to the back of this book for a preview of C.R. Everett's novel *Love, Carry My Bags*, companion to *I Loved That About Her*.

To the misunderstood

ACKNOWLEDGMENTS

I would like to thank my family for allowing me many hours at my desk putting *I Loved That About Her* together. And thank you to my fans for requesting Glenn's side of the story. Extra special thanks goes to A.J. Lape for her extraordinary help in sharpening my words and softening Glenn. I know she's got a huge soft spot for Reese, but also, a soft spot for Glenn. Thank you to Lucy Wright and Natalie Townson for being guinea-pig readers. And wow, Natalie made a cameo appearance in the drama! I'd also like to thank some other special friends, always there to lend a hand or give advice, Kelley Grealis, JD Nelson, Aneesa Price, Julie Cassar, and Mary-Nancy Smith. Love you girls!

Thanks to my Street Team for cheering me on. And special thanks to those who inspire, encourage, and believe in me. I appreciate you more than you know.

PROLOGUE

Germination

Seeds need certain conditions for them to germinate, conditions of temperature, light, air, moisture, and nutrients. Without proper conditions, germination may be delayed or may never happen at all. Some seeds, particularly those untamed, need specific influences to spur germination. For example, some species need to be exposed to fire in order to germinate. Other seeds may need freezing temperatures or to lie dormant during winters before they will sprout. Even some rare varieties need to be infected by a particular fungus before they will grow, and other seeds need to pass through an animal's intestines, be eaten alive, in order to germinate.

People can learn a lot from seeds. Perhaps we are one.

CHAPTER 1 - GLENN

I failed the entrance exam twice, the second time in early 1988. Those stupid multiple choice tests with the fill-in bubbles (blue or black ink only) trip me up every time. Even the ones requiring a #2 pencil suck because I erase so much I end up tearing holes in the automatic scoring sheet. Machines don't read holes, the holes in my mind that work their way to the page. I read slow, so the test takes longer in the first place. Then I find the right answer, say, B. My hand goes to the score sheet and fills in the circle next to C, and I can't figure out why the hell this happens. I know the fucking answer, but my hand puts it in the wrong place, and I'm screwed. AGAIN.

Mrs. Muller taught my English class sophomore year in high school. "Glenn," she said. "I know you know the material. You just aren't paying attention. You're being lazy, careless." Blah, blah, blah. I tuned out the rest. She could go fuck herself, just like all the rest of them. It's like listening to a broken record for my entire life. Don't even get me started on my parents. After my dad gave up on *beating* some sense into me, he chalked me right up there with the Prodigal Son, only never hoping I'd return, period. My mom went along with what my dad said. It was easier for her that way.

Most pass college entrance exams the first time, even if by a thread, but I manage to fail. Fail. Failure. That's what I am, a failure with a capital F. Why it's so easy for everyone else and so hard for me is the million dollar question. Wait, I just answered it. Because. I'm. A. Failure. I'm pretty sure that's what my parents had in mind when they named me Glenn F. Conroy. Yes, that's right. I only have a letter for my middle name. I get to fill in the blankety-blank, blank.

Glenn Failure Conroy.

I did manage to graduate high school by the skin of my teeth back in 1976. Oh, and by a few winks and charms for the teachers. Who could resist holding charisma like that back a grade? They passed me. Worked every time. Maybe *they* were the stupid ones and not me.

I punched the wall with my fist, venting my frustration about the failed exam, leaving a dent in the drywall. I felt better. It gave me a rush. Apparently it gave Mom a rush too because she came rushing into my room. "What the hell is going on in here?" she asked, like there's a problem. She stared at the fucked-up drywall and started to cry. Moms can get so emotional, and I had no idea why. She probably wished I'd never moved back in. You know, after my failed marriage and a failed stint in the Navy, she probably didn't want to deal with Glenn Failure Conroy back in the house. Mom put her hands on her hips in that pissed-off-mom pose. "I will not tolerate that behavior in my house. Do you understand?" She looked like she was going to blow a gasket.

"I didn't mean to," I said, which pissed her off even more.

"How old are you?" she said, which was really stupid because we both knew I was thirty. We were both there when I was born. I couldn't figure out why she changed the subject, and that pissed *me* off because she can never stay on topic, always throwing in bullshit that has nothing to do with anything, and then she gets mad at me for not following her train of thought. "*You* should know by now, throwing your fist at the wall never solves anything," she said, drilling her gaze into my head. She pointed to the drywall. "You're fixing that. With your money."

There she went with the consequences again, erroneously thinking I'd eventually learn my lesson. With me, life lessons didn't stick. "You know I don't have any money," I said. I started to panic and was hurt because she was being unfair.

"You should have thought of that before you hit the wall," she said then walked out the door.

"I didn't think. I just did it," I called after her. She stopped, spun around on her heel.

"That's your problem Glenn. You. Don't. Think," she explained like she was exasperated, but I thought she was overreacting.

Actually, I had thought this over way too much. I typically didn't sit around thinking things through or mulling them over. What a boring waste of time. My time was better spent going out, so I hopped in the new sports car I emptied my bank account for last week and left. Thinking Mitch or Ron might wanna join me for a beer, I drove twenty miles into town to find out because it was easier than looking up their numbers in the phone book.

* * *

The guys weren't home, so I drove back to the house, popped open a beer. "You want one?" I asked my dad who had just come home from work. He scowled at me. I was just being nice, offering a beer, and he freaking scowls at me. What an asshole.

"Your mother tells me you punched a hole in the wall."

Oh, that. He brings *that* up. They really ought to relax. I stared at him, waiting for the rest of his blah, blah, blah. I took a swig of beer, making his lame drivel go down better, and then my ears perked up when he said something about me getting a job at the St. Louis Arena. Gotta love hockey.

"So I'll call Blakely and set you up. You can start Monday."

I think dad said something else about buying time until I could take the college entrance exam again, and me fixing the hole in the wall, but my mind honed in on *Blakely*. He was *the* "it" man for St. Louis Blues hockey and I was already planning how to get all the players' autographs. They'd probably give me a real Brett Hull jersey on my first day, I thought, that I could have them sign. And if they didn't offer, I'd ask for one. Dad still blathered, ". . . fixed before Monday."

"Yeah, Dad," I said, looking him straight in the eye. That's how I always answered my dad because if I didn't look him straight in the eye, he'd think I wasn't listening. Most of the time I wasn't listening anyway. He didn't know that, although I'm sure he suspected as much. The direct-eye approach was my best bet, otherwise the continuing lecture was, to me, like nails on a chalkboard.

*   *   *

"If you've got any extra jerseys laying around, I'd take one off your hands," I said after Blakely's people showed me the mixing board and sound equipment I'd be working on. They kind of laughed at me for some reason, yet by the end of my shift I sported one and had gotten two players to sign. Score! I'm not as useless as everyone thought, and I had to keep giving myself that pep talk because no one else that mattered did. After work, Mitch and Ron met me at the bar where I showed off the goods.

"Awesome!" Mitch said, his eyes bugging out. He reached out his hand for a high-five. "Dude, you rule."

"Yes, I do." I took another swig. "Margaritas all around," I said, in the mood to celebrate my new job. We clinked our glasses.

"To hockey," Ron said, still admiring my jersey.

We BS'd about the season's stats, talking smack about nothing, but it was fun.

"To Brett Hull," I offered after our third round.

"Screw Brett Hull," Mitch said. "Those Blackhawks have a chance this year."

"Bullshit." That's when it got exciting, me defending the Blues like I owned the team, but Mitch and Ron got torqued, leaving me with the bill.

"Dude, you need your head examined," Mitch said as he left. Motherfuckers. Some friends.

"One more," I said, raising my glass toward the bartender. He eyed me like he had a problem with that, but I touched my index finger to my nose and bugged my eyes out at him. He sighed, pouring me a drink. "Got a light?" I asked, suddenly feeling the urge for a smoke. He produced a lighter from under the counter, flicked it on for me to light up. I took a long drag, making sure my cigarette was good and lit and then blew smoke everywhere. "You ever feel like no one understands you?" I asked him.

"All the time," he said. Bartenders are the closest I'd ever get to a shrink. Sometimes I thought I wasn't normal, but mostly I thought other people wasn't normal. That bartender eased my mind. And I knew the phrasing, "other people *wasn't* normal" wasn't normal, but it's a habit I never worried about breaking.

"One more for the road." I drained the last of my margarita, sticking my tongue way out to catch the last drop and then pushed my empty across the bar. "On the rocks this time. Extra salt."

"No can do," he said, removing my empty glass from in front of me. I gave him a look, wondering what his problem was. Then he freaked out. He raised his hand in some sort of signal; then a bouncer came after me. The bartender said something about if looks could kill. Hell, I didn't give him a murderous look; I just wondered what was up his ass.

The bouncer threw me out the door, roughing up my hockey jersey a bit too much. I smoothed it out just as a minor earthquake hit, causing me to walk unsteady. A few girls walking by didn't seem to notice what I swore was the ground shaking. Weird. I got into my car, cranked "Come Sail Away," and then sailed down the highway, using the dashboard as a drum, keeping rhythm. Blue and red flashing lights in the rear-view mirror fucked up the whole evening, which I had thought went pretty well.

"Damn," I said, pulling over. The cop appeared at my window in two seconds flat. "What can I do you for, ocifer?" I said, trying to be polite and jovial. He didn't smile.

"Did you know you were doing eighty in a forty-five?"

"I was not." Who the hell did he think he was? Probably out to get me because he had a beef with my dad. His radio made one of those white-noise farts as he called for backup.

"Ten-four." It farted back.

"License," he said, ignoring my protest. I produced my driver's license. He then scrutinized it until a second cop arrived. "Out of the car with your hands up."

What the hell? They really knew how to take the joy out of a joy ride. I got out of the car, very nonchalant, like this was all a big misunderstanding. Truth be told, I was scared as shit.

Cop two said a bunch of legalese crap, but I heard in my mind, *breathalyzer or you'll go straight to jail.*

"I'm not drunk."

After some more legalese he said, "Prove it. Deep breath," and then jammed the thing into my mouth. At least that's how I remember it. *Mommy*, a little voice piped up in my head, which was really stupid, because I was a grown man.

When they got what they needed, they put their little pea brains together and decided to take me down to the station. Where's the joy now? I didn't know, but it sure was exciting. I'd add "booked into jail" to my list of exciting life experiences. Can't get enough of those. That's what's livin's about.

Eventually they called my dad, who was less than thrilled, arriving at 2 a.m. with a look on his face that

8

said he thought these days were long over for us. Normally I didn't know what the hell type of look was on someone's face, but when the excitement revved up, I could read faces pretty well. And that's when I was really living. What a rush.

"Russell," cop one said to my dad, shaking his hand. My dad nodded, a serious look in his eye, like he had some business to take care of. They stepped out of sight. When they came back, my dad stood there with both hands in his coat pockets, expressionless.

"Come on, son," he said to me. That's all he said. Silence the whole ride home, and it wasn't until morning I learned a good chunk of my first paycheck would be going to pay my speeding ticket. Whatever magic my dad worked, I was grateful for. No charges pressed. Apparently, I wasn't driving drunk after all.

Then my mom started in. "Haven't you patched that hole you punched in the wall yet?"

"I plan on doing it when I get home from work," I said. She rolled her eyes like she didn't believe me, but it was true. I planned to do it right after work.

"I packed you a lunch." She crinkled down the edge of a brown paper bag.

"Thanks." I headed back to my room to fetch the hockey jersey for more autographs. Then I headed out the door, leaving the lunch mom packed behind. And she sure let me know it.

The second I got home, "You forgot your lunch," she said, miffed.

"I plan on taking it tomorrow," I said, figuring I couldn't undo what was done. I grabbed a bag of chips, plopped down on the couch, and turned on the TV. I glanced over at mom who was drilling her eyes into the back of my head. "Wha —?" I said, mouth half full, me confused. What did I do now?

"I thought you were going to fix the hole in the wall."

Christ, can't a man have a few minutes break? "I'll do it," I said. My head started to hurt.

"You said you'd do it right after work."

Jesus, a literalist. "It was a figure of speech."

Mom shook her head then left the room. I called after her, "I plan on it!"

*　*　*

On payday I took my jersey in, hoping to get the only signature I was missing. I made sure I had brought the jersey every day and hung around after practice, getting the players' attention. My boss handed me my check. "Man, did I get ripped off," I said well within earshot. "I was expecting a whole lot more than this." My boss looked at me like I had "crazy" written all over my face. He looked over my shoulder, pointed to the hours and wage, confirming that's what I'd been hired in at. Then I noticed the "deductions" section, which I'd forgotten all about. That stupid speeding ticket took my entire check. I had nothing in my pocket, and my gas tank was empty.

"Can I borrow some money for gas?" I asked my mom. She glared at me.

"Where's all your money?" she asked, like I was still a kid, which annoyed the hell out of me.

I went over the tax problem, reminded her about the ticket then said, "And I had to buy my lunch, so I don't have any cash."

Mom grabbed her forehead between her fingers and thumb, looking down like she was in pain and then opened the fridge and pulled out a brown lunch sack. "You HAD to buy your lunch," she said, rubbing in the fact that I'd forgotten to bring my lunch every day except the day she physically put it in my hand as I headed out the door. I thought moms were supposed to be nice, but she was a downright bitch about it.

"Since when is forgetting something a sin?" I asked her. What'd she expect me to be, god dammed perfect? Then she ripped me a new one about how I remembered my jersey every day and filled it with autographs, yet I was totally irresponsible about basic money management. She mercilessly pointed out that if I had remembered my lunch each day I'd have money for gas. And wouldn't have to borrow from her.

Easy for her to say.

More than likely, if I had money, I'd have spent it on a more immediate need anyway, like a night out on the town. She acted like borrowing from her was a huge deal and even made me sign a promissory note. "Way to show confidence in your son," I said to that. By then, all I wanted to do was go out for a beer, but with the cash problem and all, I just threw myself on my bed, staring at some hole in the wall, wondering why life was so fucking hard and why someone was always on my case. ALWAYS on my case, like I did these things on purpose.

* * *

Six months later, I was able to take the Parks College entrance exam again, and by the grace of God, I actually passed. Hoorah! I knew I knew the stuff. I'm

11

just a terrible test taker and that day was my lucky day. I think my parents broke out the champagne, celebrating the fact that I'd finally move out. Again. But I resolved I'd make it up to them. In my heart, I wanted to make them proud.

CHAPTER 2 - GLENN

My assigned dorm room at Parks College of St. Louis University had blue, concrete block walls and was the size of a walk-in closet with two dinky excuses for beds and a couple of desks. Reminded me of my compartment when I was on the ship, and I'd had enough of that. And I'd had enough of roommates. Something got hosed up in the room assignments because I'd arranged for a single, but only doubles were available. Not. Happening. I went to the Student Housing Office and demanded a refund then walked across the street to the only apartment complex nearby.

"I need an apartment," I said to the landlady while kicking the snow off my boots.

The gray-haired lady wheeled her scooter around behind her desk, checking her books. I stared at the calendar on the wall. January 1989. Hard to believe I was finally here. The lady spoke, shaking me from my thoughts, "I've got one left — a two-bedroom."

"I'll take it." I felt so lucky; I didn't even ask the price. "Where do I sign?"

I dropped off my stuff then headed back to my parents' to bring back furniture with my dad's truck. As I carried up the last overstuffed box, a lamp hanging precariously out the top, I noticed a girl and two guys moving stuff in two doors down. I wondered how this girl managed to get two boyfriends to help her move in, and since she looked pretty fine, I figured I could join them, if not oust them. After all, if she was running around with two boyfriends, she couldn't be all that serious and may just be a lot of fun. While we passed each other on the stairs, I noticed her eyes matched her hair. "Hi," we said. She was into me or else she wouldn't have said "hi." Even though she wore loose red sweatpants and an oversized shirt, I saw enough of her curves to warrant further exploration. I imagined her in tight jeans then managed to look at the rest of her. She had voluminous dark blonde curls, pulled up into a mess on the top of her head, and she wore hardly any makeup. That was fine by me because I called it fakeup, and even though it made models in magazines look stunning, the true test was how a girl looked without it. Stunning in a magazine and stunning in real life were two different things.

I went back home for another load, clearing out my old bedroom, and saw dad working on a drywall repair in my room. "I was planning on doing that," I said. "You didn't need to do that." I figured dad worked hard enough, he didn't need to spend his time fixing it.

"Your mom was tired of waiting."

* * *

So I found out this girl's name was Camryn. I helped her carry a stack of boxes up to her apartment and stood there looking around until she told me where to stick it. Well, she didn't exactly tell me where to "stick it." That would be rude, and she seemed like a nice girl. She kindly told me where to put them. Sometimes I know what I want to say in my head, but the words come out wrong. It's not until I hear what comes out of my mouth that I realize my eloquence has *failed* me, and sometimes that eloquence-detection system fails too, leaving me and everyone else frustrated five ways from Thursday. Goes along with the territory.

Camryn had nothing, not even a bed, only a mattress to sleep on. Funny thing was, she didn't even seem upset about it. She actually seemed happy. I invited her to an icebreaker event at the school, told her I'd pick her up after I did a few things, but I got there late and when I knocked on her door no one answered. I decided to go without her; after all, no sense sitting around the apartment alone. Then when I walked into Kitty Hawk I saw her talking to some guy, Raine, I think his name was. I immediately didn't like him just because he was talking to Camryn, so I walked right up to them and put my arm around her shoulder, "Sorry, I got hung up in traffic," I said even though it was a lie. I'd simply lost track of time. The sun shines on some people and everything goes their way, but I'm not one of them. Me and the "time?" We weren't friends. I fully intend to show up on schedule, but the rain cloud of lateness pours down on me for inexplicable reasons, and I'm running behind. We have a long, sordid history, and I've come up with ways to hog tie that time-bitch. Still, those ways aren't foolproof. I'm cursed. It's embarrassing. And I'd never admit it in a million years because it's truly not my fault, and the best way to deal with my curse is to fib. Lie is such a strong word. I explain the unexplainable with reasons people will buy without the blame being on me. I've had enough blame too. It sucks.

We played several games at the icebreaker, including lacing arms together while back to back. We then had to sit down on the floor and get back up, each of us standing on our own two feet again, arms intertwined the whole time. Falling down was the easy part. We pressed against each other, trying to be careful at first, but three-quarters of the way down, Camryn's legs gave out and my weight landed us on our asses in an unceremonious plop.

"That kinda hurt," she said, but she was laughing, so it was fine. Getting back up was more of a challenge. She leaned her back into mine, trying to get up, but not getting anywhere, obviously, without my help. I leaned into her but ended up pushing her back down with my weight. She pushed harder, and I backed off until we found some sort of balance and stood back up, leaning on each other the whole time. It felt like a huge accomplishment.

"That was hard," she said. She looked worn out from all the pushing and pulling between us. I felt exhilarated, having reached our goal together. I got the feeling I'd like to reach goal after goal with Camryn if it meant I'd get to touch her more often.

Our last icebreaker was a staring contest. Raine stood right next to Camryn, and Camryn stood across from me as my partner. Some homely chick stood next to me, giving me the heebie jeebies. Thankfully, she was the one staring into Raine's eyes and not mine.

"Ready, set, go," the event coordinator instructed. I was hell-bent on bringing Camryn down, having her blinking in no time, outlasting her. But when her gaze fell into mine, it felt as if she peered into my soul, which caught me off guard because I'd never had that feeling with anyone. I was shaken and taken at the same time. I had to look away.

"You're determined," I said to Camryn, making it seem like just a game, covering up my unexpected feelings. "Congratulations." She smiled back at me, seeming satisfied with her victory. Raine had taken his partner down, but in his case, his gaze seemed cold, at least to me, but when we left for the evening, he turned on the charm for Camryn and asked for her number.

"Maybe later," she told him. Was she playing hard to get? My job was to make sure later never came. I made sure I got to her first.

* * *

Our first date went great. Well, it really wasn't a date because I had no intention of getting serious with anyone. After what my ex-wife did to me, I couldn't risk becoming close to anyone again. I'd already built my walls of straw and sticks, but the vibe I'd gotten from Camryn was she might be the Big Bad Wolf I'd need extra protection from.

I took Camryn to Stooges. Everyone at school was talking about it, like that was the place to go, and my philosophy is "When in Rome . . . ." So what if the place stunk to high heaven. I had a good time, and Camryn was a good listener, like a sponge soaking in every word I had to say. A nice change from the treatment I get from most people I hang out with . . . and from my family, barely listening with one ear. She was interesting too, seemed like an adventurer who wanted to try new things.

Another night I invited her over for Chinese food, no sense eating alone. She'd already started cooking her own dinner, but I convinced her it'd keep for another day. I had made sure my bed was made and living room spotless, wanting to make a good impression. She walked in, looked around, and said, "Nice poster." At the same time, she seemed to have gotten something in her eye, rolling it up into its socket, but quickly recovered. My ex-wife hated that poster and made sure I knew it. I don't know if it was the fact that she wasn't as well-endowed as Ms. Belle and was jealous or what. I enjoyed looking at both of them and had told her as much, but she just couldn't get over it and a few other things. So hard to please. Camryn not having an issue with it, even complimenting my décor, made her even more enticing.

"Who were those guys who helped you move in," I asked, "your boyfriends?"

"Huh?" Camryn looked at me like she had no idea what I was talking about and then said, "No," while shaking her head. "They were my brothers. Boyfriends? Really?"

"Well, I didn't know," I half apologized.

"You seriously think I'd have two boyfriends help me move my stuff in together, at the same time?" she asked, like I'd missed something. Then she wasn't so enticing, but instead she was starting to make me feel like an idiot, a familiar feeling people stirred up in me.

We ate dinner and watched hockey, chitchatting all the while. At one point she attempted to get away, go home and do homework of all things, but I simply asked her to stay, and she did. Homework was for the birds.

I caught Camryn on her way to the gym the next day then spontaneously decided to join her. Always up for something new. She kept looking around the equipment, at the walls and stuff while she worked out

18

on the treadmill. It was funky, mirrors everywhere where no one could hide, but no one looked normal through those indirect images. People appear slightly twisted when looking at them through something else and not *really* seeing them. A girl looking kinda like Ms. Belle—only with more clothes on—was on the treadmill next to Camryn. I couldn't help but smile at her. The inside of my pants smiled at her too, and that smile lasted a while longer, coming back home with Camryn and me.

"Bring the taco stuff over to my place. You can cook it here," I said, unlocking my apartment door.

"You were supposed to eat at my place," Camryn said, smiling on the way to her front door.

"We'll be more comfortable at *my* place."

She couldn't dispute it, given that the only place she had for us to sit was the floor or a metal folding chair. "Fine, I'll be right over."

Camryn walked in with a sack of the taco fixin's, setting things out and getting started. I asked her about her family, and that's when I found out her dad was a minister. My happy pants deflated a bit, that lower head thinking a minister's daughter would be tough to bag. The head attached near my shoulders sped into high gear, taking it as a personal challenge and new goal.

"Oh, that explains why you don't drink," I said, switching my focus from getting in her pants to getting her drunk. That'd be fun too.

"I don't like the taste," she said.

She seemed a bit cool after I made the drink comment, but I was sure she'd warm back up with a little alcohol in her. I excused myself to make us a couple of Amaretto Collinses, sure she'd like it.

I was right. She liked it. Downed the whole thing. While we were sipping our drinks we both loosened up, talking, and for some reason I told her I was dyslexic.

I was diagnosed during an unsuccessful stint in community college when I'd written an entire paper backwards, like you could read it in a mirror. My professor asked me if it was some kind of joke. I looked at the paper; it did look a little weird. I knew there was something wrong with it, but I couldn't see what. Then when he asked me to read the paper to him and I did, just like normal, he sent me to the Learning Disabilities Center. The psychiatric quack broke the news to me privately in his office, "Son, you have dyslexia, and you may have ADHD." I knew they were all quacks because when I was a young kid, they put me on some kind of drug to calm me down, Ritalin, I think it was. It didn't fix a damn thing, only made matters worse, so after a week of hell squared, my mom took me off of it and I was written off as "that boy who has ants in his pants." So anyway, after the dyslexia diagnosis, they put me on some kind of learning plan to work around my dyslexic tendencies, and I promptly forgot about that other thing they mentioned and so did they. It never came up again.

I told Camryn about my troubles with school and this sort of personal crap. She warmed up to that more than she loosened up with the alcohol and we talked about our families and shared stuff I normally didn't talk about. I started feeling these warm feelings toward her I didn't want to feel, feelings of attraction that wasn't just lust, so I pushed her away in my mind.

*   *   *

A few days later Camryn walked by, arms loaded with groceries. I had my apartment door open while I partied with some new friends, "Come on over," I yelled over the music. She showed up a few minutes later. "Where were you?" I asked.

"I went to the store."

"You walked? It's not safe," I said, worried for her. And in that moment, I knew I couldn't push her as far away as I'd like. I had to take care of her because she was alone and had no one else helping her out. I always wanted to help, be involved, fix things. Sometimes, I guess, maybe too much.

I introduced Camryn to the others, Zac, Morgan and the look-a-like Ms. Belle. It was funny, her real name was Tiffany Bell. No kidding. Camryn seemed to give her the cold shoulder. At first Camryn seemed to take a liking to Morgan, but after Morgan asked her if she wanted a drink and asked if she went to church every week, Camryn gave her the cold shoulder too. I had no idea why. After I made Camryn a virgin Rum & Coke, and I thought everything was going well, Camryn suddenly said, "I'm expecting a call," and then left. Just like that.

The party wasn't as interesting after she left, and I kept wondering why she made such a hasty retreat. Still, no sense wasting the afternoon. I cranked the music to which Tiffany and Morgan squealed with delight to one particular song. They jumped up, raised their hands above their heads, and shook everything they had. I watched Zac pick his chin up off the floor and wipe the drool from his mouth. Being a good host, I did some moves in between them and then hip-bumped each of them at just the right time to the music's beat, moving my drink to the side when it just about spilled down Tiffany's front. Then I imagined licking it off of her. Then I wondered if Camryn ever let loose. When I got bored, I sent them all on their way.

"Time to shut it down, guys," I said to everyone as I shut the music off mid-song.

"We were just getting started," Tiffany said with her pouty lips.

"I'm sure you and Zac can find something to do," I said, watching Zac massage her shoulders, slinking his hands below her armpits and just to the sides. I could imagine him wanting to reach all the way around, wanting to "massage" the front too. Tiffany giggled, turned around and leaned way into him, running her fingers up the back of his head through his hair.

"I'm sure we could too." Her voice had a seductive growl, which I was thankful for because Zac didn't waste time taking her hand and leading her out my door. Morgan hesitated in my doorway, but not for long when she registered I was already closing the door behind her. She followed the other two downstairs, dragging her feet. Eh, they'd figure something out. Maybe a threesome . . . give them all something to do.

"Hey, we should do this again," I called after them.

Morgan's eyes brightened up as she looked back at me. "Yes, we should." She gave me the thumbs-up.

I cleaned up the mess, hoping I could get Camryn to come back over and then went knocking on her door. "Want to go out? We can't stay home," I said when she let me in. I made the mistake of letting her decide where we should go; she suggested a movie.

Boring sang in my head. I'd have rather gone to a club or back to Stooges. So I compromised in my own mind. "Okay," I agreed, "then we can meet up with everyone at Stooges."

I treated her to the movie, which I thought was mighty nice of me. She sat through the whole thing, stiff as a board, giving off this vibe that I shouldn't even put my arm around her. Somehow, I managed to keep my hands to myself. After the movie, she suggested bowling, which I thought was a great idea before we hit Stooges. I used to play on a team so I knew I could beat the pants off her; the thought made me chuckle and made my own pants smile again.

"What's so funny?" she asked.

"Nothing," I said. "You any good at bowling?"

"Not really." She shrugged her shoulders.

"Good." This time I touched her shoulder as I ushered her through the door and it felt like she instantly heated up.

I beat her at bowling even though I tried to help her out, giving her helpful tips. She didn't much seem to care whether she won or not, which I thought was weird.

Finally we went to Stooges. I had a blast. We ran into Tiffany, Morgan and Zac who were talking with a bunch of people. Camryn was sort of quiet, but I was sure she was having a good time too. How could anyone not have a good time? It was like the party at my house only bigger. And we all know bigger is better.

"What'cha doin' after this?" Morgan asked me, her voice sultry . . . and drunken.

"I'm taking Camryn home," I told her, trying to dissuade any drunken designs she had on me. Morgan reached up to the top of my shirt, slightly fingering the first button until it fell undone, and then she moved down to the next. "With me," I added.

Camryn gave Morgan an ice-cold stare. The whole room felt hell freezing over. My energy level revved with the prospect of being the cause of a cat fight. And I'd have a front row seat. The whole thing was hot. Smokin'. With those thoughts in mind, I said to Camryn, "Let's blow this popsicle stand." I marched her out the door, this time with two hands on her shoulders. She gave me the sensation of dry ice—cold, yet undeniably smokin' hot.

"Didn't that bother you, what Morgan did to your shirt?" Camryn asked while I made us a couple frozen strawberry margaritas back at my place. She hadn't had so much as a beer all night. I knew she'd like this too.

"Oh no," I said. "She was just drunk, having a good time."

"So you have to get drunk to have a good time?" Camryn said. I think she was testing me. Something seemed up. And God knew, tests and I didn't always get along.

I dropped into the chair next to her and set down our drinks. "No, but it helps." I raised my glass in her direction, indicating that she should pick hers up too. We clinked them together. "To good times." She took a sip, smiled and then admitted the margaritas were divine. Well, that wasn't exactly her word for it, but that's what she meant. We talked for a good while, even covering the mysteries of the universe. I didn't want it to be so, but it seemed like some sort of bonding was going on, like we had a connection. She threw her head back and laughed, leaned in, and listened. I wanted to reach out to her, touch my fingers to her face . . . kiss her. But while my mind seemed alert with excitement and the prospect of getting it on, I had had a few drinks too many and my body might not, ahem, perform. I might have been too drunk to get it up, and I didn't want the embarrassment of finding out in front of her. Plus, the sober part of my self (it was in there somewhere) didn't want our first time to be a drunken fuck fest. She was better than that. *I* was better than that.

*   *   *

Thankfully, Camryn had left her shoes at my place when she'd gone home the night, well, early morning, before. I was just about to return them and invite her over for breakfast when there was a knock on my door, Camryn behind it.

"Bagel?" I said, lifting my already cream-cheesed half, mouth half-full. I motioned for her to have a seat and then set a cup of coffee and bagel in front of her too. I had been up half the night thinking, a question nagging at my mind, so I just blurted it out. "Do you have a boyfriend?"

Camryn didn't answer right away, causing panic to stir inside of me, yet relief at the same time since I didn't want a serious relationship. "No," she said, looking down into her coffee cup, swirling it around as if reading tea leaves. Right then she looked beautiful to me; I felt lucky to have her in the room. And what I wanted long-term drifted quickly from my mind. Now was what mattered.

"Come here." I patted my lap for her to come sit, and when she did, I said something I don't quite remember and the next thing I knew, my lips were pressed into hers and they didn't stop. Now, I knew about juicy kisses. And this wasn't one of them, but my lips had an extra wetness . . . tears from her eyes. "You okay?" I asked.

Camryn didn't answer exactly, she nodded slightly with a little, "Mmm hmm," but I could tell she wasn't fessing up her feelings. I wiped the tears from her cheeks with my thumbs, looking her straight in the eyes. She looked so pretty in spite of the tears, maybe even because of them.

*   *   *

A couple of Saturday nights later I went to The Oz with Zac, Tiffany, and some other guys. It didn't take long for the other guys to pick up girls who were gyrating on the dance floor. I felt alone even though I got out there and gyrated too, the disco ball enhancing the booze and making everyone dizzy. I should have invited Camryn, but didn't think about it until I had already paid the cover charge and downed a couple of beers.

"Fancy seeing you here," a voice behind me said. I turned around. Morgan stood there half drunk, her shirt unbuttoned one button lower than what's normally socially acceptable. I felt a lurch in my pants and sort of wished it wasn't so because I wasn't interested in doing anything with *her* and here she was, practically throwing herself at me. "Cigarette?" she offered.

"Sure." I patted my jeans for a light, coming up empty.

"Here," she said, flicking her Bic. I took a long drag, making sure it was lit and then exhaled. Cigs weren't my thing necessarily, but when everyone else was smoking, it only made sense to join in. Didn't want to stand out from the crowd unnecessarily, I did that enough without even trying.

"Mind if I cut in?" Another voice came from behind me. Raine. Trying to steal my girl again. Wait a minute. She wasn't my girl and I didn't even want her, but something inside of me wanted to punch him out. He gave me that icy stare again, like he had issues.

"Whatever," I said, turning to catch the waitress for a refill. I downed it in three swigs then decided to head home, leaving Raine with the spoils, if you could call it that. Halfway to the apartment, I jerked the wheel back from the center line. I probably shouldn't have been driving, but too late, I was already behind the wheel. I pulled into the complex, driving extra slow, careful not to hit any parked cars. Camryn's light shone through her blinds and I wanted to run up and knock on her door, but an unusual sensibility kicked in. I liked her too much to show up on her doorstep drunk. I didn't want to scare her off.

The next morning I cooked bacon and eggs in a frying pan. Bacon first and then the eggs in the grease. They tasted better that way. Camryn came to mind, so I left breakfast on two plates and jogged over, knocking on her door.

"You have to have breakfast with me. It's getting cold," I said as she opened up. She looked like she'd brushed through her hair, no bedhead strays floating around, but she was still in her nightgown, some cute little plaid baby-doll number.

She hesitated, looked down at herself blushing. "Give me a minute. I have to change."

"You don't have to change. You can come over in that."

"No, I have to change," she said.

I found myself wishing she'd be more spontaneous and then had visions of her coming over in a French maid outfit with nothing underneath, which would be hot and exciting. "It's getting cold," I half sang and half taunted.

Camryn was over a minute later, having thrown on a sweatshirt and jeans. I was disappointed, but her jeans were tight and that almost made up for it. I gave Camryn her plate. She looked at it, not diving right in.

"Do you have a napkin?" she asked.

I handed her a paper towel from the roll on top of the microwave. She pressed it to the top of her eggs, mopping up the bacon grease.

"You're taking away the flavor," I objected.

"Grease is bad for you."

"My grandma cooked everything floating in grease, and she's still going strong at ninety." I grinned at her. Grandma knew best.

"Well, good for her," Camryn said. "Grease is still bad for you. You know, heart disease."

"Old wives' tale," I pointed out. Camryn looked at me with crossed eyes, like she was trying to figure me out and I wondered what made her question me. She shook her head then mumbled something about getting to know new people, wondering about different cultures.

"Don't look at me like that. I'm not from Mars you know," I told her. Changing the subject, I asked her what she did last night.

"Studied. Watched TV," she said. Oh my god. How boring an evening could she possibly have spent?! Poor thing. I told her I wished she had been with me at the club because other guys had their girlfriends with them and I was kind of alone. *Lonely.*

I took her breakfast dishes to the kitchen then returned, kneeling between her legs as she sat in the living room chair. "You're pretty," I said, brushing a stray strand of hair from her face. I looked into her eyes and saw the same depth as on icebreaker night. My heart did some heavy calisthenics in my chest, and the room was suddenly hot. She looked at me as if no one had ever told her how pretty she was, which I found hard to believe. Even so, I felt moved to show her just how beautiful she was. The tightening of my jeans made me want to unbutton the fly and get right down to business, but for some reason, girls like the foreplay stuff and I wanted to make a good first impression. She deserved that. I kissed her lips, which were also hot and open for more. We were in a slow-motion clip for a moment, she pulling back, looking down at my lips then up to my eyes. I dove in and tasted her tonsils. At that point, I knew I had her, her response not letting up. I reached up the back of her shirt, merely touching her skin, and then I peeled it off up over her head. I pushed her bra aside, caressing what I'd exposed with my thumb. She kept staring at me, speaking to me with those eyes, not saying a thing with her voice. My pants nearly bust open and I wished she'd reach down and at least undo my fly. I moved my mouth to her nipple, and then her legs wrapped around my ass, pulling me in close. Score. Score. Score! I had hoped she'd let me have my way with her. Dreams do come true. And she was beautiful; I couldn't wait to see the rest of her.

"Let's get more comfortable," I said, unhooking her bra, letting everything loose. I reached for her hand then led her to my bed where I undressed in front of her, it obvious I was more than ready. She lay on the bed, looking at me like she'd never seen a man before.

I sidled up to her on the bed, ran my hand over her hip then up the inside of her thigh where I cupped just under her fly. She was hot. I undid her zipper.

"You protected?" I asked, suddenly hoping to God she was prepared because I remembered I only had one condom, and it had been in my wallet for months. She replied, "yes," which was good enough for me. I didn't ask any questions, but tugged at the jeans which she was poured into. I don't mean "poured into" in a disgusting way. They fit her shape like they were custom-made, something I found exciting. "You do it." I gave up trying to peel them off of her.

Wow. She was more natural-looking than anyone I'd ever been with. Not as shaved and Brazillianed like my others. Nothing a razor couldn't erase. Still, I found her nude figure lying hot n' ready in my bed amazing. Camryn still hadn't said a word, but looked like she might want to. I figured if she wanted to talk, she would, so I carried on in the missionary position. I always wondered why they called it that, maybe because the dude was on a mission, just like me, to clean the ol' pipes. But that was so ordinary.

"You get on top," I told her. It was nice watching her on top, and she seemed to like that better. She moved in to stick her tongue in my mouth and then nibble away at the ticklish spot on my neck she didn't even know was there; plus, with her on top, my hands were free to do other things. I smiled. She still never said a word, but she felt great and I let loose, shuddering beneath her. Then with my eyes closed, I laid back flat, arms melting into the mattress at my sides, spent.

I popped my eyes back open. "Was it as good for you as it was for me?"

I saw a smile on her face and then rolled her over on her side so I could slip out and clean myself off. When I returned from the bathroom, Camryn had already gotten dressed, which gave my mind a pouty face. "Aw, . . . I liked looking at you," I said while hugging her, peering over her shoulder at her ass.

I dressed, and as the excitement was over and Camryn's "cat" still had her tongue, I offered up some sandwiches for lunch. We made boring small-talk, and the idea of hanging around the apartment all afternoon drove me stir-crazy, so I decided to visit my folks. "I'll see you when I get back," I said. It took Camryn a minute to get up and leave, but I held the door for her, and on my way out I kissed her goodbye.

CHAPTER 3 - GLENN

I knocked on Camryn's door the next evening. "Pizza at my place," I announced and then did an about face to check on dinner. I looked over my shoulder to see if she was following behind. And she was. She looked so cute following along like the puppy I didn't have, doting on me like man's best friend. *My* best friend.

"Have a seat," I told her, handing her a plate of pizza. Seems like we did this all the time. "Hockey's on." I thought Camryn rolled her eyes, but I wasn't sure. Then the phone rang. My mother. Probably calling to hound me about studying again, something I didn't want to hear, so I told her what *she* wanted to hear: that I was studying.

"Why did you tell her you were studying?" Camryn asked.

It's complicated. It's hard to explain, so I didn't. I steered the conversation elsewhere and then learned Camryn was putting herself through college because her parents wouldn't pay.

"That's just wrong," I said to this news. Camryn thought I was mad, but I wasn't. A bit miffed. And I felt sorry for her, but I wasn't mad. I wished I could help her out.

She made an excuse for her parents' neglect. I mean, she was *excusing* them and thought nothing was wrong with this picture, which I didn't understand at all. Baffling, yet intriguing at the same time. I'd never met anyone like her. Someone so forgiving, and headstrong to get through school anyway. It actually turned me on.

I turned my attention from the hockey game to eyeing her up and down, but she changed the subject, easing into it slowly, looking nervous. Then wham! "I think what we did yesterday was too soon," she said.

I had to think for a moment, what she was talking about, and then it hit me. The sex. She's talking about the sex. I wouldn't say I regretted it, but something did seem off. Then again, that could have been me because I never really know what's on or off. I just go and hope for the best. In this case I decided to err on the side of caution since I cared about Camryn. And I was struck with my realization—I cared. I said, "I was thinking that too." Then she did the oddest thing. She crawled into my lap. She sat on my lap, and if that wasn't a come-on, I don't know what would be. *Women*, I thought in frustration then kissed her on the cheek, returning my eyes to the game. "Stupid ref," I yelled at the television. I let Camryn sit on me while I watched the game since that's what it seemed like she wanted. The next thing I knew, she was staring at the sand-textured ceiling. She left shortly thereafter, not waiting for the end of the game.

*   *   *

Camryn dropped by the next day, helped herself to my lap again, seeming to be happier and more relaxed than ever. She smelled like vanilla, my favorite. I couldn't keep myself from touching her. My hand went up her shirt, touching her hot skin while I kissed her. The more I kissed her, the harder I got, so I kept going, and she didn't stop me. I tugged at her jeans and they came off along with her "His Pants for Her" girlie boy underwear. My shirt flew to the back of the couch.

"I'm getting rug burns," she said, so I fetched a soft blanket, spread it over the living room carpet. My jeans landed on the chair. I unhooked her bra, pulling it through the sleeves of her shirt to get it out of the way, and then the whole shirt and my boxers landed under the coffee table. We didn't talk much, but her body didn't lie; she was into it. She wanted me. I wanted her. And that was the common language we spoke.

*   *   *

We also spoke airplanes. "He asked you to go for a ride?" I said to Camryn after she had told me about going along on some guy's check flight where they killed the engines and everything. I felt fucking jealous. I didn't want her flying around in someone's airplane. Being in someone else's mile-high club. She said it was a girlfriend's boyfriend who asked her, which made it all the more weird in my mind. But the fact that she went showed me her adventurous spirit, and I loved that about her.

"I wanted to be a pilot," I said, keeping myself interesting.

"Why didn't you?"

"Too old," I said, joking.

She rolled her eyes. "Seriously . . ."

The truth was, I didn't know why not. I wanted to be an engineer, and I wanted to be a pilot. Why I couldn't be both seemed so self-limiting, and I'd never admit there was something I couldn't do. I couldn't shame myself like that in front of her. "I told you. I'm too old." Then to distract her, I said, "I got you something." Her eyes lit up. I pulled out a sheer red nightie that had "Remove Before Flight" printed across the front. "You'd look pretty in this," I said, and then my tongue in her mouth kept her from saying another word.

Another time, when Camryn *could* get a word in edgewise, she told me she'd like to see a movie. My brain groaned, horrified at the thought of sitting still in a chair for two hours focusing on the same movie, following along . . . not being able to see what I wanted to do with her at the movie, in the dark. Problem solved, I thought, looking at three pornos the fraternity brothers had left in my apartment — she gets her movie, and I won't be bored.

And we could never go to the clubs together since Camryn wasn't twenty-one, and she refused to use a fake ID. I swear, sometimes she was a bit too "goody two shoes" for me, but really, that's another thing I loved about her. She was honest, and trustworthy. These things you couldn't find in just anybody. Finding an honest and trustworthy hot body was almost too good to be true. And with that thought, I didn't want to wear out my welcome with Camryn, seeing her *too* much. So when she suggested spending the night on a Friday after her shift at the video rental store, and after I got home from The Oz dance club with my buddies, I said, "Maybe some other time."

Earlier, I had dropped by to see her at work, telling her my Oz plans, but just as I walked out the door, Raine walked in. "Raine." I nodded, a glare in my eye.

"Glenn," he said. A shitty grin crossed his face. I wanted to slap it right off of him, but I didn't want to keep my buddies waiting any longer. I imagined him chatting up Camryn, and it pissed me off the entire evening.

*   *   *

I went fishing on opening day of trout season with Zac, catching my limit, as always. I would have asked Camryn to come along, but it didn't seem like something she'd want to do. Maybe next year. Plus it's good to get away with the guys. Do guy stuff like smoke cigars, drink beer, and harass water moccasins — not necessarily in that order. Zac brought his hot rod, racing it up and down a dirt road with some redneck we found on the river. Zac's a redneck wanna-be, but he'd never fit in . . . too brainy. Although, sometimes he's dumber than rocks, like last weekend when he was itching to get laid. Tiffany was nowhere to be found, so he rented a dirty whore from East St. Louis. He'd gotten the personal recommendation from Ronin, who'd been quite serious with Deidre . . . or so I thought. I didn't know how these guys lived with themselves. It wasn't right. Of course, I'd been sworn to secrecy. Thankfully, I had Camryn to count on, and she could count on me. I mean we were a couple, and she had to have known that, but I'd never told her I loved her. That scared the shit out of me. Love. It was all loaded up with confusion and strings and obligations I didn't want.

When I got home, I went straight to Camryn's apartment. "Where have you been?" she asked, surprise and relief in her voice. I gave her a huge hug.

"I told you I was going fishing this weekend."

She paused. "Uh, no you didn't."

36

I felt bad; sure I had mentioned my plans. "Sorry, I thought I did," I said, brushing past the awkward moment. I didn't like the feeling that I had screwed up.

*   *   *

In class on Monday, I figured out that I had fucked up big time, totally forgetting a paper I should have done over the weekend. I crammed all afternoon, trying to get the stupid thing written. That's when I did my best work: under pressure. But I'm a lost cause at typing. It's like that bubble-test problem I have, constant mistakes because I hit the wrong keys and it takes me forever. Since it was a nice day, I had my front door open. "Hey, come in here," I yelled as Camryn walked by. I had seen her steal a glance inside. When she appeared in the doorway, her face was bright red. She could never hide it; her face lit up in an embarrassed rash. It was cute. "I'll make you dinner," I said.

"Nice." She smiled, looked awkward and then sat down. "What are you doing?" she asked, staring at the mess of papers and books spread across the room.

"Homework."

She got up, felt my forehead.

"Ha, ha. Funny," I said. "I have a paper due soon." I didn't tell her it was overdue and I'd better as hell have it in tomorrow, or I'd fail this class too. It wouldn't be my first. "I don't type very well." I stuck my lower lip out, reached for her hand. "You do." I brushed a strand of hair from her face, a curl. The curls bugged me. I know some people like curls, but straight hair was where it was at. The rest of her looked nice. I made a mental note to ask her to let her hair grow out anyway so I could see it straight and unpermed.

Camryn hesitated to answer, so I answered for her. "Here." I handed her a couple sheets of my chicken scratch. "You start typing, and I'll start dinner." She took the papers, headed into the office.

"Glenn," Camryn yelled. I popped into the room, bearing a hamburger and fries, set it down on the desk for her. She rubbed at her temples. "What does this say?" she asked, pointing to a scribble that made sense to me when I'd written it. I was a bad student. I was a bad writer. I was bad, bad, bad. But I could think on my feet. I could look at a screwed up piece of machinery and call out the fix in a minute or two when it took others hours of trouble-shooting. I was good with shit like that, but I sucked at this writing stuff.

"Uh, just say that Einstein's theory about the space-time continuum was ahead of his time, or something like that. You're good with words. You'll figure it out." Then I kissed her on the head and left before she could give me that look she gives me every time, like I've grown a third eye. Sometimes I bring her aspirin, but it always works out. I'll come home with an A or a B on the papers she types.

"I'm done." Camryn came into the living room, cross-eyed. I glanced at the clock. 3:17 a.m. "You can print out the file. It's finished."

"I owe you." I kissed her before she headed home, but all I got back was mush, no oomph in those lips at all.

"Goodnight," she said. I watched as she walked to her door, jingling her keys to unlock the door. Then she closed it behind.

I stripped off my clothes, fell into bed naked, no sheets on top. I lay there thinking about all the work Camryn had done for me. I felt bad. I really did, but when you're like me, you do what you have to do to get the job done. Sometimes you have to get creative and have someone else do it for you, or it just won't happen. She was awesome. The more I thought about it, the more my mind drifted even though I was beat. I thought about her lying in her own bed, imagined her sleeping naked too and what I might do to her, but this time I actually knew better than to go knock on her door. I reached for the *Playboy* under my bed, took care of myself and was asleep by four o'clock.

CHAPTER 4 - CAMRYN

Dear Reese,

It was so good to hear your voice when I called you. Reminded me of the comforts of home. Well, the comforts of home I have in my mind at least. We both know my mother is hard to live with, and it was time for me to leave my dad's. But I always imagined we'd have our own comfortable home, the two of us someday when you got out of the Air Force. You always put me at ease when we were together, and I felt like my whole self at those times. The time apart hasn't been easy. I feel so distant, and I'm heartbroken that things didn't work out between us.

But when we spoke the other day, we really didn't speak about anything. And that made me sad. What I really wanted to do was shake you through the phone, grab you by the collar and ask, "Why did you leave me?" I know what you said, but I'm still in a fog because what you said wasn't clear but more of a skirting of the issue. It didn't make any sense. I felt like you didn't want my help. Stupid me let you slide, letting you be. Maybe that was the right thing to do. Maybe it's a road you need to walk alone. I don't know. Throwing it all away after everything we've been through the past four years feels like I lost the most valuable thing I had.

I dreamt of you last night. You sat down at my kitchen table for lunch. You gave off a good vibe but didn't speak. I whispered, "I love you" in your ear, but you didn't answer. This is how all the dreams are and how I feel my life is: incomplete.

I wish you would have come here. I remember all the fun times we had and ache that they aren't anymore. I miss your company. I miss your touch. I miss being in the Norfolk McDonald's with you, when we never realized we were in the bad part of town. Because all we were concerned about was being together, no matter where or what the circumstances. I miss your humor and loving acceptance of me. I miss your poetry-inducing presence. I know that sounds corny, but what we had was the stuff the moon and the stars are made of: magic.

I've been seeing someone. He's energetic and pays a lot of attention to me. It's been nice having a friend when I didn't know a soul. We help each other.

Remember that time on the beach when you and I ate at that fish-and-chips restaurant, and a seed stuck on your face? I pointed it out. You said, "I'm germinating." I can't help but think that was true, and I hope you grow into a mighty oak where one day I can rest leaning against you.

Always my love,
Camryn

I glanced over what I had written. Nothing I had to say was going to change anything; it was almost the same letter I'd sent before, that letter severing ties. That letter had gutted me to the core, although I felt as if I were backed into a corner and had no choice. You can't change anyone else, only yourself.

I pulled out a second sheet of stationery, this one for my best friend, Megan. We met when I was an exchange student in Australia, and I was missing Reese then too. She was my sounding board when I couldn't sort through my own thoughts, so I poured it all out to her as well. When I was finished, I reread the letter I had written to Reese and shook my head. Gave up. Our courses were set. I wadded it up, hardly able to bear throwing it away.

CHAPTER 5 - GLENN

"Why don't we just live together?" Camryn asked me out of the clear blue sky. Well, it wasn't really clear blue, but more like blue with some clouds in it. "It'd save us both a lot of money, and I'm over here all the time anyway."

Yeah, she was over here all the time. All the time except when I wanted her to go away, and if she lived with me, I couldn't send her home. I panicked. She freaking wanted to move in with me. Just because we had sex she thought we should be together for life or something. I mean, I knew some people thought that. Well, I was taught that growing up, but I didn't know anyone who *really* took it seriously. Scared the shit out of me.

"No, it's against my moral code," I said and then told her my mom wouldn't like her if we lived together anyway. Camryn looked at me like I was delusional, but I don't know why. After that, she backed off, which I was glad for, but at the same time, she didn't speak as freely as she used to and that bugged the shit out of me. God, maybe it even hurt me.

But one night when I did want her to stay, I thought I'd spice it up a little, messing with her. "I'm going to bed," I said. I wanted to see what she'd do, see if she'd stand up for herself, speak her mind for once. A woman who could say what was on her mind was what I really wanted. I turned off the light in the kitchen and then the living room light. The only light left on was the bedroom. Camryn stood in the hallway with a deer-in-the-headlights look. Instead of following me to the front door when I went to lock it, she followed me into the bedroom, sat on the edge of the bed, and began to take off her shoes. "Aren't you going home?" I teased. But instead of taking it as the joke I intended, she wrestled with the tears welling up in her eyes. Of course I felt bad. I never wanted to see her cry, but damn. How could she be so sensitive? And how come whenever I cracked a joke, no one ever thought it was funny, but very often, just the opposite?

"Don't do that to me," she said, crashing into the pillow, wiping beneath her eyes.

I apologized. I helped her out of her clothes and held her close, listening to her talk about being unsure of where I was coming from. If I wanted her there or if I didn't. I listened. Half the time I didn't know if I wanted her there or if I didn't either, so I wasn't in any place to say anything. I listened, rubbed her shoulder, cuddled her close. She rolled to the side, clearly loosening up, becoming more comfortable then said, "I had thought you might have been married before." This didn't come out of the clear blue sky at all. This came out of a very dark sky, one with storm clouds, ferocious lightening, and deafening thunder. I hadn't told her before because it's not something I wanted people to know. It wasn't something I was proud of, and I already had a public list of things not to be proud of. And most importantly, I didn't want to scare her off. She was too good. The thought of scaring her away frightened me more than the thought of loving her— eventually—and that scared me too.

But now that she'd added a few things up, put two and two together, it was time to be straight forward and honest. She was smart. So I answered, "I was."

"You're divorced?" she asked, not entirely surprised, which surprised me.

"She cheated on me," I said. Camryn hugged me, stroked my arm. She didn't ask anything else about the divorce, which suited me, and I didn't offer any other details. Best to keep the past buried deep.

Camryn did ask my age at that point. Her jaw dropped when she found out I was thirty, a good ten years older than she. To me, age didn't matter. It was what was inside a person that counts. Then she started in with a bunch of other questions about whether I'd been in jail or not, things like that, like she was finally sizing me up. So I told her just what she needed to know, anything to keep her away from the divorce questions. She settled in next to me under the covers, keeping close. To my relief, she didn't get up and leave after what she'd just found out, and I wouldn't have blamed her if she had. I enjoyed literally just sleeping with her, knowing she was there, loyal, steadfast. These things I hadn't had much of my entire life. I'd always managed to piss someone off, and they'd push me away, but Camryn was different. If anything, she held on tighter. I loved her for that, but I still couldn't tell her. Letting that love-cat out of the bag surely would have it running wild in ways I wasn't ready to tame.

* * *

That first summer we'd known each other was one of the best and worst summers of my life. In between our summer school classes, I'd take Camryn to

45

Cardinal baseball games, out for drinks on The Landing down by the Mississippi waterfront, for romantic walks under the St. Louis Arch and plenty of afternoon naps, which didn't involve much sleeping, but instead plenty of bedroom (any room for that matter) gymnastics. I think Camryn would have done it on her head if I'd have asked her to. But, here's the weird thing, I could never get her to have a beer with me. What's pizza without beer? How can you enjoy a baseball game with no beer? I tried every which way, but on that one, she wouldn't budge, which boggled my already boggled mind — the mind that couldn't understand "no" meant no, but instead took it as a challenge to be mastered.

The Fourth of July was a day I'll never forget, and I forget a lot of things. Of the best and worst summer of my life, it was the best and worst day of my life. Well, it wasn't the worst day, but definitely in the top five. Camryn and I held hands at the VP Fair on the St. Louis Riverfront. She stared at our entwined fingers, deep in thought and then brought her other hand to the party, rubbing her thumb over my pinky, like holding hands with one hand wasn't enough. I took a swig of my Budweiser then kissed her on the lips. We'd just finished watching a Harrier jet hover over the river, disrupting the water with its turned-down exhaust nozzle. What an awesome machine, I thought. Then an F-15 and an F-18 passed by at high speed, showing off their stuff. This was why I was in school. This was why I kept at it. This was why I loved Camryn so much, because she loved airplanes too. Seeing the planes sparkle then disappear in the sun and whoosh past again was the highest high. The ultimate.

Ronin and his bitchy girlfriend, Deidre, and Zac and Tiffany joined us. Unfortunately, Raine (Who the hell invited him?) and his sweetheart of a girlfriend, Natalie, some chick from Wales, did too. At twilight, we all took our seats on the cobblestones, awaiting the fireworks. Zac had Tiffany laid all the way back, his tongue down her throat, making a scene with his public groping of her ass. Although with the enormous crowd, the riverside parking lot looked more like a rookery, everyone going about their own business. Ronin and Deidre reached through each other's arms, sipping their beers in toast to themselves. Camryn had hit it off with Natalie. Since Natalie was Welsh and Camryn had spent time in Australia, they settled on talking about all things English until Raine came back with nachos and a chili dog for their late-night snack. Thank God they were gone. Raine, at least. He was such a prick.

Camryn leaned into me, her back to my chest. It was the typical St. Louis summer night—warm, humid air. At least Camryn wasn't shivering. She was relaxed; looking up into my eyes, she made me feel like none of the other nesting couples around us was there. She made me feel loved, like I was the only one. Something, an aura, about her made my eyes sparkle from the inside and I felt with my whole being what I knew she wanted to say. I had said it myself, through my kiss, just moments before.

"Is there something you want to say?" I asked, barely in a whisper? There was something *I* wanted to say, but I was too nervous to make that leap. I wanted her to go first. Or maybe I didn't want her to go at all. She was loving me and scaring me all at the same time.

"No," she whispered back, but the love in her eyes shouted with joy. On that night, my heart heard it. And it was more than okay that she didn't actually say a thing; because with me, the words just get in the way.

"Where'd you get that scar?" she said, lifting my left hand, while gently tracing over the line where the gash in my pinky had been.

"Old war injury," I said, lifting my bottle. I took a drink then swallowed again, hoping my answer would suffice.

She brought our clasped hands to her lips, kissing the scar like she wanted to kiss away all the pain from my past, even the past I chose not to share.

I heard a *BOOM*. A pop and a crackling of brilliant color and light ripped through the sky. That's how my heart felt, having fallen in love with Camryn right then and there. We lay under the open sky and watched an explosive display of our feelings, unspoken.

Camryn stayed with me that night and the next even though they were during the week on a school night when we normally didn't sleep together, I mean, normally didn't spend the night. I kept the air conditioner set extra cold, making sure she'd stay close all night, since there was plenty of room to sprawl out in my king-sized bed. I liked her there, close to me, paying attention to me, continuing to love me, but then she actually said it.

"I love you," she said, bright fireworks love-gooiness in her eyes. I know she meant it. I know I heard it. I know I didn't deserve it. Inside I froze. The words did get in the way, and so did my goddamned past, like an eight-hundred pound weight.

"Is that what you wanted to say last night?" That's the best response I could come up with.

"Yeah," she said. "Is that what you wanted to say?"

"Yeah." There, I had said it. I loved her too.

*   *   *

I had a fishing trip planned that next weekend, and I had meant to leave Camryn with my spare key. She'd brought a lot of her stuff over, and my place was more comfortable for her, especially with her roommates running in and out at all hours of the day. I knew she liked to study and would have her nose in her books the whole weekend while I was gone, but the whole "leaving the key thing" slipped my mind.

When Camryn asked for my apartment key when I'd gotten back, going into an unnecessarily long-winded explanation about why, it was a no-brainer. I went to the drawer and handed it to her. And after dinner, she distracted me from my TV show again, right there on the living room floor. God, she missed me. She didn't even bother getting dressed afterward, but lounged around in a bathrobe the rest of the night.

"You ready for bed?" I asked her.

"Yeah," she answered, but she didn't leave to go home.

My back hurt and I wanted to sleep solo, at least that's what I told myself. I felt her Big-Bad-Wolf vibe bearing down on my walls — threateningly kindhearted and soft, foreboding of falling in love. I wasn't near ready to open the door and surrender. Instead of sharing those feelings with her, I said, "I like to sleep by myself . . . . More room."

49

She had this ridiculous look on her face, but it wasn't like we were married, where I had to literally sleep with her. She should have known this, so I didn't feel bad about sending her back to what *was indeed,* her own apartment. It didn't take a neuropsychiatric brain surgeon to figure that out.

She went home.

* * *

"I'm having coffee with Natalie," Camryn said one day, a rarity. She didn't get out much, which didn't seem to bother her, but how could a person live that way? Honestly.

"You're what?" I asked. "Is Raine coming along?"

"Don't worry. Just the girls this time," she said. "I won't be making us any double dates."

She sure as hell wouldn't be making us any double dates, not if it involved Raine.

"I don't know why you hate him so much," Camryn said. "He's actually not so bad. He adores Natalie, and he's always been nice to me."

"He's a charmer." I snorted with indignation.

"What do you mean, 'He's a charmer'? How would you know?"

"I just know."

"You don't like him because he looked at me during the icebreaker at the beginning of last semester. You and I weren't even going out yet. And he's with Natalie now." Camryn adjusted the purse on her shoulder. "They moved in together."

"In that case, I'd rather you didn't see Natalie anymore," I said. Camryn's face fell, but I wanted to keep her safe, far from Raine. That kid was psycho.

50

One time I was hanging out with some seniors working their Bernoulli's-principle assignment in the wind tunnel lab. Sometimes the guys would bring refreshments to get them through the night. I'd even seen some of the professors get wasted right along with them. Anyway, this one night, Raine had about four too many, and on a bet, crawled up into the wind tunnel to break the speed record. The wind tunnel filled up a large chunk of the room and looked like a long dragon or a vicious creature with shark eyes, a mouth, and teeth painted on the wide end, similar to the nose art on old fighter jets. Zac cranked it up to, I don't know, 125 miles per hour. Raine was hanging on for dear life, his face nearly peeling off in the hurricane until Ronin, who was standing watch outside, sounded the alarm and made them stop before Dr. Raviswami walked in on everybody. Close call. I personally wanted to see Raine's face peel off, maybe even get all caught up in the fan, but no such luck. Unfortunately, it wasn't dangerous enough to get caught in the fan. What an asshole. And even worse than that was — so I heard — when he strapped a live cat into the wind tunnel and cranked it up. He didn't kill it in the tunnel, but the thing couldn't walk straight and keeled over as soon as he took it out. The cat belonged to Raine's roommate at the time and Raine said he was just trying to get the loose fur off of "the beast" since it shed all over his furniture.

If I'd have seen him doing this, I would have stopped him. I mean, I hate cats, but you don't treat animals that way. I never told Camryn about Raine's psychotic streak. I didn't have to. Honoring my wishes, she severed ties with Natalie on her own, making their coffee dates fewer and farther between until they soon lost touch, at least I thought they did.

*   *   *

I felt bad having left Camryn at home so many weekends, so I suggested a road trip to visit friends of mine, Jason and Lori, on our next three-day break.

"When ya gettin' married?" I asked Jason as soon as we walked in their door.

Jason froze. Lori looked at her feet, while twisting up the hem of her shirt. Camryn glanced around, looking for the nearest rock to crawl under. "What?" I asked. "I was only trying to help."

I pulled out forty dollars, handed it to Camryn. "We need a guys night out. You girls go shopping," I told her. Jason was a good guy, but such an idiot for not seeing the great girl he had right under his nose. Make a perfect wife for him. We needed to have a talk.

When Camryn and Lori got back, even later than we did, it was like they were new best friends. "Wine cooler?" I asked, twisting off the cap. I sat one bottle in front of Lori. Camryn nodded, taking the other. I liked seeing Camryn happy like that, and she'd seemed so excited about the new coat she'd bought. I liked that she bought something for herself besides gas or groceries; she was *so* careful with her money, almost like she budgeted down to the penny. Me, I spent it until it ran out and then waited for the next paycheck so I could spend some more. Worked for me.

Camryn and I settled in to Jason and Lori's bed after we'd finished playing cards. "I finally talked some sense into Jason," I told Camryn as she peeled off her shirt. She was exceptionally affectionate that night, pressing her naked self into my chest, causing me to get hard . . . and making it hard for me to think, so I forgot all about thinking and instead reached between her legs.

"I love you," she said. Just enough light streamed in from outside that I saw into her dreamy eyes when she said it. Instead of the hairs bristling on the back of my neck at the scariest words ever spoken, a tenderness overcame me, and I rocked into her slowly, meaning something with every stroke. It wasn't just a fuck, and then it was over. I kissed her hard, wanting her so much I could have eaten her face. She pulled me into her, her legs wrapped around mine, not letting me go. I melted into her completely. After my talk with Jason and him telling me he was going to propose to Lori, and my sudden clarity that I had a great girl too, I said, "I love you, too." I meant every single word, and in that moment, with her desperately loving me back, I wasn't scared. I was excited to be making love to my future wife.

*   *   *

Camryn stole my family's hearts at Thanksgiving when she first met them. My mother especially, treated her as one of her own, which made me happy. What made me sad was that Camryn couldn't spend Christmas with us as well, instead visiting her sister, Karla, in Savannah. When I dropped her off at the airport, I'd given her a necklace I'd spent quite a bit of time picking out. She looked hot in it, but then again, she looked hot in anything . . . or nothing. Maybe next Christmas we could go away together, just the two of us.

While she was away, some lady from her work called asking for her, which I thought was weird because obviously they knew she wasn't around, not being at work and all. I gave them Karla's number. Good thing Camryn's so organized, leaving me a list of important numbers taped on the fridge, or I'd have never found it.

"Hello." I picked up the phone on the first ring.

"It's me," Camryn said. She didn't sound so happy, kinda serious, but I was happy to hear her voice no matter what. Then she dropped a bomb. "I lost my job."

Camryn then went into a full-blown panic, going on about how she needed the money and now what was she going to do. I knew she'd be fine. She's always fine. Hell, she could wait tables at PT's, make a lot of money there and I told her so, but I guess she didn't like the idea of working in a smoked-filled strip club.

* * *

The food stamps Camryn got tided her over until summer break when she moved back home with her parents and got her old job back at Hallmark. I couldn't think of a more boring job than working in a card shop of all places. Well, maybe a bookstore, but she seemed to like it.

I missed her, and my apartment was a morgue with most people gone for the summer. Without her here, I had to find other things to do, and coincidentally, I flunked one of my classes. She kept me on track, and I needed that even though I complained every time she said we should do homework instead of heading down to The Landing.

"I love you," I said at the end of a long-distance phone call. It was easier to tell Camryn how much I loved her when she wasn't actually here. She'd written me several letters over the summer, which I liked, but I couldn't reciprocate. I'm a terrible speller. It's embarrassing. And collecting my thoughts and arranging them on a page is torture; I cringe just thinking about it. Plus, I've got foot-in-mouth disease bad enough the way it is; I don't need a pen to help it along. She wanted to come and visit over the 4th of July, asked if I'd split the plane fare with her. I missed her and wanted her with me, but later it slipped my mind that she needed money for the ticket, and I never sent her a check. By the time she asked about it again, I'd spent the money.

"You needed your space, I guess. Time apart," she said after she came back for the fall semester.

"What are you talking about?"

"Well, you didn't send me any money for a plane ticket, so I figured you really didn't want me here," she said and then sang, "Actions speak louder than words."

I threw my hands up to my hairline then slid them down slowly over my face, realizing what I had done. "I forgot all about it. I'm sorry," I said and then started making up a believable excuse to cover up the real reason which was that I'm a dumbass and forget things all the time—the overdue bills, missed appointments; do an assignment, forget to turn it in, beg for forgiveness; turn it in late—which only works about half the time. The other half the time I end up flunking the class. I'm lucky I hadn't flunked life. I'd paid a late fee on some overdue bills, even had to pay a reconnection fee when I'd blown off my electric bill one too many times, and then I didn't have any cash. Paying bills is boring, and boring jobs don't get my attention. It's only after the electricity is turned off that bill-paying becomes exciting, and I don't plan it that way, it just happens. "I had a tough load this summer. The classes were so hard. I had to study all the time. It was barely all I could do to keep on top of things. In fact, I had to drop a class before I got an F. I'll take it again next semester." In my mind, it was the truth.

Sometimes forms have a disclaimer at the bottom that says "I swear this is true to my knowledge at the time." My life should have that disclaimer at the bottom because I live my life true to my knowledge at the time, even though it doesn't often appear that way to others. I'd swear to it. And so would my grandma; she'd vouch for me. She's the only one who unconditionally believed in me, but in her old age, she didn't have my back like she did when I was ten.

"I'll make it up to you," I said, kissing Camryn on the forehead. It seemed like I was always making something up to someone, a fact of my life. Camryn was an easy forgiver; I could see it in her eyes when she looked up at me, hugging me tight. I loved her for that too.

* * *

I nursed my hangover from the night before Homecoming day. The bright sunlight made the pounding in my head worse. Zac and Ronin had brought the keg to the football field for the alumni football scrimmage where current and past fraternity brothers duked it out. My position was team photographer, getting all the action shots.

"What's the water bottle for, Raine? Ya wuss," Zac said, slapping his shoulder. Most everyone else was freely watering themselves at the keg, plastic cups everywhere. Some had their own flasks as well, for the occasion.

"Run, Zac," I yelled as he caught the pass and took it in for the winning touchdown, where I captured every frame.

Ronin sloshed the keg. "Gettin' low," he said.

"I got it." I grabbed my keys, heading off for a beer run. That was my job as well, since half the fraternity wasn't old enough to purchase liquor.

When I got back, Ronin and a few others grabbed at their necks gasping, "Thirsty . . . ."

"Took ya long enough."

I gave them the finger, poured myself a cold one. Even though it was fall, the sun was unusually hot, beating down on the field, encouraging everyone to drink more.

"Oh my god," Zac said, "I think I'm going to be sick."

"Me t—," Ronin almost said, but instead hurled a pink mass all over the field, followed by Zac and at least a couple more. My quick thinking put the camera in my hands. You don't see this every day.

I laughed. "You idiots." I kept snapping pictures of mid-air action hurl for the boys to enjoy when they were sober. What dorks.

After we rolled everyone off the field, I ran the film down to Walgreens. An hour later I was passing them around the frat house, grossing everyone out. In the commotion, a few photos disappeared, and not long after that I found myself in the dean's office providing an explanation.

"Do you realize how this reflects on the University?"

"Yes, ma'am," I said, scared as hell.

"And do you realize all parties could be expelled?"

At first I was too scared to answer, my future flashing before my eyes, envisioning cleaning the johns in an airport rather than engineering the planes that fly there. That is, if I didn't screw that up too; boring as it was, I probably couldn't handle the position. "Ma'am," I said. "I wasn't throwing-up drunk. I only took the pictures." Then I negotiated a deal: turn over all the evidence, probation and community service for the entire fraternity, and the administration would pretend this episode never happened. Sweet.

"You saved my ass, man," Ronin said, cleaning his pants because he'd been scared shitless that he'd be kicked out of school.

I saved more than one ass that day including my own, one of my prouder moments.

"They let you all off the hook?" Camryn said to me, shaking her head.

"I worked a deal," I said oozing a cocky confidence that I actually felt and was aware of this time. I'd done good. I patted myself on the back again since hardly anyone does me that way very often.

"You'd get away with murder, but I'm glad no one got kicked out, especially you." Camryn leaned into me as we sat on the couch. She looked more worried than glad, but that all fell away when we dozed for an afternoon nap, really napping in the wake of all the unfurled drama.

*   *   *

The homecoming dance rocked the roof off the hangar, but rather than a mere mix of modern tunes, we played bugle-boy WWII era beats as well, honoring our alumni war heroes. Camryn chummied up with one of the old geezers' wives (and I mean "old geezer" in the fondest way), which I thought was weird. Why would she rather talk to an old lady than mix with her own kind? Wait, Camryn didn't really have a kind. She was different, weird in her own way because she didn't follow the crowd, and I loved that about her. Weird is good, I always say.

I sidled up to some of the vets, listening in while they swapped war stories and admired the old P-1. "Thank God we didn't have to fly that old thing," one of them said. "Don't think we'd have made it back alive."

"We're going to restore it," I said, speaking on behalf of Parks College. I decided right then and there that *I* was going to restore it. Sounded like fun. Who wouldn't want a chance at preserving history like that? That sucker was over 60 years old at the time, back in 1990. And even though I drug Camryn onto the dance floor when no one else was out there, getting the party started, all I could think about was getting my hands on her, the P-1, making her good as new and maybe even better. Nothing better than a new challenge. But even with that distraction, I looked into Camryn's eyes as we danced solo, all eyes on us, and said, "I love you."

It was the best thing in the world, hearing it back.

CHAPTER 6 - GLENN

When Camryn told me I'd thrown away the hockey tickets, I freaked. Not only were our tickets gone, but Jason and Lori's too. And they were coming in for the weekend. We'd been planning it for months. "You should have told me they were there," I yelled at Camryn when she said they were on a pile of papers I thought was trash.

"I did," she said, stressing out over not only the missing tickets, but also my outburst. She explained the whole scenario and exactly what she had said when she put them in a pile of other important papers. She claimed I even answered her, but apparently I'd had another cognitive malfunction, and I didn't recall any of it. Deep in my psyche, where all the important stuff resided, I knew she was right; she was telling me the truth, but that "in-between space" that betrays my intentions *all the time,* wouldn't allow that particular knowledge to emerge. Instead it made me lash out and deny everything. It's like my being was made of layers; my inner soul was taken hostage by my mind and thrown way off in the corner. Meanwhile, my mind paraded around, out of control—an imposter impersonating *me.* And this is why people couldn't tell the difference between me and the real me. I was all rolled into one, and most of the time, I couldn't tell the difference either; I only sensed it.

Finally, I rationalized the only thing that settled in my mind. We didn't have the tickets. The box office was supposed to make sure we had the tickets. So that's exactly what they were going to do. I'd make sure of it. "Give me their phone number," I said to Camryn, all business and focused on the task at hand. I figured she'd have it since I didn't. Later, she told me my demand sounded insensitive, but the nonexistent voice in *my* head didn't hear anything. I merely had been getting the information I needed, directly, no beating around the bush. And when I was done improving the box office supervisor's mind over the matter, we had will-call tickets. Problem solved.

Camryn looked at me like I'd just kicked a puppy.

* * *

"Blues, Blues, Blues," I yelled from the grandstand. Hull made the winning score. "Whoo hoo!" I turned to Camryn then said, "See, I told you they'd win." She looked unimpressed, so she turned back to Lori, resuming their girl-talk.

When we got home, Lori made the big announcement, "We're pregnant!"

"That didn't take long. Haven't even been married two months, have you?" I asked Jason. Before he could answer, I said, "Been busy, eh?"

Lori slapped me and it actually sort of stung, but I was truly happy for them. I watched Camryn as they shared their big news and thought that we could share big news like that too, one day. I sat on the couch next to her, put my arm around her shoulder and rubbed my hand along her arm. I squeezed her closer as I thought about making love. Then when my *cooler* head prevailed, I thought as nice as a family might be, I wanted nothing to do with being tied down any time soon, although you never could get enough practice. No harm in that. No strings attached.

* * *

A few months later I found Camryn kneeling by my bedside, my stash of porn magazines at her knees. Wow, watching her stare at those covers was hot. What guy wouldn't think so?

"What's this?" she asked, holding the latest issue of *Cheri.*

"A magazine," I replied. She asked a question, and I answered, although a little something nagged at me that she knew it was a magazine, particularly *that* kind of magazine. But she asked, so . . . .

I invited her to flip through the magazines with me. "What do you think of her?" I asked. Camryn really didn't answer, wouldn't say, even though I wanted to hear her opinions. So I had to ask more pointed questions. It's not like me to give up, but when Camryn didn't have much to say, I pushed the magazines aside, focusing on her body instead. Why bother with the magazines when I had the real thing? Although I did think she'd look great in what those models were (or weren't) wearing, and wished she'd wear them for me. Camryn was more of a jeans-and-a-T-shirt kind of girl, and while that was good, I liked variety and encouraged her to like variety too. "Do it for me . . . wear it for me . . . please, *for me*?" I'd ask her, and she'd almost always say yes, wanting to be thoughtful *for me.*

There was this one time when she said no. "How about a threesome?" I asked. "We could get Morgan over here. I hear she's into that kind of thing."

"Where'd you hear that?" Camryn asked me. She looked like some sort of gears were turning in her mind, but I could never figure a woman's mind out, so I didn't bother to try.

"Some guys. Guys talk," I said. "You never thought about a threesome?"

"No," she said, and I could tell she was serious. Then she teased, "Maybe with two guys."

"Hell no, I'd never do that."

"Why not? If a threesome's okay, what's the difference?"

"Well, that's faggy. I'm not doing that shit."

"Well isn't two girls lesbo?"

"No, it's hot," I said. Then Camryn just couldn't see the difference, and it started into an argument about double standards, and this one wasn't worth it to me. Since she put up such a stink about it, I backed off and let her have this one. Sometimes she seemed so touchy, and even though she thought I was pissed off about it, I was happy to give in. It wasn't that big of a deal.

*   *   *

I took Camryn to happy hour the next night. We often went. For a couple of beers we could get a whole meal; some spreads even included oysters, crab legs, nachos, tacos. You had to know where to go. We met up with other guys from the fraternity along with sorority girls. I was just goofing around when I asked Camryn, "Why don't you look like that?" while I pointed to her roommate, Casey. Casey was cute, slightly smaller than Camryn, and I thought that with not too much effort, Camryn could look that way too. She was always trying to lose a few inches or pounds,

63

stressing about it, so I thought I'd help her out, give her some encouragement. Talk about ta-uch-chy. Touchy. Geez. She slid the last of her cheese and crackers onto my plate.

"Not hungry?" I asked, noticing she hadn't eaten much.

"Not really," she said. She gave me the silent treatment. We watched Casey and some guys having a good time on the dance floor, and since Camryn didn't seem in the mood for dancing, I asked her out for ice cream instead, something more her speed. I thought I was being nice. She freaked out. "Are you nuts? Blah, blah, blah."

That just pissed me off. Why was it every single time I tried to do something nice, it backfired in my face? I knew in my heart that Camryn was a good person. She was hardly ever sassy, always trying to be polite, but every once in a while she'd blow up like that. Between her freak-out and the outcome of my intentions constantly undermining me, I'd had enough. Maybe I was better off alone. Maybe *she* was better off alone in her own la-la land where people don't gain five pounds at the mere mention of eating ice cream, because she acted as if that's how it worked here.

"Let's go." Then when we left the parking lot I said, "And I didn't tell you that you were fat."

Somewhere along the line she thought I said she was fat, but I never even said the word "fat." If I was going to call someone fat, I'd say it out straight, not dance around it. Call a spade a spade. Call fat, fat. I would have come straight out and said, "You're fat," just like when she had morning breath, and I said, "Your breath stinks." Direct. To the point. Camryn was

64

always reading stuff into things and I told her so. "Stop doing that," I'd say. "Listen to my *words*. Quit reading things in that aren't there. My brain doesn't think that way. I don't think like you do." I'd had enough of that too, living like we were from two different planets that had nothing to do with Mars or Venus. I felt inside that I was from Jupiter where I was stupider. And if being around Camryn made me feel stupid, it was better to push her away.

My mom always spoke in these goddamned riddles, and I vowed never to play games like that. She'd tell my sister, "Maybe it'd be better if you didn't wear that striped shirt with those plaid pants," and then expect my sister to go change. I said, "That's fucking ugly. Go change." My sister didn't like me very much, and I never could figure out why. She was standoffish. I was direct, unambiguous, honestly spoke my mind, yet she'd be all upset about it, like she'd rather hear a message that *wasn't* to the point. That was unfathomable and confusing as hell to me. Lots of people, usually guys I worked with, appreciated when I shot straight with them. They never gave me shit about it. I wished everyone appreciated how I operated. Accepted me as I am. Even my mother couldn't give me unconditional love or understand where my heart was coming from. "Stop being so mean," she'd correct when I only had the kindest and best intentions. If I didn't *care* that my sister was about to walk out the door looking like a freak and most likely get made fun of at school, I wouldn't have bothered to say anything. Mom, always the one *picking on* me. And I thought moms were supposed to *pick you up*. Sometimes I wished I could have traded mine in . . . gone to live with Grandma instead.

As all of this built up inside me, I exploded into a rage. I pounded my fist on the steering wheel and said, "You know what? I can't do this anymore."

Camryn burst into tears, and it tore me up inside to see her cry because of me, but I didn't know what else to do but end it between us. In the glow of the dashboard lights, I watched Camryn wipe at her eyes during the ride home. Soft music from the radio and an occasional sniffle from her side of the car was all I heard. By the time we pulled up to our apartments, I'd collected myself on the outside—inside, I was still a mess. I resolved to put us out of our misery, hers at least, my inner pain would continue just as it had my entire life. It felt worse when I was with someone because I spread the pain around. That old saying about when two are together their pain is halved and joy doubled didn't apply to me. Why me? Why was I the cursed one? "We need to take a break," I said. "Break up."

Camryn nodded. She looked at me with bloodshot, puffed-up eyes full of pain. The opposite of that old adage applied to me. The opposite of tons of things applied to me. The pain here was doubled, pain caused by me, and our joyful times had been halved because she was always reserved, wary of what I may say or do next. I'd told her at times to loosen up and live a little, but she lived in a tight turtle shell, afraid to poke her head out because of the rambunctious animal inside me.

* * *

Natalie stopped me a couple days later in front of my apartment building. "What'd you do to her?" she said.

"Do to who?"

Natalie gave me a look that cut right through me, a look that made me feel like a moron. But she didn't say who she was talking about, so I had to ask. How else would I know?

"Camryn, you idiot." This time she blurted it all out, which made me like her a lot less, made me think she was rude for assuming I'd be a mind reader. And I'd had Natalie pegged for a nice girl.

"I didn't do anything to her. We broke up."

She gave me that idiot face again. "She loved you, you know. You're making a huge mistake, letting her go." Natalie shook her head. "You're such an ass." The way she said "ass" in that Welsh accent made it sound a whole lot worse than a typical American ass. She bent down, picked up a rock and then tossed it away, like she was contemplating saying more. "There's not a lot of girls who'd put up with your shit. I've seen how you operate. For some reason, Camryn puts up with you, and if I was you, I wouldn't let someone as rare as that go."

Natalie had a point. She was direct and to the point, which I appreciated. Camryn was rare, and that's what I still loved about her.

* * *

I bit at my lip as I dialed Camryn's number. She picked up after four rings, and I wondered why it took her so long, but managed not to ask. "Camryn, I was wondering if you wanted to come over for supper," I

67

said into the phone, trying to sound as if all was okay with us. I mean, how do you recover your footing with a person when you've been told that you broke it off like an ass? You wing it. Who cares? Well, I did care what Camryn thought of me, but no sense getting bogged down in yesterday's news. This was today.

Camryn thought for a moment, and I high-fived myself in the mirror when she said yes. "See you at five thirty." I hung up the phone then looked through the fridge, wondering what to cook. When Camryn showed up, I had grilled cheese and salad all ready to go.

"Sit down." I motioned to our usual dinner seats in front of the TV, but this time, I didn't turn it on. We *talked* during dinner rather than our usual staring at the set. "I like talking to you," I said.

"Me too." Camryn smiled, and I think we were both hopeful we could get past this. It already felt on the mend.

The conversation steered around our summer plans, and when Camryn said, "I can't afford to stay. I'll have to go back home," my stomach tied itself into knots, worse than when I had broken up with her three days ago. At least with a break-up, she and the possibility of rekindling were close. "Back home" was hundreds of miles of too far away.

I'd told Camryn I was going to school over the summer, and then I said, because it had slipped my mind all weekend, "Speaking of school, would you mind typing up my term paper tonight?" I'd beg if I had to; passing or failing the entire class rode on this paper.

She shook her head no then said, "I need to study."

Her words stabbed through me. Panic set in, but then, just as fast, I realized she hadn't *said* no. I needed to get this assignment done, and I knew I couldn't do it on my own. I kept at her, finally resorting to a guilt trip even though I didn't mean to. "If I don't turn this paper in, I'll fail the class," I said, leveling with her. She wasn't the type to leave me high and dry even if it was my own fault. I loved that about her too, even though if I had been in her shoes, I would have told me to take a hike. I guess I wasn't as caring as she was, and being around her, I hoped some of those traits would rub off. Isn't that what the shrinks say, "surround yourself with those you wish to emulate?"

"Yes," she said with a sigh. "I'll do it."

We worked on the paper, all business, well into the early morning hours. Camryn tapped the stack of papers onto the desk, straightening them and set them down. She headed to the front door, eyes crossed.

"Thank you for doing this for me," I said. "I owe you one."

She flicked her fingers up, counting, while her eyes looked somewhere between the inside of her head and the ceiling, half thinking aloud. "I think you owe me about five now."

I pulled her into a hug, kissed her head through her hair. "I'll make it up to you, promise."

"I need some sleep," she said. She looked like a zombie as she reached for the doorknob.

After she left, I stared at the door a few minutes wondering why she hadn't stayed like she had after other all-nighters, except for that first one. I crawled into bed, patted the space next to mine. It felt too empty. I'd have to fix that.

CHAPTER 7 - GLENN

Camryn and I had made up by the next day and I'd solved that empty bed problem, although it saw different sorts of action until she could start taking the pill again.

"Why would I need it if we were just friends?" she said, after I asked why she'd stopped taking it. "You dropped me like a rock. You were so angry. Why would I have thought you'd ever want me back?"

I hated when she answered my questions with more questions. I also hated that she thought I was *so angry* when I was instead frustrated, mainly with myself. Rather than get into it and answer her questions, I kept quiet this time and let my lips and mouth, not my voice, do the talking. And from the sound of her, she liked it.

* * *

Camryn lay on my bed, resting on her side. The sun streamed in the wide-open window. I ran my fingers down her side and over her hip, touching her gently. I loved looking at her. "I want you to go to the formal with me," I said.

She reached for my face, pulling my head toward hers and kissed me with everything she had. She pushed me to my back, showering me with kisses. I hadn't known an invitation to a formal was such a turn-on, but I wasn't arguing. Camryn stopped, looked me in the eyes with such depth, like she was seeing right into me . . . seeing the real me. My heart melted right then because in that moment, I felt understood.

"I love you," I said and nipped once at her lip before ravishing her with a full-blown, face-eating kiss, losing myself in her, leaving her no chance to utter a word.

*   *   *

I bought Camryn a wrist corsage to go along with her gown. She wore a satiny strapless dress with a drop waist and a skirt that was higher in the front than the back. I'm not sure what color it was. I'm not good with colors, but it fit like it was custom made—because it was, by her. That blew me away. How someone could have the patience, I didn't know.

"You cut that wrong," I teased. "It's lopsided."

She smacked me.

"It's beautiful, just like you," I said and then took advantage of the short hemline in front and ran my hand up her thigh.

She smacked me again, gave me a terse, "Later!" Camryn didn't have much patience for interruption, especially from me while she put last minute touches on her hair and face before a big date.

The formal was held in the back room at Paqueños, an upscale restaurant in downtown St. Louis. When we passed through the main dining room, the thought crossed my mind that it'd be a great place to propose.

A sea of people packed the dance floor, heads bobbing up and down. This wasn't like the homecoming dance with oldies mixed in. It felt more like modern wedding-reception music. Half the people were dancing, and the rest were either in the buffet line or already eating.

"Wine?" I asked Camryn even though I knew she'd say no. It was polite to ask, wasn't it?

"Get me a whiskey sour," she said, taking me by surprise. I liked surprises.

We settled with our dinner and drinks at the only table with space available. No wonder. Raine sat there scarfing down his food, Natalie by his side. Some other couples were there, talking amongst themselves, no one we knew well.

"I see you've come to your senses," Natalie said to me, nodding toward Camryn.

"I don't have senses," I said. Everyone thought I was making a joke, but for the most part, I didn't joke and felt it was true. My mother had always said, "When are you going to come to your senses?" Hell if I knew. I was still waiting.

But, I had managed to change my mind about Camryn, and I think that is what Natalie was getting at. Natalie and Camryn chitchatted about their flowers and dresses, while I made uncomfortable small talk with Raine.

"How'd you do on that Calc III test?" Raine asked. As if he cared. "Those word problems were pretty tough."

Those word problems were more like impossible. I'd gotten all but one wrong, failed the test. And since the exam was worth half the semester grade, I'm sure I flunked the class. I had been busy not thinking about it until Raine brought it up.

"I think I got an A," he bragged.

Would he not shut up? Raine was an idiot. How could he have gotten an A and I fail? Oh yeah, I forgot my middle name. If I was into self-analysis, I'd have a lot to consider here, but I chose not to torture myself any further. I stood from the table, "I need another drink. Anyone else?"

Camryn still had half of hers left. "I'm good," she said. Everyone else waved off except Natalie, another surprise.

"Bring me one of those frou-frou drinks. The ones with the little umbrellas," she said and then called after me as I walked away, "One with a cherry!" Then she winked at Raine.

I wanted to throw up.

While in line for my drink, that Calc test tugged at my mind. Pissed me off, really. Another beer would help take the edge off, at least for now. I gathered our drinks, returned to the table and set Natalie's umbrella-adorned drink in front of her. Camryn and Raine's chairs were empty.

"They went to the dance floor," Natalie said.

Huh? Camryn and Raine? My mind jumped to a thousand conclusions, and it felt like my face burned as red as my tie.

"Raine wanted to dance, but I wanted my drink, so I sent Camryn off with him. They'll be back."

No sooner than Natalie fished the cherry out of her drink, Raine and Camryn sat back down at the table. I pulled Camryn's chair closer to me. Natalie tipped her head up, puckering her lips at Raine. She kissed him on the mouth while dangling the cherry stem between her fingers. "Let's do this together," she said into Raine's face, barely pulling away. Then she crammed her tongue in his mouth one more time before making a display of placing the maraschino right between her front teeth, inviting him to take it. Raine leaned in, smashed his lips to hers and then bit down. Cherry juice squirted across the table. They both laughed, faces still pasted together, chewing and sucking face at the same time. But they looked more like penguins from a documentary, sharing their food. I turned away before I barfed too.

"I don't want you dancing with him again," I said to Camryn.

She shook her head, dismissing my concern. "He's not as bad as you think," she said. "Don't worry about it." Camryn picked up her whiskey sour, now watered down with melted ice and took a sip. She leaned in to kiss me, putting an end to the conversation. "You wanna share a cherry too?" she asked, thinking it was funny. It was and it wasn't.

"Someone already beat me to that," I said, not playing along. I rubbed Camryn's shoulder while I uninterestedly watched a conga line form in the room, too many things on my mind. Camryn looked away as if her eyes were burrowing a hole through the table, while her right hand absentmindedly twisted a nonexistent something on the ring finger of her left hand.

* * *

I helped Camryn load her things into a storage unit for the summer. All of her roommates had moved on, leaving her apartment almost as empty as when she had started. Her plan was to move back home, work at the card shop and then find a new place to live in the fall, somewhere smaller and less expensive.

She checked her compartment in the community mailbox one last time, and while there, I checked mine.

"I got my report card," I said, pulling it out.

"Wha'd ya get?" Camryn asked.

I shielded the paper from view, not wanting to divulge right away. Some B's, C's, and that f'ing F. I knew it was coming, but seeing it there on the page . . . . I punched the mailbox. "Dammit!" Then I paced back and forth, running my stressed-out fingers through my hair.

"What happened?" Camryn asked, although I know she suspected. She's not dumb.

"I don't want to talk about it." I wadded the report card up and crammed it into my front jeans pocket, treating it with the respect it deserved.

"Maybe if you talked about it, we could figure this out," she said.

"I said I *don't* want to talk about it."

"You're mad."

"No shit, I'm mad. And you keeping on pestering me about it is *not* helping."

She had a didn't-see-that-coming look about her, and I'm sure she was wondering what she'd done wrong, which was nothing. But in that moment, in my mind, it was all about me and my feelings. After all, I deserved my angry pity party for one. I had the curse, not her. I wanted to scream. I wanted to cry. I didn't want to go around punching things, but failure after failure put a chip on my shoulder—no, a huge chunk on my shoulder that I walked around with nonstop. And besides, Dad told me from as young as I can remember that grown men don't cry; so I got angry instead. "Buck up," he'd say. It was okay to behave like an angry buck rather than let something outside of yourself kick your ass. What I didn't realize was that this thing that was kicking my ass was inside of me. So in ignorance, I spread the blame around. It was Camryn, pestering me. It was the stupid teachers who had it in for me. It was my parents for not sending me to the right high school. Sometimes it was even God. Damn you, God.

Speaking to Camryn about my flunky status was the last thing I wanted. I wished I could be more like her, getting nearly all A's. I loved that about her, but it also made me frustrated and angry because I couldn't do the same thing, even though I knew I wasn't stupid. Proving it to the world was another matter.

"I need to get going," Camryn said, fiddling with her keys.

"Yeah." I looked down. Awkward. Not the sendoff I would have liked to have given her. I hugged her, my chin resting on her head. "I'll see you in August."

"See you in August," she said. Camryn ducked into her car, started the engine and then unceremoniously drove off. This time she didn't cry.

As soon as Camryn was out of sight, I unwadded my report card from my pocket. My next stop was the dean's office. Last time, she'd given me my last warning before expulsion.

CHAPTER 8 - GLENN

"Hello Glenn." Dr. Brewster's secretary greeted me. "What can we do for you today?"

I'd been in and out of the dean's office so many times, it's like we were old pals. Sort of.

"I'd like to see Dr. Brewster, please."

"Sure, darlin'. Take a seat." I didn't like the sound of that, like she could see right through me and knew she was the gateway to my end. I actually didn't *like* to see Dr. Brewster. Shaunda Brewster, PhD was former military, worked her way up, did twenty years and was now the first African-American female dean at St. Louis University, let alone at the engineering college. She carried herself like a drill sergeant, and part of me was sure she could chew me up and spit me out, but that other part insisted she was a pussycat.

A few moments later, Dr. Brewster came out holding a carafe. "Coffee?" she asked. I'd have rather had a cigarette, but since Camryn didn't like it, I'd quit.

"Sure. Black," I said, even though I never drank it black. I needed it full strength for this.

"I thought you'd be paying me a visit," she said, motioning for me to follow along to her office.

I felt a fucking ulcer coming on.

"Have a seat."

I took what felt like the hot seat, sipped my jet fuel. Dr. Brewster stared at me, waiting for me to start.

"I suppose you've seen this." I tossed my rumpled report card on her desk.

She picked it up, almost like she was afraid to touch it. I felt the same way, like it might burn me twice.

"We've talked before," she said, "and I told you—"

"I know you told me that I'd be expelled," I interrupted. I took another sip of coffee. Between the coffee and the immense stress of being on the brink of being thrown out on my ass, I was in top form. "But, let me tell you this. I'll pass it next time," I said, confident and on a roll, "I'll study hard. I'll join a study group. I'll get extra help. Whatever it takes."

She, in turn, studied me, deep in thought, so I went on.

"And this summer—" I started, ready to wheel and deal, "—I'll make it worth your while. I'll head up the P-1 restoration."

She scrutinized me some more, looking interested in my proposal, so I took that as a yes and motored on.

"I can do this. I'm good with blueprints. I'm good with the mechanics. That theoretical bullshit has already been done," I said. Oops.

A slight smile crossed her lips.

"All I've got to do is put the thing back together," I explained, recovering my faux pas.

She nodded, still not saying a word.

"I'll give you as many hours as it takes. Volunteer hours," I specified.

"You know my reputation is on the line," she said. This was good. She was at least considering giving me another chance. That's the thing about going to a small school. Things could be worked out with some one-on-one negotiation. None of that by-the-cookbook, rubber-stamp-by-committee crap.

Dr. Brewster went on. "You remind me of my son," she said, but didn't elaborate. She rested her elbows on her desk, folded her hands and then set her chin between her knuckles, contemplating my fate.

Holy crap. I didn't know if this was a good thing or a bad thing, me being like her son. No wonder her hair was thin.

She leaned back in her chair, elbows and hands on the arm rests. "I'll give you a last chance, Mr. Conroy." Her eyes narrowed. "Don't make me regret it."

Her words miraculously cured my ulcer. I wanted to leap for joy. "Thank—"

Dr. Brewster cut me off. Her former military-brass, no-nonsense demeanor took center stage. "Report to the hangar. P-1 restoration starts now."

"Yes, sir," I said, shocked into submission. "I mean, yes ma'am," I corrected, too excited to be embarrassed. "Yes, ma'am."

I downed the rest of my coffee, set the empty cup on her desk, and reported for duty.

* * *

The next Monday I reported to my emergency make-up class of Calc III. Well, it was a practice run in the grand plan of making Dr. Brewster proud. Call me a glutton for punishment, but I was just sitting in on the class during the summer and planning to take it for real in the fall to make double sure I'd pass. Sometimes you had to do what you had to do.

"Hey," I said to Casey, the first one I recognized as I walked into the classroom.

Her eyes lit up and she patted the seat next to hers, so I took it.

"I thought you took this last semester," she said.

Ouch. "I'm taking it over, trying to get a better grade." It was the least painful version of the truth.

"I'm pretty good at this stuff," Casey said. "We should study together. Kinda dull doing it alone."

I didn't have to think. I fist-bumped Casey in agreement. It sounded like a good idea to me, plus I'd just swore on my mother's grave—if she were dead— that I'd do whatever it took to make sure Dr. Brewster didn't regret her decision. "Deal."

Turns out Dr. Brewster already had a talk with my Calc III prof, Dr. Presson, about me. "Stay after class, Conroy," Dr. Presson said, as he wheeled his chair up to the overhead projector. "I'm your new private tutor."

Great, just what I needed. I sulked down into my chair. "Yes, sir," I said. Dr. P. had his own issues. His mother must have dropped him on his head too. My family always joked that way with me, growing up. But my mother never dropped me. No one ever dropped me on my head: I was born this way.

Dr. Presson, on the other hand, wasn't born that way and actually had a severe accident leaving him in a wheelchair and barely able to use his arms. With his left hand, he palmed a home-fashioned penholder onto his right. Then he scribbled our assignment with the attached dry erase marker onto the overhead transparency. Since his hand didn't function any more than a crippled up tool, he had to leverage his entire arm to write.

"Could you read that, please?" I asked. Even *I* felt bad about asking a cripple to read his own indecipherable writing, writing that most people in the class seemed to comprehend except me. I suspected there were a few others in class who were happy I had balls enough to ask. But Dr. Presson never minded me asking. He understood his "condition" made it harder on us too.

So I stayed after class. And the class after that and the class after that with Dr. P. Two cripples helping each other out, me crippled mentally . . . somehow . . . with a condition called . . . . Well, I don't know what it was called, but "stupid" was the closest thing I could peg. At least Dr. P. had a concrete name for his ailment — paraplegia and then some.

"How's the P-1 restoration coming along?" Dr. P. asked.

"Perfect," I said, "Wanna see?"

It wasn't often I could say something I was associated with was perfect, so I was eager to show it off, and Dr. Presson was excited to have me show him, as he was limited to scholarly book things and calculations. When I took him to the hangar, he could see those calculations applied, the real deal, in action. Plus, being somewhat of a fossil himself, he enjoyed seeing history restored, could identify with it even though restoration of his crippled body (at the present-day state of science) was wishful thinking. Sometimes when seeing things, associations unexpectedly click. I think he was hoping for some kind of Lazarus-effect inspiration to strike, observing the P-1 come back to its glory.

Aside from hanging out with Dr. P. over the summer, I also studied with Casey. She knew her stuff. I felt with all the extra help I was getting this summer,

Camryn would be proud when I could wave an A from Calc III in her face.

"I think I've had enough for today," I said, rubbing my temples. I checked my watch, beer-thirty on a Friday. I wrapped the long neck in the bottom of my shirt, twisted off the top and threw the cap on the counter. "Want one?"

Casey closed up her textbooks, stacking everything up. "No. I think I'll wait for the races tonight."

"Races?"

"Stock car. Every Friday night. Wanna come?"

Hell, yes, I wanted to come. Why didn't I know this sooner?

*   *   *

Casey had already planned on going to the races with Ronin and Deidre, so I joined them. Deidre sat there picking the polish off her nails, looking bored. Casey and Ronin had their favorites, cheering them on. I couldn't possibly root for the same drivers, so I cheered for the most aggressive driver I could find, liven it up a little. Rivalry was always fun, gave me a reason to debate, rather than let some random event light my debate circuits. At least I had a semblance of control this way.

"Your guy's a *loser*," I said, taunting Ronin. "I'll bet you a beer at Stooges afterwards."

"You're on, loser." Hearing him call me *loser*, even in fun, stung a little bit. Twenty years later I could still hear the kids on the playground all over again. *Loser, loser, Conroy is a loser.* Sometimes they had called me a *poor loser*, mainly because I'd had a reputation for throwing tantrums if I didn't win. I liked to think I'd

82

outgrown those impulse-control issues, but truth was, it still snuck up on me sometimes.

Three-quarters through the race, my driver, Evans, took out #67, Casey's pick, and in the process, wrecked himself too.

"All right!" I stood up and yelled from the grandstands.

"What are you cheering for?" Casey asked. "Your guy wrecked."

"Yeah, I know, but he took you out too. Plus, now I'm not a loser. My guy didn't even finish the race."

Ronin, Casey, and Deidre looked at each other, confused expressions on their faces.

"What the hell?" Deidre said to Casey, still looking confused. She glared at me.

The white flag came out. Ronin's guy roared past the rest of the pack, beating them to the checkered flag. While #55 was taking his victory lap, driving around the track in the opposite direction, Ronin said, "You owe me."

"Hell I do," I said, "I didn't lose. I didn't even finish, so how could I have lost?"

Then we got into a heated discussion about what a loser was, and according to Ronin, a loser was anyone who didn't win the race. By that definition, the dog sitting at the end of the row was a loser and so was my grandma who wasn't even here.

"You make no fucking sense," Ronin said.

Ronin was the one not making sense, but since his guy won the race, and Ronin thought everyone else who didn't win was a loser, I caved. I really just wanted a beer at Stooges anyway even though Ronin was clearly wrong. Even I had my limits arguing about things with idiots.

* * *

At Stooges, Ronin started his shit up again after I'd bought a round explaining to some friends, "Yeah, Conroy owed me. His guy lost."

Unfortunately, Raine and Natalie were within earshot. "Doesn't surprise me, Conroy, you loser," Raine said.

By that time I'd had enough of people throwing around the *loser* term. They had no right. They had no clue what they were talking about, and I didn't have to take it from anyone. Not my brother, not my sister, not the kids haunting me on the playground, not Ronin, and especially not the personification of *loser* himself, Raine.

Raine had a look on him like he'd just shit his pants when I slammed the schooner down on the table, beer sloshing over the edges and spilling down the sides. I got up, walked over to Raine. Sometimes my feet had a mind of their own and so did my fist, which hurled itself at Raine's left eye, leaving him crying for his mommy.

Natalie looked at me like she'd seen a demon possessed. "What the bloody hell, Conroy. Can't you take a joke?" Then she turned to Raine, "Need some ice, baby?" she said, while gently pressing Raine's sure-to-be shiner with her fingertips.

Joke? I didn't see anyone laughing, especially me. "F'ing hilarious, Natalie," I said, while Ronin grabbed me by the collar and threw me out the rickety front door. The screen slammed shut and I stood there in the grass alone. Rejected.

"Take a chill pill, Glenn." Ronin wasn't the first person to tell me that, but they were the ones who needed to chill – watch who they ran around calling *loser*.

I walked home, decided to call Camryn.

"Hey," I said after she picked up.

"Glenn, are you drunk?"

"No, baby. I just had a few." Why would she even ask that? All I said was "hey." I may have had one too many, but it was like she was psychic.

"Oh. It's past midnight. Did you know that?" she asked.

"I didn't think about it. I just missed you and wanted to call. I'm sorry, did I wake you?"

I told her I'd gone out, but not where or who with. I certainly didn't tell her I'd punched Raine in the face. "I saw Natalie over at Stooges. It got boring over there, so I came home." All that was true. To a degree.

"I miss you," she said.

I loved hearing that. "I miss you too."

*   *   *

Casey and I suffered through the summer, regularly studying Calc III together and then hitting the races for a rewarding break.

"I can't wait for Camryn to come home," I said to Casey as I popped *Beverly Hills Cop II* into the video player. A sudden thunderstorm had cancelled the races, so we decided to hang at my place instead. It sucked staying home watching movies, but I had a drinking buddy, so I'd deal. "One more week."

85

"That's just 'cause you're horny," Casey said.

That was true, but not the only reason. "No it's not. I miss her company too."

"Yeah, sure," Casey said. "Then why don't you ever take her out?"

"You've seen us at the dances. We go out to eat. We do stuff," I said, defending myself.

"You haven't taken her to the races. You hardly ever take her to the bars."

"She doesn't really like bars," I said.

"Figures." Casey sat there pulling her bubble gum out in strings and then chewing it up again. She annoyed me sometimes.

"Well, I didn't know about the races before, but I'll take her now. She'll love it," I said, figuring if Casey loved it, then Camryn would too. I mean, who wouldn't?

"Got a beer?" Casey asked. The movie previews kept rolling, seemed like forever.

"Yeah." I got up to get her one, handed her the bottle.

"How many times have I been over here?" she asked.

I started to think, four, maybe fi—

"You're such a dipshit, Glenn. Every time I've had a beer over here, I ask for a glass, but you keep handing me the dang bottle."

"I don't remember you asking for a glass," I said, hurt that she'd called me a dipshit. I had thought I was being nice, serving her a cold one. I sulked back to the kitchen.

"You seriously need your head examined," Casey said as I handed her the last clean glass from the cupboard. She emptied her beer into it and took a swig. "Much better."

"Now look what you've done," I said, noticing the lipstick mark left behind. "You know that shit doesn't come out in the dishwasher?"

"So wash it by hand."

Casey had a way of talking back to me that Camryn didn't. Camryn was always afraid she'd offend me. Casey didn't give a shit. In a way, I liked that about Casey, but she was kinda rude. Camryn was polite, the kind of polite I wished I could be, and I loved that about her even though I wished she'd speak her mind and not worry so much.

*   *   *

Camryn returned home the next Friday afternoon with a homemade chocolate cheesecake. The kind of cheesecake that was better than sex. Well, almost. "It's great," I said. I planted a huge kiss of appreciation on her, taking my time. Mid-kiss, taking her to the races popped into my mind. "There's a race tonight."

"A what?"

"I couldn't wait until you got back so we could go together. Going with Casey was fun, but going with you will be funner," I said, shoveling in more cheesecake. Damn, it was good.

"We'll give it a try," Camryn said, hesitating. It almost seemed like she didn't like the races, but I was sure she didn't know what she was talking about.

Camryn had her fingers in her ears before the race even started. Next time, I'd try to remember earplugs.

"I shouldn't have worn a white shirt," she said, trying to brush off the dust that settled every lap.

This was nothing, just time trials.

Camryn said, "I like the white and blue one, number sixty-seven."

She couldn't have picked a crappier driver. I couldn't have her rooting for him, sitting right next to me. "He's no good. Second to last in the standings," I told her. I stood up and yelled, "Go Thompson!" as the #33 car sped past.

No sooner than the race started, the official threw a caution. I jumped to my feet. "Black flag him!" I yelled. Stupid ref. Camryn just sat there watching the cars parade around the debris field.

"Fuck you," some moron in front of me said.

"He cut him off!" I yelled back, throwing my hands up in the air, disgusted.

Camryn's face looked a little bit green, but it might have just been the kicked-up dirt. "It's only a race," she said, tugging at my arm, trying to get me to sit down. Like hell it was "only a race." It was an experience. You were supposed to get into it. Experience some excitement. It was good for the ol' ticker. Got the blood pumping.

I'm pretty sure Camryn had a good time by the end of the race. She didn't complain and even suggested going to Blarney Stone for our fave beef dip sandwich. We talked more over dinner, catching up on the summer and then walked the riverfront. I almost told her I loved her, but something held me back. Seemed like too much of a commitment even though I wanted to say it. I decided to show her instead. That'd be good enough. I reached out, caressed her jawline with both hands and kissed her under the moonlight. I wanted her bad. Couldn't wait to get back to my apartment.

"What's your fantasy?" I asked.

She took a little too long to answer, like she was conflicted inside. "I think it'd be fun to take a shower together," she finally said.

I was hoping for something like doing it in an elevator or having me shave her whole crotch bald, but for now, I could make this fantasy come true. I kissed her again then whispered into her hair, "Let's give it a try." I reached down, slid my hands up the back of her thighs to give her ass a good squeeze, firmly planting the idea in her mind.

Back at the apartment, I started the shower, fully intending to fulfill Camryn's fantasy. She walked into the bathroom naked, looking around while the water was warming up. I couldn't help but touch her. It had been all summer long, by god. I went straight for the parts that count, feeling her up. She was wet, but wriggled away.

"No foreplay?" she asked. Camryn wanted to take it slow. I just wanted the action, never thinking about what was satisfying to her. It never crossed my mind. The here and now. *This* moment crossed my mind, and that was how it was for every moment, no planning ahead, no looking back. That's how my brain worked, which was normal for me, all I'd ever known. When other people said, "learn from the past," I'd get confused. Hell, I could hardly remember the past, let alone learn from it. And planning for the future only served me well when it'd help get me stuff now, like graduating college would help me buy that new CD changer now. I could get a good job and pay for it later. That's what credit was for.

"Foreplay, smoreplay," I said, more interested in the main course. "But speaking of s'mores, dribbling chocolate all over your body and licking it off might not be a bad idea." I thought it sounded like an enticing idea, but the drinking glass Casey had left in the bathroom last week distracted Camryn.

"What's this?" she asked, holding it up to the light.

Cripes, way to ruin the moment. By that time the bathroom had steamed over. I flipped on the vent fan and opened the door, letting some cool air in. "Casey and I watched a movie over here the other night. She likes her beer in a glass," I explained. I wasn't about to admit Casey had been here plenty of times, helping me study. This was good enough. Camryn still gave me a disapproving look, which frustrated the shit out of me. "Come off it. We're just friends," I said.

Camryn stood there, biting her lower lip, which looked like it was quivering.

"Let's just do this shower thing." I picked up the white T-shirt she had worn to the race, handed it to her. "Wear this."

"We're taking a shower," she said.

"I know." I waggled my eyebrows at her. Then I slid off my boxers while she put on her shirt. I pulled her into the shower with me, making sure she was soaked before I smoothed out her then almost-see-through top. "You don't have much there," I said, cupping her breasts in my hands, but you'd win a wet T-shirt contest with those nipples. At that point I bent down and nipped at them through her shirt.

*   *   *

90

A couple days later I woke Camryn with my hand between her legs. We slept naked. Easy access. Clothes got in the way, at least I thought so. I kissed her neck and down over her shoulder. She seemed to like that better than the whole shower thing. I knew it was a lame idea when she brought it up. I kept kissing all the way down her body until my lips ended up where my hand had been, and then my imagination took over with thoughts of chocolate sauce dribbled all over a nice bald pussy. Like a warm cream sundae. Not an ice cream sundae because there was nothing cold about her. She was downright hot. She seemed to like that idea too because all I felt was her hands in my hair and her hips getting into it like she was fucking my face. She pulled up, tried to wriggle away, but I held her close doing more of the same. She writhed and moaned a few seconds more then fell back, spent.

"You like that?" I asked.

"Mmm hmm." She had a smile on her face.

"I love you," I said, without thinking.

"I love you too."

Too bad it couldn't be like this every day. I knew I wasn't good enough. I knew I wasn't ready, and didn't know if I'd ever be ready to make us a real and forever couple. A few days together would be all it would take before I totally blew it, and she wouldn't want me anymore. Keeping her at a distance was safer.

"When are you going to find your own place?" I asked, ready to plan the day.

"You know I've been looking," she said.

Something had changed from how she had looked in the bedroom to how she was looking at the breakfast table. It was almost like her bedroom-hot switch had been flipped to cold, but it wasn't like I was asking her to break up. I was just asking her to get out, which was no surprise since she already had plans to find her own place. Nothing had changed.

Camryn had made plans to move in with some guys from Jamaica, rent a room from them. I didn't like the idea of her rooming with a bunch of guys, and thankfully the Jamaicans thought the better of it, letting her down easy. But still, she had to find somewhere to live besides with me.

Camryn ended up finding a small house to move into. It was cute, and since she didn't have much stuff anyway, I thought she could store some of my things over there. The day I helped her move in, I playfully threw her onto her mattress and began tickling her, all in good fun. She laughed and screamed, "Stop it!" like girls always do even though they are having a good time. I loved seeing a good reaction out of her especially since she was so reserved, so I kept it up, but suddenly she tried taking a chunk out of my arm with her teeth.

"Wha'd you do that for?"

"I told you to stop," she said.

I never thought for a minute she meant it. To me, she looked like she was having a good time. I felt bad that I'd done something to make her want to, and actually bite me, so I decided to make it up to her. I ran my finger gently from her chin down across her chest to her jeans. She must have been thinking the same thing because she reached for my zipper and all else was forgotten, at least in my mind. We christened the new place right, and times like these made me think having her around all the time wasn't such a bad idea, but then thought the better of it. She was always there when I needed her. And I loved that about her.

I kissed her, thinking how lucky I was and then offered to let her have some time alone to settle in. "I'll come back in a couple of hours and take you to dinner, my treat."

I returned with a small fan for Camryn to use, staving off the brutal St. Louis summer heat. It sucked that her AC was out of commission, but on the other hand, that made her appreciate the fan I'd brought over and that made me feel good. It was always nice to be appreciated, and since I was always screwing something up, it felt extra nice to me. "Wear something nice," I said to Camryn, anxious to get to dinner.

"Where are we going?" she asked.

"Paqueños."

I could almost hear her thinking from the other room, perhaps too stunned to speak. She flipped through the hangars in her closet, looking for something in particular. When Camryn came out, she looked hot, and I couldn't keep my hands off of her, but that tight denim miniskirt wasn't leaving her house. She could put it on later for me to enjoy, but having the rest of the world enjoy it too, wasn't going to happen. "Nice," I said. "Now go get dressed for dinner."

"I am dressed for dinner," she said in protest.

I explained my position, and I felt bad that she was upset about it, but I really didn't want her looking like a whore out in public. Private, for me, yeah. I was all over that because I knew she wasn't one, and it was just fun. But the public didn't know her, and she didn't need to look like something she was not.

"We're having tapas," I explained when we sat down at the dining table.

Camryn curled up one eyebrow and scrunched her forehead in question. It was fun showing her things she'd never heard of before. We laughed all through dinner. Camryn relaxed more each time the waiter came by with a new dish.

"This mousse is *so* good," she said after downing two of the four mini dessert cups in front of us.

I gave her one of mine.

"It's as good as that chocolate cheesecake."

A look of ecstasy came over her face. And when the waiter came by offering coffee, Camryn was so relaxed, she nodded. "Bailey's coffee with whipped cream," rolled right off her tongue. She shivered, the air conditioning turned too cold for her liking. I motioned for her to come sit on the same side of the booth beside me. I put my arm around her, keeping her comfortable as she sipped her warm drink.

* * *

I was mad at myself because I'd forgotten Camryn's birthday. It fell on homecoming weekend, and I was busy with the fraternity and school and the P-1 and stuff. Not that any of those things were a good excuse, but they were the only excuses I had and I'd use them. I certainly didn't want Camryn to know I'd forgotten, but remembering the night before her birthday, which also happened to be the night of the homecoming dance, didn't give me any time to do anything about it, so I made more excuses in a desperate attempt to slide my shitty memory by, undetected.

"I'm going out with the guys," I told Camryn, "I'll meet you at the dance about nine."

Spending the least amount of time with her was probably the best game plan, less exposure to me getting caught.

When Camryn showed up at the dance, I said, "There's drinks over there," sending her on her way. I was in no mood for dancing or anything else with her, besides, she moped around, bummed even though she had told me she'd just come back from having drinks with friends. Having Camryn around right then didn't make me feel good at all; her presence only reminded me of my middle name, Failure, this time by forgetting. I kept busy helping the DJ and didn't have much time to spend with her anyway, I told myself, which dovetailed into my plan of non-exposure quite nicely.

Camryn returned with her drink followed by Ronin and Deidre. "We just got engaged," Ronin announced, his eyes glazed over with drink. On the outside he tried to portray happy, but knowing what a bitch Deidre could be, I didn't see how he could be happy on the inside. I'm sure the booze helped him fake it. I wanted nothing to do with that kind of "happiness" and decided my plan of non-exposure to Camryn needed to be intensified: no exposure.

"Why don't you go home?" I said under the guise of having to clean up. "I'll call you tomorrow."

Camryn left just as bummed or more so than when she'd arrived. Good thing she left because someone that down was a drag on me too. Why couldn't she lighten up a little, have some fun? The more I thought about it, the details making sense in my mind, the more I thought she should be history.

"Where's Camryn?" Deidre asked. I didn't know why she'd even care since she didn't like Camryn much. Hell, she didn't like anyone very much unless she could use them.

"She went home," I said. "We broke up." As far as I was concerned, we were broken up because I'd just decided she was history.

"Aw, I'm sorry to hear," Deidre said, although I knew she wasn't sorry at all. Window dressing was all that Deidre was, and even that was a stretch because she was a touch homely. She did what she could. The friend she had along with her was another story. Courtney looked hot; didn't even need beer goggles for her.

"You should come out with us, Glenn," Deidre said, lacing her fingers between mine.

"Yeah, come with us," Courtney said. She had on a denim miniskirt with a crop top showing off her abs. And she did look a bit slutty, but I didn't care in this case because she wasn't *my* girl. She was just *some* girl throwing herself out there for all to see. So I may as well look. And she noticed me looking.

"You moving in on my fiancé?" Ronin came up and asked.

"Not at all, man. Congratulations."

I felt free. No girlfriend, just a few friends out to have a good time. I handed Deidre back over to Ronin where they made newly engaged kissy face. Courtney and I stood there with a smoldering tension just below the surface, yet both feeling like third wheels until I said to hell with it and put my arm around her shoulder. "What are we waiting for?" I said. "Where we headed?"

96

Somewhere between bars, we lost Ronin and Deidre. The temptation from being alone with Courtney was harder to fight because I *didn't need* beer goggles; and worse yet because I found myself wearing them. She was fun, dancing all over the place, joining me for a few drinks, touching my arm, reaching for my thigh. When we went to the dance floor, at times holding her close, she felt good. She flicked her brown hair back over her shoulder, and I figured she had to have brown hair everywhere. And right after I thought that, I thought of Camryn, feeling a twinge of guilt. But we were broken up, so I could do what I wanted. And when we closed down the last bar and the streets were deserted, I kissed her under the corner streetlight and kept kissing her, my hand touching the small of her back just under her rumpled white shirt that looked like she'd been out all night.

"Come back to my place?" she asked.

Finding out and falling into what was under that denim skirt sounded like a fine way to top off the night. Very tempting. My loins even said I should go for it. I checked my watch, stalling to answer and then noticed the date. Camryn's birthday. Camryn, who I know didn't stay out all night partying with friends. Camryn, who I was sure, was asleep in her bed, probably waiting for me.

"I'll drop you off," I said, giving her one final kiss on the head. I let my hand fall from her back.

When she got out of the car, she slipped her phone number into the cup holder. "Call me," she mouthed through the windshield.

I waved, drove home to the rhythm of my beating headache, and fell into bed lonely and alone.

The sun shining in my windows woke me at eleven. I'd wanted to sleep all day, but at that point, I was too wide awake. The night before was a blurry sludge in my mind, and my head still ached. What was that girl's name? A vision of me kissing her sat front and center. Did I do that, or was it a bad dream? I felt guilty even though I'd mentally broken up with Camryn. One way or another I'd have to tell her, but not today. Today was her birthday and, well, I guess there was no good break-up season, but birthdays weren't the days to do it. I showered before giving her a call.

"What do you want to do?" I asked. Since I didn't have anything planned, letting her decide sounded like a nice gift, but when she suggested a picnic in the park under bright sunlight that my hangover could not take, I said, "I was thinking we could go to the mall." Girls liked malls. "I'll pick you up in half an hour."

I checked my watch, careful to leave in plenty of time so I wouldn't be late. When I was a kid, I missed the school bus one too many times and had to brave the wind and ice and snow and all that shit to get to school. I'd get into trouble all those times for being late. That scarred me for life. A lifelong incentive to be early, just to be sure, burned into my brain. I left in plenty of time.

"You're not ready yet?" I asked Camryn when she answered the door, curling iron wrapped around her hair. Women. Then she started splitting hairs (ha ha, I made a funny) about how much time had elapsed since I'd called and that I was early. How the hell could she not know that early was a good thing? On time is still too late in my book, and I had a long book on *Glenn's Unwritten Rules That Everyone Should Abide By*. Too bad it wasn't published because then I could hold people more accountable. I flopped down on her couch, waiting, strumming my fingers on the end table, checking my watch. "Hurry up," I yelled into her bedroom.

She came hurrying out, grabbed up her purse.

"So, are you ready?" I asked.

"Yes."

"About time." I looked at my watch, rolled my eyes up at her, and creased my forehead for emphasis.

"I'm right on time. Quit acting like I'm late," she said, which sounded all snotty to me. Damn.

Camryn settled into the passenger seat, the same seat where—oh yeah, Courtney, that was her name—sat last night.

"I thought I'd take you to the store and let you pick out your own gift," I told her, laying out the plan.

Then she started in with the silent treatment, like she was pissed about something, but she couldn't have been pissed about Courtney because she didn't know. Traffic slowed. We followed behind some piece-of-shit low rider; the driver slouched sideways so his head was in the middle of the car, rather than on the driver's side. I got frustrated because he was going slow, like no one else mattered but him, and I couldn't get around, so I rode his ass instead.

"Back off! You're scaring me," Camryn said.

I shot her a glare, annoyed she bitched about my driving. Even worse, music blared from his windows, the bass pounding through my chest. "Damn nigger," I said.

"Why do you say that?" Camryn snapped. "I've asked you not to say that."

I shrugged, not seeing the big deal. "That's how I was raised. My dad says it all the time."

"Doesn't mean you have to." It sounded like she had a nasty sneer in her voice. Look who was talking now.

We rode in silence again after I squealed the tires in disgust, getting around the low-riding jerk, until Camryn brought up a new subject. "When did you get home last night?" she asked.

"About one" slid right off my tongue, not even giving my mind a chance to think about it, but when my mind caught up, it reminded me I'd really gotten home closer to four. Some people might call things like that lies, but that was my MO and I didn't do it on purpose. You had to say a mistruth on purpose for it to be a lie. "Tom and I went out for a beer."

That part was true in the truest sense. Tom was along for part of the night after we'd run into him at a bar, and we did have a beer. I left out the Courtney part, seeing it as irrelevant information.

"Oh," she said, and then just over the Mississippi river she asked, "Do you ever wish you could see your ex again?"

What the hell kind of question was that? I hadn't thought of her since the last time Camryn brought it up shortly after we'd met. The ex left a bitter taste on my soul, remembering what she'd done. Then a tiny little bit of my conscious gnawed at me about last night. But that was different. Camryn and I weren't married. I didn't sleep with Courtney, and I was almost breaking up with Camryn anyway.

"No," I answered. "Do you? I mean do you wish you could see an ex-boyfriend?"

Camryn didn't answer right away, like she had to think it over and I, for a split second, wondered what that was all about. "No," she said. This was another case of "no" which might really mean "yes," but at that point, I didn't care. I just wanted to get through the day.

We strolled the mall like awkward strangers, worse than that because awkward strangers might actually be happy, yet still awkward.

"You like this?" I asked Camryn, holding up a shirt.

"No."

"You like that?" I said, pointing to something else.

"No."

That's all she could say, was "no, no, no." Hell, she's the one who acted like she hadn't slept all night, and to top it off, she was damn picky about picking out her own birthday present.

"Flowers would have been nice," she said.

Finally, something positive out of her mouth, but when I suggested going to find a flower shop for her to pick some out, she said no to that too. I couldn't win. Then she said, "Why don't we just have lunch and call it good?"

"Fine."

We sat down to Camryn's favorite Asian soup, and she barely sipped it. "Don't you like the soup?" I asked.

"I just can't eat it right now." She didn't even answer my simple yes or no question! She didn't even acknowledge I'd asked a question. Instead, she changed the subject to something else. It's common courtesy to answer a question when asked, and she was pissing me off.

"You're hard to please, you know that?"

Camryn's face went green, but I didn't care. She brought all this on herself. I laid into her with a rant the size of Texas. Feeling defeated, I said, "Can I do anything right?"

She didn't answer that either.

"Bill, please," I said to the waiter, but he took too long to come back, so I slammed some cash onto the table. Camryn started in with the tears.

"I should be the one upset," I said, pissed off at—I didn't know who I was pissed off at—her, myself, the waiter, God, the world, or all of the above.

"Let's go," she whispered, streaking the tears across her cheeks.

It's a good thing we didn't crash on the way home because I was out of control on the inside, like a thousand demonic squirrels were scratching away at my brain, driving me crazy and pressing all my "angry" buttons. If God had made me any less of a man, and I felt like a lesser man often, I would have hauled off and punched Camryn, just to let off steam, but the man I was didn't hit, not physically at least. I was raised old-school with the "sticks and stones" theory, letting the words fly. Questioning the theory's validity never entered my mind. I felt like one of those demonic squirrels had morphed into a full-blown demon and reached across the front seat with its sordid hands around Camryn's throat. And I was powerless to help her at all. Something else was in control. Camryn had fear written all over her face, and I couldn't help but catch a glimpse of my own reflection in her eyes. It scared me too. "You know what? We're done. I can't take this shit anymore," I said, loud enough for an entire jam-packed gymnasium to hear, so I'm sure Camryn got the message.

*   *   *

I pulled the keys out of the ignition and then noticed Courtney's phone number sitting there in the cup holder. Thankfully Camryn hadn't seen it, but I was confused as to why I'd care anyway. We were broken up now, for real this time. I grabbed the number as a course of cleaning out the trash from my car then threw it on the kitchen counter when I set everything down in the apartment. That was another of my MO's: pile shit up until the shit was deep then sort it out when I couldn't stand it anymore. It wasn't a learned skill; it was instinct.

A few days later, Camryn called. I was glad to hear from her, yet surprised she was even speaking to me after ruining her birthday. So much for my plan to break up with her on a non-important day. I couldn't help myself at the time, and just said "to hell with it," but when she called, I wondered if I had made a mistake. The past few nights were lonely and boring in my apartment, and I found myself going out every night, just to be around people. Anybody. Didn't matter if I liked them or not. I even tolerated Raine and Natalie at Stooges one evening, Natalie giving me an earful about how tacky it was to break up with someone on their birthday.

So when Camryn said, "Come over tomorrow," my spirits lifted for a few seconds until she said, "I have some of your stuff." It felt like a sort of death march, finalizing shit. I hadn't even thought about getting my things back or returning any of hers. I'd only thought

103

about being free, yet being free wasn't what I wanted either. Not today anyway. Some people may call me hard to please. I thought it was pretty simple. I wanted what I wanted when I wanted it, and it may change from one day to the next, but I always knew what I wanted in that moment. Simple.

When I showed up at her house, she had a couple of bags of my stuff ready to go, but I didn't grab them and leave. I sat down to talk. "I'm sorry," I said, "about breaking up with you."

Then Camryn fell apart, going into a teary-eyed rant about never getting her fairytale, having to start all over and possibly never seeing her 50th wedding anniversary. I was a sucker for mush like that too, but it rarely showed on the outside. My mind kept it hidden within my soul where it only did me any good and no one else. Camryn handed me my house key, returning it again. I wished it was a key to my heart that would let all the goodness on the inside come out—a key that would open the door between my world and everyone else's so we could live in the same space. But it was just a key to my apartment, effectively shutting her out in both my realities. Her returning the key felt like a nail in my coffin, but I didn't let on. Even though I hadn't thought it through, I'd asked for this.

I pulled a tissue from the box on the table and handed it to her, offering a semblance of support. She dabbed her eyes and whispered, "I wish you loved me," but I told myself I didn't hear her correctly. It was easier that way.

* * *

For the next week and a half I pretended I was fine without Camryn. I'd heard some geek had asked her out. Rather than being happy for her, I found myself wishing the geek would drop dead, and I was relieved that rumor was, she'd turned him down. I called Casey, went out for drinks with her and some frat brothers, but never asked her back to my place. We actually studied at the library together, a place that typically made my skin crawl, but I'd aced my Calc III midterm and was determined to give Dr. Brewster a reason to believe in me. Somebody had to. But when Deidre asked if I'd called Courtney, I found myself wanting to call Camryn. And when I came across Courtney's phone number on the kitchen counter, I stopped for a minute, remembering we'd had a fun night out and thought about giving her a call. Instead, I threw her number into the junk drawer.

Then, the night Jason called everything changed.

"It's a boy!" Jason yelled into the phone. "Man, I can't believe I'm a dad."

"Congrats, man," I said, sharing in his joy, wanting some of that joy for my own. Who was I kidding? There wasn't anyone I'd rather share the joy of parenthood with other than Camryn, and the only way I'd have a family of my own with her was to patch things up. I'd try again.

Camryn answered the door wearing a towel. She opened the door, turned, and headed back to her room to change into some clothes, leaving me to let myself in. I sat on the floor in front of a couch I'd never seen before.

"I saw you at the party last night," I yelled.

"Yeah, I saw you too."

I took that as a good sign; at least she'd noticed me. At the party she looked like she was having a great time, even had a beer in hand, which I'd never seen her do before. After I thought about it, I wondered if she was as miserable as I was. Sure there were sorority girls crawling all over the place, but most of them gave off the "sleaze vibe." Even though I wished Camryn partied more, I didn't want a sleaze to mother my children. She was good and wholesome and honest. I loved that about her.

Camryn walked out wearing jeans and a T-shirt, combing her still-wet hair. She sat on the floor beside me, and all I wanted to do was kiss her and make love to her right then and there. I told her about Jason and the baby, looking her in the eyes and holding back my own tears for possibilities I had thrown away.

"I know I've made some mistakes," I said, "and I'm sorry."

Camryn began to cry.

Oh, great. I came over to patch things up and all I managed to do was make her cry again. I pressed on with the apology and reconciliation. "I was wondering if you'd have dinner with me. We could try this thing again."

Camryn didn't answer. She hugged me for what seemed like forever, and I liked that. Very much. I took that as a "yes."

CHAPTER 9 - GLENN

"TWA is interviewing on campus. You should go," I said to Camryn.

She named off five lame reasons why she shouldn't bother, including an internship she had lined up that required she be in school.

"Do you want to be in school your whole life?" I asked. "It won't hurt to go and interview." She could have graduated that December, but "reenlisted" because her only viable meal ticket at the time was a paid internship with Meeting Planners International.

I could think of nothing worse than being in school longer than you had to. Taking Calc III three times sucked, but the third time was a charm and I came out with an A. That A made the pain worth it, but I still hated every minute. The whole purpose of suffering through was to get out there and get a real job, a real good-paying job. I was still in school for three reasons, 1) I loved airplanes, and I knew this was the only way I was going to get my dream job working with them. 2) I changed majors part way through college, extending my sentence. I had learned that brainiac aerospace engineering behind a desk was boring compared to hands-on aircraft maintenance engineering where I could actually touch a plane. And 3) Camryn helping me see it through. I loved that about her. Without her, I didn't know where I'd be, and I hated to think about it. She'd talked me out of quitting school more than once. At times, I'd thought of being a truck driver, alone on the open road, no one to piss off or inadvertently hurt, yet I hated being alone. I hated being alone so much that I'd even go to the grocery store for groceries I didn't need just to be around people. I hated being alone more than I hated the risk of screwing up someone's life, and deep down, this was the tap root of my commitophobia (at least that's what Camryn called it). The "once bitten, quadruple shy" was the other reason and the only reason Camryn was aware of. I kept these fears to myself. I didn't need anyone leading me off to get my head examined or some quack telling me what was wrong. I got enough of that for free— you're lazy, you're stupid, you're crazy. I didn't need to pay anyone to dish it out.

Camryn went to the TWA interview in a navy blue skirt and a white blouse. She looked professional, maybe a little school-marmish, but professional and that's what counted.

"So, how'd it go?" I asked as soon as I spotted her in the student lounge.

"If you graduated Parks and breathed, you were good. He said he'd be in touch."

"If he's not back with you in a week, call him," I said. It was always good to follow up on a hot lead, not let it get away. That's how I'd landed a few jobs, although a couple of employers told me they'd hired me, so I'd quit bugging them. Persistence pays off is how I viewed it.

But Camryn didn't follow up at all, content to do her thing with the Meeting Planners internship, setting up trade shows and stuff. So when opportunity strikes . . .

"You can get us free tickets, right?" I asked Camryn as she typed the umpteenth term paper for me.

She looked at me like I'd grown a third horn (obviously adding to my devilish charm). "Does Schnucks give its employees free groceries?" she answered, going there again, answering a question with a question, which she should have known pissed me off. How much more confusing can you get? Some people might speak that "dodge the point" language, but I was a linear kind of guy. In my book, answering a question that way was just wrong. And frustrating.

"No. What's your point?" I said, all three horns glowing red, not at all charming anymore.

Camryn said something about not being annoying, something I ignored.

"Fine. Don't ask. You're cutting yourself short." I knew she deserved at least free tickets as a bonus, with all the extra work she put in. Ask and ye shall receive.

*　*　*

"What the hell, Camryn," I said, seriously wondering where she was going, leaving me lying naked and hard as a rock on the couch. Yeah, I'd had a few beers. Yeah, she was crying, and I didn't know why, but still. "Get back here."

Camryn wiped under her eyes and returned, lowering herself onto me, picking up where we left off minus the dirty talk part. I'd asked her to talk dirty to me and, well, she sucked at it. "Come on, it isn't hard," I'd said, meaning talking dirty, not my dick, because *it* was, "Just say a few words. It turns me on."

She tried, taking forever to spit it out, ruining the mood I'd had playing in my mind. She'd never make it as a phone sex operator, which was good because I wouldn't want her to. But for me? She couldn't even do it for me?

"Don't you love me?" I asked. That's when she really lost it. The stilted expression that had been on her face, as though she had been enduring something, turned into full blown tears. Why was she so pent up? Why couldn't she just enjoy things? She got off of me, looking like she'd head straight for the door, but couldn't, not wearing a thing. I'd gotten her shirt off her earlier, talking her into posing for a few shots for my camera. I always had to talk her into stuff. She never jumped right in, suggesting anything fun and kinky herself, so I encouraged her. I encouraged these things all the time, but I encouraged more when I was drunk. The only reason she was even at my place was because I'd called her up, drunk after a party that she didn't want to go to. She didn't want to come over after I'd gotten back either, but I'd encouraged that too. "Come on, you're no fun," I'd said, playfully. "I miss you. Please. Do you love me?" That's all it took. And I did miss her. I'd wished she had partied with me, so I didn't need to call, but I didn't press her on that one. I pressed her on other stuff. She was too reserved for her own good.

I passed out after that, and in the morning when I woke, Camryn was gone.

*   *   *

"I got the job! I got the job! I got the job!" Camryn yelled into the phone a few days later, nearly blasting my ear off. I loved hearing her so excited, but I had no idea what job she was talking about, forgetting about

110

that four-month-old interview. I knew it was big news because it takes a lot to get that sort of reaction out of her. And this big news seemed to have erased any lingering unease from the morning she'd up and disappeared. I'd apologized for being drunk, but I'm not sure my apology had been accepted and turned into forgiveness for the entire drunken evening. At any rate, I was glad for the diversion and good news about this scheduling job with TWA. I was happy for her. Happy for us.

"I knew you could do it!"

Later, we sat around the dinner table with Camryn's father and Jo, her stepmom, discussing Camryn's new position. They happened to be in town visiting when the good news broke.

"Will you stay in town?" Jo asked.

Jo's question scared the holy crap out of me. I'd never entertained that the job offer might be for a job out of town. Panic flashed through me. What would I do if she left? "The job is in St. Louis, isn't it?" I asked, almost out of breath.

Thank God she answered, "Yes. The job's here."

"Good. You won't have to go," I said, the relief obvious in my voice. I squeezed her thigh under the table, just above the knee, willing loving vibes into her. I wanted her to know I didn't want to lose her.

Crisis averted, the next order of business came up which had nothing to do with anything we'd been talking about, but it lodged in my head and I felt compelled to say it. "About the Greek formal," I said and then explained the frat rules as I understood them: you had to be in a fraternity or sorority to attend.

"You're going stag then, since I'm not allowed to go?" Camryn asked. The pendulum in her mood shifted. One minute happier than I'd ever seen and the next, almost bitter. God, she was moody.

"I was thinking of taking Casey."

Camryn looked like she was about to pass out, probably from not saying what was pent up in her mind. I quickly said, "Only because she's Greek." I held my hands out and shrugged an apology, since technically this wasn't my fault, and I could do nothing about it. I had to go, couldn't let my brothers down.

* * *

Camryn had to quit the internship and get her diploma in order to accept the TWA position. She awed me, graduating with two degrees, half way through a third, while I schlepped through one. She was someone I admired, and I loved that about her.

To celebrate her new job, Camryn invited me out for beer and chicken wings, a favorite staple of ours, her treat. "You know we wouldn't be here right now celebrating if you hadn't made me go to that interview," she said.

I hadn't thought of it that way at all. I'd always thought it was all her. She got the good grades; she was poised for the interview and projected herself, and she graduated. I'd only mentioned the interviewers were on campus. Once I mulled it over, I saw it was true. She wouldn't have this job if it weren't for me, a crucial link the the chain. I felt good about that.

"Yeah, you owe me," I teased. I ordered the first pitcher of beer. "How many kids do you want?" I asked her, reaching under the table and touching her thigh, higher up this time.

Camryn went blue in the face. "What?"

"I was just wondering." I had been wondering. Now that Camryn was set with a job and I had my major sorted out, I'd thought about a future, although not until I graduated, which was still a couple of years off, so I didn't have to think too hard.

"No more than two," she said.

"I want three. Three times the fun!" Camryn turned blue again, but she was still smiling. We clinked our glasses together, while I signaled the waitress for another pitcher. I winked at Camryn. "There's power in threes."

I refilled Camryn's glass then whispered, "I have some good news. It's not a Greek-only formal. You can go!" With all the talk of future and children and the warm vibe of celebration, I reached behind Camryn's neck and pulled her face to mine, planting my chicken-wing lips all over hers, almost tasting the chicken wings she'd already eaten. We abused the alcohol, leaving the rest on the table going to waste. Camryn didn't need any encouragement from me. She placed her hand high on my thigh in the car, squeezing gently, tongued my tonsils once we parked, and pulled my hands to the buttons on her shirt while she undid mine in the living room, where we stayed, celebrating the rest of the night.

*   *   *

Camryn's car was a piece of shit. Yes, it ran, but not perfectly. It got her where she was going, but it had

113

some rust. New job. Cha ching! New car. "We're going car shopping," I said.

"I'm not ready."

"We'll just look around. See what's out there."

She agreed to just looking, but if she was anything like me, she'd be unable to resist, and buy in no time. I'd buy myself a new vehicle for a graduation present as soon as I got a new job. No doubt.

I took her to the Chevy dealer, looking at the Corvettes first.

"I don't want a Corvette," she said. Oh Lordy! Was she nuts? Everyone wants a Corvette.

We looked all around at the Corvettes anyway, me explaining all the features and what I'd like. She might not get one now, but I'd get one later.

"I want this one," she said after making another round of the dealerships on her own. She handed me an Acura brochure.

"Honda product. It's no good," I said. My uncle had one several years back, and it was nothing but trouble.

Camryn tried showing me a Consumer Reports on it, but I didn't need to bother.

"They suck," I said, resolute.

She tried every which way to get me to change my mind, showing me data, graphs, and articles. Then finally she got so fed up with me pushing a sports car and not giving her research the time of day, she threw the magazine at me at walked out. That got my attention. I had no clue she was that set on her Acura find. I thought she was being stubborn and not listening to me. But she didn't often blow up like that. In fact, she told me she's never gotten so mad like that with anyone until I came along. What a claim to fame . . . um, NOT. Well, she did say she'd hurled a Barbie at her sister once when they were little, but that was because her sister was being a total rag. Barbie's leg broke off at the hip.

I realized I must have screwed up big time. It would be nice if I could see the screw-ups coming, but again, Fate threw me in apology mode. This happened way more often than Fate granting me grace ahead of time. I took off out the door and past the cornfield looking for her on the neighborhood streets. I wasn't about to sit in the apartment waiting for her to come back. I had to *do* something. "I'm sorry," I said as soon as I found her.

She sniffed her tears away, nodded.

"We'll go see it tomorrow," I told her, hating to see her unhappy.

It turns out that the little Integra she picked out wasn't half bad. It wasn't bad at all. I actually liked it.

"Why'd you shoot it down before even giving it a chance?" Camryn asked me.

"I don't know. It's just what I thought." You only knew what you knew, and I knew I thought it sucked. There was only so much room in this brain for questioning things I already thought I had a handle on. Really, why waste the effort? But if I didn't have a handle on it, the questions came one after another. Some people said I asked questions like a kid who asks, "Why? Why? Why?" and that I was being annoying, but if I didn't understand, how else was I supposed to find out?

One time I was told I asked stupid questions. "It's common friggin' sense," they'd said. Maybe common to them, but not to me. I felt different. Unwanted is more the word. People are cruel whether they know it or not. My mom had said, "You're trying my patience!" My teachers and principals said, "You are trying my patience!" Camryn never said it, but she acted that way sometimes. How good does that feel, knowing you were put on this earth to try people's patience? It doesn't. It feels no good at all.

"How much for the car?" I asked, taking over negotiations. Negotiations were fun. It was like playing verbal "uncle." And when I played uncle, I always won. No mercy.

The car dealer shot back a price. I said, "Thirteen-five, spoiler and floor mats."

The dealer went to consult with his manager when I said to Camryn, "You have to play hardball. Get mad."

"Why are you telling me this?" Camryn asked, perplexed by my methods.

Without a thought I said, "So you're strong in case you need to handle things for the kids." Even after I said it, I still didn't think about what I had said. We'd never talked about kids anymore after chicken-wing night, and I figured if we continued on like we were, it'd probably happen someday, but I didn't see any reason to go into that now. Literally, it was not a conscious thought in my mind. Camryn had that blue look on her face again, but I chalked it up to first-new-car-buying nervousness. She was a wreck.

When the salesman said, "Sold," I felt let down. No haggling, no fighting back and forth. It was downright boring. He gave in too easy. There was nothing like a healthy discourse to fire up my usually sluggish brain. Sitting around having peaceful discussion was boring, boring, boring. The most entertaining thing that happened was watching Camryn shake with nervousness while signing the paperwork. Poor thing.

"Why would you want to fight?" Camryn asked when I explained my disappointment.

"It's fun," I said, big smile on my face at the thought.

Camryn looked at me like I'd grown the third horn back.

I'm not a hostile person, really. There's nothing worse than bad juju between friends, but sometimes people accuse me of arguing for arguing's sake and enjoying it, even calling me sadistic. My confrontational nature was like the moon producing werewolves, where the tame turn into out-of-control, seething monsters by night; only my internal moon didn't have a regular schedule. I didn't enjoy it, but I needed it; if I didn't get that rush, I didn't feel alive. I didn't *want* to hurt anyone. Heavens knows I knew what being hurt felt like, and I wouldn't wish it on anyone. At the same time, if some weakling couldn't take conflict, then too bad for them. I thrived on it, even prided myself on it, that I could take the heat others avoided.

*   *   *

Camryn had settled into her job and was making nice money for almost a year now even though she claimed that between her rent, car payment and gas, she had hardly anything left. Things would be easier on her if she wasn't so hell bent on saving ten percent for retirement. Already! Retirement was 40 years away. Hell, I could barely plan into next week. In my mind she had plenty if she could afford to save.

I, on the other hand, couldn't afford to save. I mean, how often do spring breaks come up? I wouldn't have the full college experience if I didn't do spring break. I set my sights on South Padre Island. Yeah, it cost me about $1000 and I was short on rent the next month and had to borrow from Camryn, but it was so worth it.

"Seriously," she said when I asked her for a loan. "You manage to go on spring break, but can't pay rent?"

"When will I ever get to do this again? You only live once," I explained.

The fraternity brothers and I had a great time down at the beach, drinking too much, chatting up girls. Some guys even brought the girls home then sent them away in the morning, but while I fell into bed alone, I missed Camryn instead of bagging some girl I just met. That's one thing I didn't like about the fraternity, how so many of them were unabashedly loose, but it didn't bother me enough to not hang out with them. We all had our weak spots, so who was I to call them out. Besides, watching everyone get stupid was fun.

I later found out that Deidre filled Camryn's head with a bunch of crap while I was away. It wasn't entirely untrue, but it was crap that happened over a year ago that didn't need to see the light of day.

"Who's Courtney?" Camryn asked.

"I don't know," I said, honestly not knowing who she was talking about.

Camryn got this look in her eye like she was taking in a pile of shit.

"You don't know?" she repeated and then added, "The girl you made out with two homecomings ago. You don't remember that?"

A blazing inferno flashed inside as I remembered exactly who Courtney was and what Deidre may have told her. Camryn pulled out a slip of paper, the one with Courtney's phone number on it. "Where'd you get that?" I asked like I had something to hide. I knew damn well where she'd gotten it—from my kitchen drawer where I just throw junk. I'd never used or planned on using it, but the "evidence" sure did upset Camryn, which upset me even more. Deidre, what a bitch!

She'd pay.

I don't know how I calmed the raging beast. Probably the prospect of losing Camryn jolted me into having sense enough to take the high road. Most of the time life was so boring that taking the low road was the easiest and most entertaining course of action. I functioned at a higher level when shit hit the fan, especially the one with extra turbo-boost.

"I kissed her, and it felt weird . . . . I never called her again," I said after Camryn pressed me for details. The hurt expression on her face worried me. I was afraid she would walk, and then what would I do? If the tables were turned, I wouldn't have listened to a word I had to say. I'd have just left, no questions asked. Amongst my worry, a moment of rage flashed back toward Deidre. I felt my fists clench.

"Deidre said you made out," Camryn said calmly, like she'd exorcised her demons about it and was merely taking care of business.

"It was more than one little kiss," I admitted, "but it wasn't right. It wasn't you."

Coming clean worked wonders. Forgiveness is a well-oiled machine when you admit the deed instead of fight it. Camryn still had some warming up to do, but at least she was still there, still forgiving me; I know I required more than my fair share.

There was no way Deidre was going to get away with what she had done. No way. I pulled up to the apartment where she lived, ready to rip her head off, and then beat her with it. On my way up the sidewalk, I ran into Raine. "Get out of my way, you fucking bastard," I seethed, deserved or not. He was in my way. He deserved it.

"Fuck you too, man," he said. "You're crazy."

I stopped in my tracks, taking the same low road Raine frequented. "What I am is none of your business," I said into Raine's face as I grabbed him up by the shirt collar. I shoved him into the apartment wall.

I didn't wait for Deidre to invite me in when I knocked on her door. She answered and I stormed through into her living room, shouting. "You had no fucking right to tell Camryn about some shit that happened two fucking years ago. Who the hell do you think you are?" I said, yelling at her until she backed into a wall and couldn't go any further.

Deidre opened her mouth to answer.

"Shut up," I yelled. "It was your fault in the first place, introducing us. Camryn almost *left* me because of you." I pinned Deidre to one spot, my arms on either side of her head, my hands flat against the wall. Ronin hadn't made an appearance, and I didn't care if he did. "You are a no-good little snob. It's no wonder Ronin was drunk and nearly backed out on your wedding day. How could he stand a bitch like you? Huh?

Answer me!" I screamed into her face, almost making my voice hoarse.

"I thought you were broken up at the time," Deidre tried to explain. "I thought Camryn knew what happened, and you patched things up. I wanted her advice." Tears ran down Deidre's face. Good. That bitch needed to feel some pain too.

"Well, that's what you get for thinking, you moron. Think a little harder next time if your shit for a brain can even handle it," I said, the demon inside of me helping the words along. "If Camryn leaves me, *you* are going to be responsible, and I won't be as nice next time." I knew I wasn't being nice now, and I had no intention of being nice, but I wanted her to get my point loud and clear. I wanted to hit her. Slap her into the next apartment, but I didn't hit girls, so I pulled one hand back and put my fist through the wall instead, right next to her face. Deidre screamed. And cried. Her wedding picture fell from its hook, the glass shattering into a thousand pieces from the impact. I didn't care. My hand throbbed, but I didn't care about that either. I left without another word, slamming the door behind me, sending another memory shattering all over the floor.

*   *   *

"Deidre told me you went to see her today," Camryn said.

I had no interest in talking about it, so I continued watching TV, trying to pacify her with a "yeah." It didn't work.

"She said you made her cry."

"She deserved it," I said, cold and bitter. Forgiveness hadn't even entered my mind. "Look, what she did pissed me off. I don't want to lose you. I love you."

Camryn took my hand, saying nothing. Then she looked into my eyes with that same 4th-of-July gaze. It dawned on me then, what I had just said. "I love you" had spontaneously slipped off my tongue, but this time instead of loathing myself for letting it slip, I let it hang there, because deep down, I meant it.

"That was two years ago. I wouldn't leave for something that happened . . . back then," she said.

Forgiveness wasn't something I was well versed in. Camryn overflowed with it. I loved that about her.

"You love me?" she asked.

"I've loved you for a long time," I finally admitted aloud, and after the expression on Camryn's face, I wondered what took me so long. Twinkles lit up Camryn's eyes like she'd gotten long-awaited-for confirmation of what she'd suspected, but it was more than that; it was like we were meant to be.

CHAPTER 10 - CAMRYN

I hadn't mentioned this before because I didn't think it was important, and then later, I was too traumatized by it all and wanted to forget. When life dishes it out, there's only so much you can regurgitate from memory, reliving it, before going full-blown crazy.

Natalie and Raine announced their engagement in the fall of '92. I'll admit I was more than a tad bit jealous. Raine treated her like she was the Queen of England herself, always respectful and adoring. He'd do anything for her. No doubt Natalie came first with him.

Things with Glenn and I were much better ever since he finally admitted to loving me and started acting more like it, but the overt adoration and respect wasn't there like it was with those two. I figured they were the exception and not the rule and that I shouldn't expect exceptional. It wasn't realistic in my mind at the time.

Natalie's mother came as soon as she heard the news. "He's gorgeous, Nat," her mother said in front of the both of them. "If I was twenty years younger, I'd collect him for myself." She pinched his cheek then gave him a motherly congratulatory hug, welcoming him to the family.

"Thank you Mrs. T.," Raine said.

"Oh, call me Prudence, Raine."

She didn't say call me mom or anything else, just Prudence. I thought to myself it was funny her initials were PT, like the the strip club down the street. And from the looks of her, and her suggestive remarks about Raine, I wondered if it might fit. I also wondered how Natalie turned out to be so nice. Maybe she was a savage in the bedroom, but she was too much of a lady to divulge behind-closed-door secrets. Her mother had the flamboyance of a '50s movie starlet; the only thing missing, the long cigarillo with cream-colored filter on the end.

"Come dear," Natalie's mom said, tugging her elbow toward the door. "Your dress will be exquisite."

Nat and her mom planned an all-day, all-night shopping spree, preparing for the upcoming nuptials. Natalie let out a nervous giggle when her mother suggested stopping at Frederick's for a wedding-night negligée. I guess some moms were game and hip like that and more power to them; I couldn't imagine it with mine.

Glenn headed out for the night, "Guy stuff," he had said, which was fine. I usually found plenty to do while he was away, but that night, I was flat-out bored. I picked up the phone and called Raine, something I'd almost never done. He was always nice to me, and I admired him for being that "real man" for Natalie. He was the whole package, smart, funny, polite. He was the kind of guy, well, he kind of reminded me of Reese in those ways. "Raine, it's Camryn. What'cha doing tonight?" I asked, trying not to look desperate for company.

"Nothing. I'm just sitting here watching TV."

"Well, come watch it with me. Glenn's out. Natalie's out. And we're bored. Might as well be bored together," I said.

"Yeah, be there in a few."

Raine came in, made himself comfortable on the couch.

"You want some cheesecake? I just made it."

"Sure," he said, flipping channels like a typical man.

I plated a serving for each of us, handed him his slice and then settled in on a chair.

"Oh, yum, chocolate," he said. "I see why Glenn keeps you around."

I gave him a dirty look.

"I didn't mean it that way," he said, backpedaling. "I mean, this is great cheesecake. You should go into business or something."

"Thanks." We fell silent, staring at the television and stuffing our faces.

"I need your advice, Camryn," Raine said. I figured he'd ask something about Natalie or the wedding, but instead he threw me a lefty. "I found a gun."

My eyes bugged out of my head, and my mouth turned down into a fearful grimace, not knowing what to say.

"It was under the floor mat of one of the rental cars I was cleaning out," he explained, "and I kept it. Enterprise doesn't need to know, but maybe I should turn it in to the police."

"Was it loaded?"

"It had some ammo."

His answer sent a shiver through me. "Maybe you should turn it in. You know, it might have been used in a crime or something."

"Yeah, I thought of that, but I don't want to get into trouble. I mean, I've had it for a couple of weeks now."

"Does Natalie know?"

"No, I haven't told anyone."

Why he decided I was a safe confessional, I have no clue, but there it was, laid on me like a sworn secret.

"Don't tell anyone," he said.

"I won't." Not only wouldn't I because he asked, but I wouldn't tell because I didn't want to get involved. This was too scary and none of my business.

We spent the rest of the night discussing their wedding plans and where he was whisking her away for their honeymoon. "I'm taking her to Fiji," Raine said. I wondered where he got the money for that *and* her huge rock, but I didn't ask. I was sure his job at Enterprise didn't pay *that* well.

"I'm so lucky," he said. "Natalie is my dream girl. I know that sounds mushy, but it's true. I couldn't imagine anyone better."

"I'm glad for you," I said, really meaning it. They worked well together. They fit, like whipped cream on a Starbucks Mocha. Both great on their own, but phenomenal together.

A couple hours after Raine left, Glenn called, checking up on me, inviting me over. He'd had a bit to drink, but not too much like he had sometimes, and when I told him I'd just see him in the morning, he didn't beg. "I'll see you tomorrow then," he said.

"Love you," I said.

"Love you too."

I didn't tell him about having Raine over to the house. In a way I felt guilty, like enjoying another guy's company was wrong, but he was my best friend's fiancé. *My* friend. I didn't feel the need to tell.

CHAPTER 11 - GLENN

Ever since I'd "let it all hang out" so to speak, openly declaring my love and letting myself buy into it this time, I felt free. And the ironic thing is that I called Camryn more than ever, even at work.

"Dinner tonight?" I asked when she picked up the phone.

"Love some."

"I'll pick you up at six," I said. I had ulterior motives and made sure we ate out at the mall, so we could "accidentally" go window shopping after dinner, even stop by some jewelers. I'd looked on my own, trying to be sneaky about the whole thing, but I didn't know what type of ring she wanted, let alone her ring size.

After dinner I said, "Let's take a walk."

"On The Landing?" she asked, suddenly horrified I'd want to walk outside in the winter. She froze even thinking about it.

"No, right here. Walk around the mall."

"I don't have any money," she said. "The last time we did this you talked me into a new pair of shoes."

I hadn't remembered that. Instead of disputing it, distracted by my other task at hand, I said, "I won't talk you into anything. This time." I knew myself well enough that talking people into things was my norm, a gift, if you will. I should have gone into sales, but unless you were selling race cars or Harleys, sales sounded a bit boring.

"Thank you," she said with too much relief. In my view, her relief was disproportionate to the promise. I filed that away in my head, leaving it there for safekeeping. Sometimes the things I filed away in my head for safekeeping got misplaced. They weren't lost though; they were still in there. I just couldn't locate and use them. It sucked. Forget things, lose things — different disgusting fruits on the same f'd-up tree.

"Let's go in here," I said, pulling her into Zales.

"What are we in here for?" Camryn said, heading to the opal section, her favorite.

"We're looking at diamonds today. Just in case."

"What? Just in case we *have* to get married?" Camryn said, attempting a joke. Her jokes usually weren't funny, especially this one.

"That won't happen. Just look," I said, steering her by the shoulders to the wedding-set section.

I was no secret-keeper. I tried, but when things were extra juicy, they came spilling out. Some people called that poor self-control or even inconsiderate. I called it exhilarating, and I honestly could not help it although most people didn't believe me about that fine detail. They said I was being manipulative and making lame excuses even though I was telling the truth. Sometimes people purposely didn't share things with me because of my "diarrhea mouth." Then I'd feel left out which made me feel even worse because I liked to be part of the group, especially the group "in the know." To me it was exciting. My middle-name letter should've been "E" for Excitement, which would've been much better than Failure. It was weird though, because when I was in the Navy I kept those Top Secret secrets secret. No problem. I guess there was something compelling about being charged with treason and being thrown in the brig that kept those secrets safe with me. That, and honor. Not that I didn't think other kinds of honor weren't important; it just wasn't compelling enough glue to keep my trap shut. I realize it doesn't make any sense, but it wouldn't be the first or one-hundredth time someone said, "You don't make any sense" to me. After a while I numbed to it, at least on the outside. Inside, it was like when the dentist puts that nasty pasty shit with the horrible smell on your gum to numb it for the needle. When he jabs it in, it still hurts like hell. Only my mental Novocain needle was empty. It poked around, hurting on the inside and sure as hell didn't offer any relief.

Camryn looked at me wide-eyed, like she couldn't believe we were looking at diamonds together.

"I just want to know what you like," I said, trying to cover up the obvious. It was obvious to me, but she held back, like she thought it was too good to be true.

"Let's see that one," I said to the saleslady. I pointed to a 2-carat stone that caught my eye.

"That's too big," Camryn said, bending around, trying to eyeball the price tag.

"Try it on," I said.

She didn't even want to, knowing the price was too high, but I made her try it on anyway.

"It's too big," she said again while holding her hand out in front of her, watching it sparkle.

"You don't like it?" I asked, finding it hard to believe a girl wouldn't like such a rock.

Later she told me that "don't like" and "price too high" were virtually synonymous with her, but to me, there was a huge difference, two completely separate issues, and I never did comprehend or accept her take on it. Maybe if I had, instead of questioning her every time, we would have gotten along better, but I couldn't help the urge to dissect her opinions thoroughly so I truly understood them—another truth no one believed. It drove me nuts not to understand something, and it appeared to drive other people nuts having to explain "the obvious" to me. It was a serious point of contention. My probes for answers mirrored back as "impatient asshole behavior," people blowing me off because they were exhausted with my incessant questions. Some said I should have been a lawyer because I asked questions "prosecution style." One time Camryn said "prosecution style" was an understatement; it was more like "execution style," but I didn't see it that way. I certainly didn't want to execute anyone. I only wanted to understand, and have understanding. But how could I explain to others, what I couldn't explain to myself?

We narrowed the ring selections down to two that we both liked. At least I could make the final decision, and it would still be somewhat of a surprise. I had her go through the ritual at a few more jewelry stores even though I'd already made up my mind at the first— more secrecy and suspense. Every selection Camryn made was a non-traditional, asymmetric design, the gold or stone arrangement slightly twisted. I'm glad she liked things that way.

I went back the next day, putting a down payment on the ring. I would have liked to have gotten her a bigger diamond, but she insisted it was big enough, which was a good thing because the first time I looked at the price was when I went to buy. I nearly choked.

Thank God for layaway. The only reason I didn't propose the next night was because it turned out I had to make payments and couldn't take possession for a while.

I called up some of my Blues buddies, asking if they needed extra help the next weekend, a couple long shifts on contract would take care of the balance.

"I'm glad you called, Glenn," Blakely said. "Two guys just bailed on me. Those two equal one of you. Sure, love to have you."

Made me feel good, what he said. It gave me a boost and made me feel like I was good at something. Some people regularly know when they do a good job, but a reliable, built-in self-congratulator must have been on backorder when God made me, and then he forgot to retrofit. Or did God make me? Sometimes I thought I was demon spawn. Anyway, I needed those missing self-congratulations—from outside of myself.

The day I paid off and picked up the ring, I called Camryn at work. I couldn't wait. "Dinner tonight?"

"You're taking me out?" she asked, already surprised.

Thanksgiving Eve might not be the most common night for a night out, but then again, it might be for an engagement, turkeys being the theme and all . . . and biting the dust. After Camryn explained her unusual carpool arrangements for the holiday—the hourly workers spending the afternoon at the bar where she'd have to meet her ride—we agreed I'd pick her up at quarter to six.

"Love you," I said, brimming over inside, feeling like I was *this close* to winning a prize.

Camryn wore her brown leather jacket, neatly tapered at the waist over her work clothes to dinner. Perfect for Paqueños. We lucked out. Not only was it the perfect setting for my big plans, but they also had an all-you-can-eat crab special. I couldn't have planned it better if I tried. The extent of my plans was to make reservations because I hated waiting in lines.

Camryn laid into a crab claw, pulling out the meat, getting her fingers messy with melted butter and crab juice. She wasn't afraid to get dirty, and I loved that about her.

I wiped my own crab fingers on the napkin on my lap, ready to do the deed. I reached into my inner jacket pocket and said, "I need to ask you something."

"What's that?" Camryn asked, intent on her crab, oblivious to the jillion nerves pulsating through me.

"I was wondering if you'd marry me." I guess that didn't exactly come out as a question, but I didn't want to do the same thing everyone else does, and that's all I could come up with on the fly.

Camryn freaked, recognizing the ring we'd picked out together. "Yes," she said. I knew she would. She'd been hinting around about it for years.

I reached for her hand, slipped the diamond on up to the knuckle where it got stuck. Awkward. Camryn offered to help, rescuing me, for which I was grateful. "Here, I'll do it," she said, twisting the ring slightly and then on the rest of the way. She held her hand out, admiring her engagement ring as our waiter walked up with two glasses of champagne already poured. I'd planned that too. I wouldn't forget the celebratory booze. "A toast," I said, raising my glass to hers.

"When did you decided to marry me?" she asked after downing half her champagne.

"When I was on spring break," I said.

She looked at me funny, again. "What took you so long?"

"No rush," I said, still elated that I'd managed to surprise her.

I usually rushed into everything, wanting everything now, and not wanting to wait: my first marriage, signing for my car before figuring out how to make ends meet, committing myself to every club, sport, and party that came along without realizing there wasn't enough time in the day. Then I'd have to do damage control, which took up even more time, but I never learned my lesson, and I'd do it all over again. "Maddening" is what my mother had called it. Down the road, Camryn had other choice words.

And now I wanted to rush home to celebrate between the sheets or on the kitchen counter or maybe a little action in the car on the way home, but Camryn said, "I don't feel too good."

"Why not?" I asked. How could anyone not feel good on one of the most significant nights of their life?

"I think it's the champagne."

Camryn alternated between shades of red and green, like she was distressed and might actually barf.

"You just want to go home?"

"Yes. I'm sorry," Camryn said. She did the chameleon thing again, this time adding in "clammy" to her appearance. "I don't feel good."

We discovered a newly fallen snow when we left the building. I held Camryn's hand as we walked toward the car when she suddenly pulled away and heaved up dinner into a snow pile.

"I'm sorry," she said again, looking as if she'd faint.

We came back to my place where we snuggled on the couch, and I tucked her all in with a blanket, making her comfortable. She leaned into my shoulder and fell asleep. It was kind of like curling up with a warm, helpless puppy. If a guy had a mothering urge, I had one as I sat there stroking her hair, thinking the evening over.

"Way to start our new life," I whispered. It'd get better. I shoved away fleeting thoughts that this was an omen of things to come.

*   *   *

Camryn went full force on the wedding plans, even going to the library, of all places, for ideas. She and my mother shopped for fake flowers, assembling them at the kitchen table while chitchatting like they were mother and daughter of the year. Then the phone rang, interrupting the whole thing.

"The what?" I said into the receiver. "The who?" I asked, not fully comprehending the most unbelievable message I'd ever heard. "What burned?"

"What burned?" Camryn echoed, pestering me while I was trying to hear.

I shooed Camryn away, paying close attention to the phone call then hung up. "Our church burned down. Electrical fire. Total loss." I wanted to run up there right away to see for myself and was frustrated with Camryn when she couldn't see the importance of heading right over. She wanted to finish up the flowers instead. "Flowers can wait," I said, leaving her no choice but to go with me.

"We could rent a tent," Camryn said as we looked over the rubble of what *was* going to be our wedding venue.

"I'm not getting married in a tent," I said. Our wedding day was supposed to be the most beautiful day of our lives, and I was going to see to it that it was. Clear open sunshine would be better than the innards of a tent. Camryn didn't agree and kept getting upset with me when I insisted on the most beautiful arrangement possible, even calling me selfish, but I was only thinking of her when I said that our guests could stand for an hour in the heat for *our* wedding. So what? We'd have great pictures and great memories, ugly tent not included.

Our wedding plans went downhill from there, and it's a wonder we had a formal wedding at all. Camryn's parents kicked in what they could, but her mother put up a stink about serving alcohol at the reception, pissing me off and upsetting Camryn. Camryn later told me she felt like she had to take sides, siding with me even though she didn't care whether we had alcohol or not.

"We should have eloped," I said after we dropped the last of the invitations in the mail. I don't know why I said it because I didn't mean it at all.

"I thought about it," Camryn said, quite seriously, taking me aback.

When the wedding did come, I thanked God we didn't elope. Camryn walked down the aisle. My hands broke into a sweat. She looked like a Barbie, and I was thrilled to show her off and couldn't be more proud to marry her and call her mine. Score!

I looked over the crowd. Everyone we invited seemed to be in attendance. Even Natalie showed up. I was half-surprised because I made it clear her other half was not welcome. No Raine at my wedding. No siree. Camryn wasn't happy about that, but, after all, it was my wedding too.

The minister said, "Repeat after me," and I parroted back all the words, but my mind was abuzz and I couldn't tell you what I'd just said. All I knew was that I loved her and wanted to honor and cherish her until death do us part. That was my honest intention.

Taking wedding pictures in the summer sun just about did me in. All I wanted to do was to get out of the tux and into my wife. It felt good to say—wife. My wife. That means I was her husband. I was somebody. I could do this.

At the reception, Jason proposed a toast, "To Glenn and Camryn." Everyone clinked glasses. "Glenn, I'm happy you found someone to trust." He could say that again. Camryn was indeed someone I could trust— trust to be loyal and trust with my life. I loved that about her.

*　　*　　*

I hit the books the Monday after our wedding, on the home stretch toward graduation. A few weeks later, when it came, it was like heaven and earth moved. When I floated across the stage, proudly wearing my graduation cap and gown, Dr. Brewster held up the show, making a special point to give me a congratulatory hug. "No regrets," she whispered into my ear, pulled back, looked me in the eyes and then embraced me again saying, "You'll do great things." She moved to hugging me 'round the shoulders, addressing the crowd. "Let's hear it for Glenn F. Conroy!" Applause and wolf whistles filled the air, nearly bringing tears to my eyes. Dr. Brewster belted my name out again, "Glenn Fantastic Conroy!" she said, sending a jolt through my heart. I marched off the stage, more proud of myself than I had ever been, sought Camryn in the crowd and gave her two thumbs up, which she returned with a look of pride, and relief, on her face.

* * *

"I got a job!" I said to Camryn, ready to celebrate. It had been a rough few months dinking around at an aircraft mechanic job since graduation. But this was a real, professional, engineering job at XB Aerospace. The interview was a cinch. Chat up a fellow alum at a bar one night, and voila: job landed. "Let's go celebrate."

I took her to the 94th Aero Squadron, the same bar where I'd secured my new position. "This is so awesome," Camryn said, proud of me. She was already making calculations, appropriating my future paychecks, figuring out how we could buy a house, save for retirement. I loved that about her, planning for and securing our future. Someone had to do it.

After another beer and another toasting to our good fortune, the bill from dinner arrived. Camryn nearly keeled over, but I didn't care what it cost. This was a celebration.

When my first paycheck came in, I wanted to celebrate that too. Camryn put on the brakes, much to my disgusted surprise. "Why not? How many first paychecks do you get to celebrate?"

Then Camryn went into some confusing, lengthy spiel about having charged the first celebration and now having to pay the piper or some other shit like that. Whatever. Talk about a wet dishrag. Maybe she was concerned about our finances, but did she have to be so extreme? All her rambling on about a budget did was piss me off. But Camryn was all into *planning*, which was good in theory. In practice, it sucked shit.

"Why are you doing this to me?" she cried out, crumpled up on her knees, pulling her fists through her hair. This was after I told her that if it wasn't for her, I'd be saving for an airplane instead of a house, and that marriage was about give and take and she wasn't giving enough by controlling the budget to stuff just *she* wanted. Yeah, she babbled about paying rent and student loans and griped about me spending a twenty here and there on whiskey. "I thought you wanted to save for a house too," she said, mystified, tears streaming down her cheeks. "You're such a Jekyll-Hyde!" Camryn threw her hands in the air.

"I said I wanted a house. I didn't say I wanted to save for one," I clarified, not sure why I'd have to do so when it was already crystal clear.

"How the hell do you get a house if you don't save for one?" she asked, quite nastily, I might add.

"I don't know. You want a house so bad, you figure it out." I was done with her nonsense, and by that time, I didn't want to celebrate. That first paycheck was a downer if I'd ever seen one. How ironic. Then somehow the ruined evening became all my fault, again, but I wasn't having it. There was no way in hell this could have been all my fault. It takes two. What I didn't know, was which two.

CHAPTER 12 – GLENN

"They want me to get a top secret clearance!" I said to Camryn, handing her the paperwork. Top secret meant I was important. I was someone. Top secret also meant a ton of paperwork in triplicate five times over. Camryn was so much better at that sort of thing; it was only natural I give the papers to her. I didn't even think to ask. After all, she was my wife—my other half.

I loved my job. There couldn't have been a more exciting job, working with airplanes. And the aerospace community was small, like family. You never knew who you might run into. Zac had gotten on at XB too.

Camryn asked me a bunch of questions from the form. "Your mother's birthdate."

"May 4th," I said, proud of myself for remembering.

"Year. I need the year too," Camryn said, exasperated.

"I don't know. I don't even know how old she is. About—" I said, thinking, "—about fifty-seven I think."

"Forget it. I'll call her and ask," Camryn said, moving on. "Your first wife's birthday."

Geez. "Hell if I know," I said. It felt like thistles were poking me from the inside out, and then my head started to pound. Was this ghost from the past always going to haunt me? "It's all in the file," I finally said, referring to the place where our important documents were stored, annoyed.

Camryn flinched. "It's no picnic for me either," she muttered.

My first thought was that she was a screwball, and what did picnics have to do with anything? Then I had presence of mind enough to run it through my interpreter and realize she was using another one of her stupid, confusing, and annoying expressions. I wondered, again, why she couldn't speak plain English and make things easier on the both of us.

*　*　*

Shortly after our first anniversary, when we ended up feeding stale cake to ducks on the river, my clearance came through. Camryn was elated that along with it came a raise, and we could finally build a house of our own. I still had pangs of wanting my own airplane, but she had a point: we can't live in an airplane. So to make her happy, I jumped in with full force, making sure everything was perfect. I wanted to make her happy. Seeing her happy made me happy too.

I wanted the bigger, roomier, and more expensive home. We'd be more comfortable there.

"This other one's fine," Camryn said. "It's twice as big as our apartment."

"But this one has even more space," I argued. "I only want to do this once."

Camryn started in again with her budget, bean-counter business. Blah, blah, blah. Who cares? I'd get another raise next year and it'd all work out. She had a good job. I had a good job. Finally, after she was being all stubborn about it, I said, "I won't be happy in the smaller one." That shut her up and made her see things my way. I mean, she got to live in it too, so it's not like it was just for me. Plus, I really wanted an airplane, not a house, so I was already giving in. Give and take.

After we signed the papers and finalized the house plans, I reached my arms around Camryn's waist, sliding my hands south.

"Not tonight," she said. She may as well have stabbed me right through the heart with a sword. I thought she'd be happy. I just signed for a house that she wanted, and she didn't even want to celebrate with me? Didn't want to give me what I wanted, which was to be close to my wife?

"Fine," I grumbled. I left her alone. When I glanced back, I saw her with her head in her hands. I think she was crying, but for the life of me, I couldn't figure out why. She made no sense at all. She was difficult, but I still loved her. She was lucky to have me because a lot of men wouldn't put up with that shit. I'd seen my uncle raise his hand to my aunt plenty of times for less, but that was just wrong. I'd never raise my hand to her. I patted myself on the back that I at least *knew* right from wrong.

We visited the building site every day. "Contractors, can't trust 'em," I told Camryn. And it was a good thing we went every day too, because they'd already screwed up the size of our basement window. Sure, it wasn't a huge screw up, but on principle, I reamed Mr. Reynolds a new asshole, making sure he knew the customer was always right. Actually, I was doing him a favor because if I made him do it right, then he'd have more business because his reputation would be in good standing.

At one point, Camryn took their side about changing the window. "It'll cost them a lot to change it now, and probably delay closing," she said.

Who did she think she was? She was supposed to be my *wife*, supporting *me*. I felt betrayed, but she didn't see that at all. What frickin' blinders did she have on? She went on about being reasonable and compromising, and mistakes or *misunderstandings* happening. She was getting things all twisted up in her mind, which really surprised me because normally, she's so smart. She's the one who needed to be reasonable and see that they clearly weren't delivering the end product they said they would, a three by four window, not a four by three. She's the one who needed to learn to stand up for herself. "Dammit, Camryn, whose side are you on, anyway?" I yelled, trying to make the error of her ways clear, but instead of going on the full-on attack with me, she mousied up and didn't say a word.

Being a man, giving into my wife's wishes, I finally let Mr. Reynolds off the hook about redoing the basement window, already poured in cement, but insisted on a free carpet upgrade for my trouble. I thought Camryn would be happy with that, but she clutched her arms to her ribcage, almost like she was comforting herself with a hug, rather than hugging me for saving the day.

"You gotta know how to deal," I told her on the way home. "They'll run all over you if you don't." She didn't say anything, but turned all green again in the passenger seat.

I certainly didn't want people running over my sweetie. She had to learn. But again, when we crawled into bed that night, instead of appreciating my genuine concern, she pushed me away, blaming it all on a headache again, but somehow it felt like she was blaming me.

*   *   *

Camryn had a freak out just before we moved. It was all over a stupid box that I'd opened while searching for my drafting pencils. Yeah, the box was all taped up, which I thought was kinda weird, and it said DO NOT OPEN all over it like a warning if it was opened some sort of evil spirit would come out and wreak havoc on the earth. But I wanted to find my pencils and didn't think much about what was written all over an old box.

"Why did you open this?" Camryn asked, all out of breath like she'd been punched in the stomach. She pointed to the open box.

What she was getting at didn't register at first. I'd been minding my own business for a change. Then I recalled that as I had dug through the box and found things from a time before me, I might have stumbled upon sacred ground and angered some kind of god. Love letters that I hadn't written left a bad feeling on my hands, like I had to wash it off. I stopped rummaging through and put everything away, not wanting to look anymore and certainly not finding my pencils. There was nothing of mine in that box except pieces of Camryn's heart. She hadn't been whole since before we met and that made me think of her mother. I felt bad; bad for her and bad for me, but I wanted to help.

"Sometimes you can be just like your mother," I said, hoping to open a conversation of healing. Instead, I'd unleashed the gates of Camryn's personal hell, which came forth in a fury only a mild-mannered introvert could unfurl.

"I AM NOT LIKE MY MOTHER!" Camryn screamed like I'd never witnessed before. From anyone. Ever. She reached toward her throat as if she'd damaged something inside. And people said I had a bad temper. But I knew this was more than overreaction to a mild slight. This was serious.

"I'll never say that again," I apologized. "I didn't know you'd freak out."

Camryn curled into a ball, bawling on the floor for forever, leaving me feel helpless and almost hopeless.

"When are you going to let me in?" I asked out of frustration.

Camryn didn't answer, but continued to cry, clearly in some sort of emotional pain I was ill-equipped to heal and maybe had even contributed to, but that had never been my intention. What I wanted was to make it all better.

CHAPTER 13 – GLENN

I called home to check the answering machine. Camryn picked up.

"What are you doing at home?" I asked.

"I wasn't feeling good, so I called in."

I wondered about that. It wasn't the first time. I knew she didn't like her job, but there was something more. That's all she talked about though: work. Whenever I asked her about us, she'd say something like, "It makes me feel like an object when you feel me up in the kitchen." Then I'd say, "You're my wife, you shouldn't feel like an object."

I thought she was beautiful and sexy, and I wanted her to know it. I wanted to rip her clothes off 24/7 and make love to her and show her how special she was, but even a simple grab of the boobs she rebuffed. It made me feel like she didn't want me, wasn't allowing me to express my love. It sucked. It hurt.

Then she'd talk about this, that, and another making her feel used. Wasn't a wife supposed to do certain things? Camryn would say it was the way I said it, that I *expected* it. I tried to listen, but what the hell? Wasn't a spouse supposed to want to do nice things for their partner like have his meals on the table? My mom always did. Never complained. Finally Camryn would say, "You don't understand," and shut me off. Shut me out. That was the worst. I understood a lot more than she gave me credit for. Why I couldn't prove it, I had no idea. I chalked it up to "women." Can't live with 'em; can't live without 'em.

"What's wrong?" I asked, holding the phone in the crook of my shoulder against my ear.

"Nothing."

Nothing. I knew that was bullshit, but she wouldn't spill, and that hurt too.

"I'll talk to you tonight," she said then hung up, leaving me worried.

* * *

When I got home, Camryn had supper waiting—chicken soup, which didn't sound good at all. "Let's save that for another night," I said. "I'd rather have pizza."

"Glenn, I don't feel good, and I don't want to go out."

"Pizza will make you feel better."

Camryn looked different, not her usual self. Maybe she did feel ill. I wanted to make her feel better.

"I'll put the soup away, and then I'll order pizza so you won't have to go anywhere," I said, kindly making the offer, compromising like she always said we should do.

Camryn stared out the kitchen window for an unusually long time then looked down into the sink. "I'm not that hungry." She then buried her head in her hands like she'd developed a headache.

After she flopped over on the couch, eyes closed, I brought her some Tylenol and a glass of water, which she took then laid right back down. And she stayed that way until well after the pizza was cold, and my beer was gone.

Finally she resurrected. "Glenn, we need to talk."

Even though the news was on, I wanted to hear what she had to say, so I gave her my attempt at undivided attention, glancing back at the news sometimes.

"This isn't working out. *We* are not working out," she said.

I was glad she threw that last bit in there because I thought she might have been talking about her headache medicine in her own weird way. I turned off the TV.

"What do you mean?" I asked.

Camryn's face turned red as a beet. Her lip quivered like it always did when something was really bothering her, and her eyes became glassy with tears. "I think we should separate," she said, so distraught that I could barely understand.

No way! No fucking way! I said to myself in my head, which didn't happen all that often, only when shit was really hitting the fan; otherwise, I didn't have much company in there. That's when I knew shit was serious, when that inner voice decided to join the party. Sometimes I wish that voice would have a talk with me ahead of time, but it never worked out that way.

"Why?" I asked, terrified. I wouldn't let this happen. I'd do anything.

"We just don't—" Camryn paused, searching for words, " —click."

Don't click. What the hell did that mean? I wish she'd give me something to go on, but again, she was speaking in riddles. So I asked her. She massaged her temples while quiet tears dropped onto her knees, and then she let loose with a list of things she liked but I didn't and a list of stuff I liked but she didn't. She said this like it was a problem, but it wasn't a problem and I'd prove it to her. "Isn't that what people who love each other do, stuff they don't like just because the other person does? To be loving?" I caught her on that one. She looked at me, confused and then went back to rubbing her head.

"And supper tonight—I didn't even feel good, but I cooked. Then you inconsiderately suggested pizza even after you knew I'd fixed something."

How that was my fault, I didn't know. No one asked her to cook when she didn't feel well. That was her own doing. And I couldn't help it my stomach wanted something else. How was a change of plans a bad thing? Then she started in about some girlie magazines I had under the couch and how when I touched her just the wrong way, at just the wrong time it made her feel used. But if I did the same thing in the right way, at the right time, it was fine. Whenever I felt like it was always the right place and time in my book, and she shouldn't have any gripes about it. Her whole argument had too many stipulations to make me feel comfortable. Besides, I loved her, and she knew that. I told her every day.

Camryn had worked herself up into a heaping, sobbing ball, crying ugly like she was eking out a spitting demon, trying to get rid of something. She was seriously going off the deep end. Someone had to bring some sanity to the situation. This wasn't happening to me twice.

"What do you need me to do?" I asked, eager to comply. She was in some sort of fantasy world where "they all live happily ever after," and everyone knows that's not how it works. Everyone has troubles, but they deal with them. "I'd pay anything to get you the help you need, get you fixed," I said. I wanted my Camryn back. I wanted her fixed now.

My loving offer only met with more violent sobs and weeping. "You're not hearing me," she almost screamed, anguished. She looked as if she wanted to pound her message right into my head, and then she jerked the other way and buried her face in the couch, completely losing it.

"We talk every day," I said, showing her that I did, indeed, hear her. She looked up at me, her eyes swollen to the point that she looked as if she'd been stung by something. Before she could say anything more about the needs she wasn't getting met, I said, "What about what I need?"

Then that demon finally burst forth and laid all the cards on the table, putting it all on the line, "I can't be who I'm not," she said.

"You were before. Is that fair?" I said, frightened I was losing the one I loved most, but whoever was left, I wanted anyway. I didn't want to be alone.

"No!" Camryn wailed, insurmountable pain pulled at her, ripping her to pieces, and I could tell it wasn't just pain from me, but something being pulled up by its roots. There was as much or more anguish beneath Camryn's surface.

"If that wasn't you, then why'd you do it?" I demanded. Part of me wanted to know. Part of me felt robbed.

Camryn thrashed some more, looking for something to throw or punch, tears ravaging her all the while. She threw herself back into the couch, looking tortured, like maybe she was hitting herself on the inside, and then she cried out, "Because I loved you, and I wanted you to love me." She sniffed up some tears, breaking the surface of composure. "I tried to be who you wanted me to be because I wanted you to love me." Camryn's tormented soul went limp, and there was no light in her eyes when she said, "I wanted to be loved."

Her words hovered in the air and then sank into each of us like blood from a near-fatal wound seeping into the earth.

"You don't think I'd love the real you?" I asked, taken aback.

"No."

"Try me."

"I have!" Camryn cried out again, undoing her tentative composure. She listed fifty examples of the real her that she claimed I never listened to nor accepted, and then she berated herself for having let it happen. "It was both our faults," she said.

I didn't remember having heard any of her fifty examples. My first instinct was to call her a liar. One of us had a serious memory lapse. Perhaps she needed help. Or I did. Somewhere inside an undercurrent feared the memory lapse could have been mine.

"I'll go to counseling if you want . . . with you," I said as a last ditch effort, fear of being alone forefront in my mind, right ahead of my fear of psychologists who didn't have a fucking clue.

"I can't think right now," Camryn said while blowing her nose. "My head hurts." She bent over, cradling her head back into her hands, trying to drain away the pain.

It felt as though my heart was being clawed open, but my head was just fine, even better than normal. I had a sudden clarity, almost like the stress cleared my head rather than clouded it. I hated the thought of losing my wife, but the cloudiness lifted from my mind felt like the "wash me" fingered onto a dirty windshield had been cleaned away. It was as if mind-blowing stress was the heavy duty, super strength cleaner my head needed to think straight, and I naturally gravitated toward those situations. Even unconsciously I created them for myself, which was an idiotic thing to do. The pleasure of a clear head also gave me the pain of unforeseen consequences. The story of my life.

"I won't pressure you anymore," I promised. "I want the real you. That's all I want. That's all I've ever wanted. I'm sorry if it hasn't come out right." I sighed and shook my head. "Obviously it hasn't or you wouldn't be this upset. I've never wanted anything other than you." I spoke from my soul. "Just you."

I sent up a little prayer asking that Camryn please know my sincerity. This time silent tears fell from her eyes, like the last drips from a fire hose as it's being rolled up and put away after dousing the flames. They were tears of relief that the worst was over, for now. With my brain fully charged, I pulled her onto my lap, not saying a word, just holding her, showing her my love.

"Let's go to sleep," I whispered into her hair.

She nodded and then followed me upstairs and fell into bed. At first she lay alone on her side, but I pulled her close, kissing her neck then up her jawline to her lips. I needed her to want me. I'd come much too close to losing her, the person I needed so much. She kept me on track. I kissed her mouth again, and then it was as if two savage animals let loose, pawing and clawing at each other, fierce and primal. I don't know if it was making love, but more of a making up, perhaps a vicious way to numb our pain.

Then I made a confession, hoping to drive home just how important she was to me. "Did you know I used to smoke?"

The moonlight shining through the window revealed a shocked look on Camryn's face, but she didn't say a word.

"I quit because of *you*. I knew you didn't like it, and I didn't want to lose *you*."

Still she said nothing, but the look in her eyes told me a thousand things were going through her mind. She stared at me as if expecting more, so I went on. I told her I wanted *our* kids and how I adored how she was and appreciated her tenacity and her undying support of getting me through school. It's like she had some unshakable belief that it was the right thing to do and that my graduating was more than what was best for me or best for her or best for us. She had conviction about things that were larger than the sum of the parts and a complexity of her thought that never really made sense, yet did. She had great faith, and even greater than that, she had great faith in me. I loved that about her. "You saved my life," I told her and meant every single word.

Camryn wiped fresh tears from her eyes. I didn't mean to make her cry. She seemed so strong, yet was so fragile. It hardly made sense. She gave me a peck on the cheek and rolled back to her side of the bed, wiping her eyes on her pillow. I wanted to cuddle and hold her. She hadn't said a thing. But I let her be and prayed she'd get some rest. I knew I wasn't an easy person to live with, and I knew I was far from perfect. "*Trying*" is what my mom had called it. I didn't know how to be another way, and I never meant to be the end of anybody, although Mom had often said, "You'll be the end of me" and "I'm at my wits end!"

I rolled over, thinking about these things, feeling helpless, tears falling onto my pillow too. I certainly didn't want to be Camryn's end: I wanted to be her life.

I felt deep down that I was a walking contradiction, mostly because that's what other people told me; what did they know? But also in that deep-down place, I wondered, what *did* they know? What did they know about me that I didn't know myself? And why didn't I?

Didn't some famous person say, "Know thyself?" Yeah, I knew myself. I knew inside that I only wanted to love and care and be kind. But those times when I saw tears on Camryn's face after something I'd done, I wondered what kind of a monster I really was. How could I ever know myself if I couldn't get a handle on myself? Just like I couldn't get a handle on typing and bubble tests even though I knew what was right. Most of the time, I didn't even like myself because of these things. But all of these thoughts were *so* deep down that they barely registered in my soul, let alone my conscious mind — and they never saw the light of day.

* * *

I knew I was in the cold, damp, back corner of the doghouse basement. I would have been "happy" to have been in the doghouse, upstairs, but this was serious. Camryn wasn't into jewelry and expensive perfume, so I couldn't win her over like that. Plus, I wanted to do something for her that she wanted, that she would like and that would bring her joy.

On Valentine's Day, after weeks of getting the lukewarm shoulder, I took Camryn on a date to the pet store, right after a dinner out. She hadn't completely given me the cold shoulder, but what a better way to warm her up and earn a space in the upstairs doghouse than with a kitten.

"You don't like cats," she said.

"No, but you do." I hugged Camryn, kissed the top of her head in a moment of tenderness.

It's true. I hated cats. They hissed and clawed and spat, especially when you chased them around the barn scaring them and picked them up by their tails. They didn't like being thrown either. Finicky things. I just wanted to play. I was kinda like a dog when I was a kid, sticking my nose where it didn't belong, rambunctious, just wanting to play. Cats weren't the only hissers and spitters when I acted like that; people too, even my friends who didn't stay friends very long. And I was kinda like that dog who kept getting into the trash and getting into trouble no matter how many times he was told no. Like I couldn't help myself. Like I wasn't in control. And after being scolded so many times and feeling like I could never do anything right, no matter how hard I tried, I stopped caring. I'd get into trouble no matter what, so I may as well meet their expectations of me, Glenn Failure Conroy.

But Camryn was different. She had a high tolerance for my dog-like behavior; it took her six years before she got fed up. Most people didn't last two. Because of her saint status, I still cared, and I knew a kitten would make her happy.

At the pound, Camryn picked up a black and white fur ball while his brother mewed in the background, trying to make me feel guilty for not taking him too. "We're only getting one," I said, drawing the line.

I paid the pound for the cat along with a nice tip. I didn't know why I left the huge tip. I just did. Maybe to help keep that other one alive, so it could find a good home too. Rain poured down outside, so I offered to zip kitty up into my coat to keep him dry. The damn thing thought I was its mother after that, until it landed on my face one too many times in the night, and I hurled it across the room. From then on, it was Camryn's baby, following her around like a dog, cuddling with her at night, almost like I'd bought my own replacement.

"What are you going to name him?" I asked as we settled in to watch X-Files.

Kitty hopped onto the couch, padded across me then settled into Camryn's lap. They sat there a few moments, staring into each other's eyes, bonding or spacing out into some sort of dreamland. Camryn stroked his fur and scratched under his chin with an unusual tenderness and affection for a cat. She said, "I'll name kitty David."

"David?" I asked, raising my eyebrows. She was nuttier than I knew.

"Yeah, like David Duchovny."

"Why don't you just call him Fox?" I asked, trying to persuade her to a name more fitting for an animal.

"I can't name a cat Fox," she said to me like I was the crazy one. Camryn turned to fur ball and said into this face, as if she were addressing a baby, "No, we can't name you Fox, can we?" She nuzzled his nose to hers as she cooed reassuringly to him, "No."

David let out a mew as if they were on the same page, which brought a huge smile to Camryn's face. I loved seeing her happy. Still, I shook my head. I knew she was an X-Files freak, but naming your cat David? I gave up trying to figure her out.

*   *   *

My job ticked along way better than expected. Once I was on the inside, had my clearance, and put my naturally excessive curiosity to work, doors opened. And I opened them.

I popped my head into the lab while walking back to my desk after an aircraft inspection. "Any little green men in here?" I asked.

"Glenn," my boss, who happened to be in the room, said. "I was just talking about you."

"Yep, my ears were burning. That's why I stopped by. Whatcha need?" I asked.

My boss looked like he didn't know quite what to make of me, but overlooked any reservations he may have had, just like anyone else who saw my potential and took a chance on me had. For those folks, I was grateful. A flashback to my fourth grade teacher, Mrs. Emerson, came to mind. She was the only one who took the time after class to sit down with me and re-explain each day's lesson, because sitting there in a room full of quiet kids, listening, drove me ape shit. Instead of listening, I fidgeted in my chair wondering what was for lunch, sometimes getting out of my chair for a better view out the window, especially when a plane flew overhead. Mrs. Emerson was nice. "I have one just like you at home," she said. I'm not sure what she meant, but at the time, I was thinking "nice little boy." During our one-on-one's, she'd speak to me like I mattered and never criticized me for not being like all the other kids who could sit in their chairs, listen, and understand, going off to do their homework by themselves after class. We did my homework together, and she gave me M&Ms after each problem I did right. Once I figured that out, I aced almost everything because there was a good reason to do the work. M&Ms right away, not some dumb letter grade handed back on a page three days later. When she explained to my folks that I knew the material, they laid into me about why I couldn't do it at home in my room, but they clearly didn't understand the power of M&Ms . . . or one-on-one.

"Conroy," my boss said, "we need you in Seattle. You're the first guy I thought of when this assignment came up—right up your alley."

I was intrigued. My ears perked up when the words "need you" hit the air. Plus the fact that he thought of *me*, and "right up your alley" sounded phenom. Having gotten my attention, I listened intently as boss man outlined the particulars of the job, throwing in words like "top secret" and "special clearances" and "national security." I was all over it and would have accepted right then and there if I didn't need to consider Camryn.

"We need you ASAP," he said.

"Let me talk it over with my wife," I said, somehow managing to stifle my excitement. I hoped she'd like the idea too.

"What do you think of moving to Seattle?" I asked Camryn.

She sat there, thinking it over while petting David on her lap. Her and that cat; they were inseparable.

"Fine. When do we go?" she said.

I almost had whiplash from her quick response. There was no fussing over leaving our brand new house, no griping about having to quit her job, leave her home state, no nothing. Total agreement. I had half a mind to feel her forehead, but I knew she wasn't ill. She even perked up and looked happy about it. She didn't even ask why I asked, which was unusual for her, not gathering all the particulars before making a decision. Reckless. On second thought, maybe she was ill.

"I take it this is for work?" she asked.

I nodded. "Classified project," I said, keeping it close to the vest as instructed.

Camryn leaned in, excitement starting to ooze into the space around her as she hung on my every sparse word. She looked like she'd start packing in that moment. "When do they want you?"

When I said, "As soon as we can get there," she gave me a hug like I'd saved her life, clinging to me like she was grateful I'd given her the best gift in the world.

CHAPTER 14 - GLENN

It took twenty minutes just to walk into the factory from the parking lot at XB Aerospace, Seattle. A cold misty rain peppered my Seahawks jacket on the way in. Camryn and I went shopping the day before, and I bought it to show my support of the locals and to blend in. I knew from experience that while I enjoyed being different, sometimes it didn't serve me well. Sucking up at the right moments made up for a multitude of sins. When Camryn objected to the pricey coat, I justified it to myself as "paying it forward." Or maybe it was an indulgence like the Catholics did, doing a little something to make a wrong right. Supposedly, paying ahead of time for future sins was a myth of how the whole indulgence thing worked, but I'd take it; I probably needed it.

After orientation, another ten minutes passed going through the bowels of the place until my corporate "buddy" and I arrived at the secret lair a few stories underneath the main building. Buddies were supposed to make you feel welcome in your first weeks of work. We talked airplanes; it couldn't feel friendlier than that.

"Here's what you'll be working on," my new boss, Corey Stockwell, said. "Ain't she a beauty?"

The streamlined ship resembled a chevron. In the biz, planes were called ships even though they weren't. "Sweet!" I said. "Stealthy. Pilotless?"

"Absolutely. Cutting edge."

Music to my ears! I managed to fist-pump only in my mind, quite an achievement. I'd died and gone to heaven.

Stockwell showed me to my desk, leaving me with a stack of software manuals and corporate policies to read. Seriously. At that point, the buddy system failed. This was torture. No way in hell could I sit there and read that stack. I got up and found my way back to the ship, chatting up a few union workers who were busy installing carbon fiber honeycomb panels.

"Sweet, isn't it—" I looked for a nametag. "—Fill."

"Sure is. You're new here," he said, looking me over.

"Transferred from St. Louis."

Fill didn't say anything to that, but instead said, "Wanna see how it's done?"

"That's what I'm here for." I was over the moon. Engineers could learn a lot from the union folk, a trick I learned that most didn't. And they called me stupid. Right. Working with the blue collars was one of the smartest things I did; my career ran circles around the engineers' who didn't. "Fill, I've never met a Phil whose name wasn't spelled with a P. Short for Fillmore or something?"

"Nope. My parents didn't think it made any sense spelling with letters that didn't sound like themselves and I don't either. Makes life easier if you spell things like they sound."

"You're right there." I liked this guy more and more.

Back at my desk, Stockwell stopped by. I had a software manual laid out, more for looks than anything. I learned better getting my hands on things, having someone else show me. "I hear you wandered out talking to Fill."

"Yep. Needed a break," I said even though it wasn't a break, because I hadn't started reading at all.

"He's our top mechanic. Really knows his stuff."

"Seemed to. He showed me the composite fasteners and how the installation differs from traditional. Can't wait to see more," I said, almost bouncing in my seat with excitement, but then I changed the subject. "Hey, while you're here. You know of any openings in scheduling? My wife needs a job."

Stockwell made some calls, giving me a few contacts to pass along. Camryn wasn't at the apartment when I got home. Still pumped from the day, I flipped on the computer and cranked up the Internet. I wished Camryn was home, help me blow off *steam*. Eh, a little online action couldn't hurt. Help me relax. With a quick browse to a few choice pictures that left nothing to the imagination, I took care of myself.

Camryn walked in as I got up from the computer chair. I went to hug her, but Camryn's return hug felt like cardboard. Then David walked by, rubbing up against my leg, reminding me that I was barely out of the doghouse. I decided to let Camryn's cardboard disposition slide and not start shit up with her. Instead I said, "I got you something," and then handed her the list of job contacts at work. "Call them up. They're hiring."

"Thanks," she said but didn't seem very thankful, like she had more in her head that she'd never share with me. I wanted to tell her about my kick-ass day at work, but the way she said "thanks" was the proverbial last straw.

"What's your problem?" I asked, direct and to the point.

"Nothing." Oh, the big *nothing*, which was an outright lie. She squirmed.

"Just spit it out," I said, ready for whatever she dished out. We weren't going to get anywhere if we didn't talk. That's what I learned when Camryn dragged me off to that damned marriage counselor, who honestly didn't fix much of anything.

"You were looking at porn on the computer again. I don't like it," she said. "It's like you're addicted. And I feel like I'm not good enough. You need more, more, more, just like everything else."

The hair bristled on the back of my neck. I didn't know if the feeling was guilt or hurt. I do know she was criticizing me, and that's not what spouses are supposed to do. I wouldn't stand for it. "Get a grip," I told her. "It's just a computer. It's not like I'm cheating. You know what your problem is? You are too damn sensitive."

Camryn winced. I didn't mean to hurt her.

"This is just stupid. It's like that time you made a big deal over my dirty socks on the floor."

"I asked you to pick them up, and put them in the basket."

"It's just freaking socks! You want them in the basket so bad, you put them in there. See what I mean? You're making a mountain out of a mole hill," I told her.

Camryn rubbed her head, letting my message sink in.

"Just like that counselor said, we need to cut each other some slack," I reminded her. "I agreed to let you do dishes after dinner rather than insist you sit with me on the couch. Now you need to back off picking at a little Internet browsing. I'm not hurting anyone. I'm not cheating," I said again, making sure she got the message that I was not and never would be unfaithful. I can't imagine anything worse, and I'd never do that to her. "Is that fair? I let you do what you want after dinner, but I can't do what I want after work? This relationship doesn't just revolve around you, ya know. Isn't what I want important?"

Tears welled up in Camryn's eyes, yet she still had nothing to say. She held her hands together, fidgeting with her fingers like they were some sort of substitute rosary. I didn't like to see her cry, yet her silence infuriated me.

"Damn, Camryn! When are you going to talk?" I stalked off to the bedroom. "Let me know when dinner's ready," I said, "unless you want me to take you out to dinner." I threw that last part in, trying to fix what I might've screwed up.

*   *   *

"I'm home!" Camryn announced as she walked in from her first day on the job. "Time for house hunting," she said with a glow about her that didn't happen often enough. That glow was contagious, and I wished it happened regularly.

I sat down in front of the computer, and turned it on to start browsing the real estate listings. A vixen appeared, spread eagle onto the screen, so I quickly X'd out of the browser, wishing I'd thought to have shut down earlier. But I wasn't quick enough. Camryn glanced down at the empty trashcan, her glow had disappeared, and what took its place was also contagious.

"You threw the trash out," Camryn said. She had a way of saying things without really saying things. It pissed me off, and we had another infectious discussion leaving us both downright sick. Honestly, all I wanted to do was make love to her, celebrate our upcoming home, and start that family she only recently agreed to try for. I wasn't getting any younger, and it killed me when she had stopped the project over a year ago, taking birth control pills again, right about the time she almost left me.

Whoever said marriage wasn't easy was a fucking Einstein. I'd moved Camryn from a job, city, and home she didn't like, hoping to put an eternal smile on her face, yet she still wanted more. She drove a hard — and in my mind, unreasonable — bargain. But I'd never give up; I could and I would make her happy.

*   *   *

Six months later, Camryn was happy most of the time. We'd had plenty of practices, trying to get that family going, ready to fill our new house that we barely argued over at all. Life was good.

"When you gonna get pregnant," I asked her, anxious to get this party started. Party of three, maybe four if we'd have twins.

Camryn scowled. "I don't know," she said. "Like how am I supposed to know?"

"Just asking."

"Well, I'm bleeding," she said.

Nothing new. "You say that every month."

"No, I mean, I'm not supposed to. Not now."

165

I registered what she had said as no biggie. Average woman troubles, and nothing I cared to concern myself with, yet, having to fix everything, I offered my advice. "Go see a doctor if you're so worried about it."

That's exactly what Camryn did. Back and forth to the doctor for a few days, them drawing her blood, checking for hormones and other stuff I regarded as too much information. The only thing that mattered to me was Camryn and the baby that didn't make it past the size of a pea.

Camryn wept onto my shoulder. I held her tight while she fell apart telling me the news. "I don't know why I'm so upset," she said, surprised and embarrassed by her vulnerable state.

She wasn't Mrs. Tough Guy like she wanted me to think, never needing my help with stuff that matters — the soft stuff on the inside.

"I didn't even know I was pregnant."

"It's okay. We'll try again," I told her, letting her cry all she needed and not once asking her why the tears. It wasn't like those times she cried when we disagreed, and she said she wasn't being "heard." This was important. I didn't have to ask why.

Sometimes tough times draw two people closer, and even though I grieved the loss of my child too, I celebrated being a comfort to Camryn: she needed me.

CHAPTER 15 – GLENN

Six months later, when Camryn was three months pregnant, for keeps this time, she came home from work bursting with excitement.

"There's no way you'll guess what happened to me today."

"You got a raise."

"No," she said, as if that were way too easy of an answer.

"Little green men showed up at the lab," I said, my turn to be excited.

She rolled her eyes. I stared back at her expectantly, rather than continue this guessing game.

"I ran into Kurt. At work!"

"Kurt who?" I asked, not sharing her excitement as I had no idea who or what she was talking about.

"You know, my friend Sarah's brother. You met him."

"No," I said, still lost.

"Well," she said, thinking, "maybe not, but still. How coincidental is that to run into someone from high school two thousand miles away? I haven't heard a thing from him in years."

"Old boyfriend?" I asked, half teasing.

"No," she said, like I'd said something outlandish that I should have known. "We were just friends." She still bounced around like this was the best news she'd had in ages. "We're going to meet up with him and his wife for dinner."

This was a first. Camryn almost never made plans with friends. She had a handful of close friends, but none of them lived close by. I had tons of friends, going to happy hour with them often, but we never had heart-to-hearts like Camryn and her crew did. During those rare times she actually got to see them in person, they'd pick up like no time had passed. My friends seemed kinda like strangers, and this dynamic, this difference between her friends and mine, I never did understand.

"Good," I said, always up for plans and eager to support, "when?"

* * *

I told Camryn to plan a trip, just the two of us. That belly of hers was a constant reminder "baby made three" and we'd have company for the next eighteen years. Normally, I didn't plan ahead, but a weekend away seemed like the thing to do. I thought she'd like that, me coming up with a nice surprise. I told her I didn't know where we'd go and left it up to her to plan and make happen. She was better at that stuff than I was anyway. But Camryn wasn't as overjoyed as I thought when I suggested a getaway.

"You mean I have to do the legwork?" she said. "You say, 'I'd like to take you away for the weekend' like you had something all planned, but then I have to plan it?"

Jesus, put that way I felt like shit. Still I tried to joke it off. "I had the idea," I said, which, in my opinion, was the most important part: getting the ball rolling.

Camryn planned a great trip — off to Canada. The ferry ride through fog-shrouded waters dotted with evergreen-covered islands calmed my three-ring-circus mind. I never noticed the chaos in my head until moments like these when it settled to a smooth and steady pace. We had a great time that weekend in Victoria admiring the Butchart Gardens, watching artisans on the streets, and enjoying each other, one of the best weekends of my life.

*   *   *

I went with Camryn to every single OB/GYN visit during the whole pregnancy. I wanted to be a good dad. I wanted to be involved. Besides, it was exciting and new. Each time we went, I asked when they'd tell us boy or girl. Each time they reminded me they'd check around week twenty, something like that.

"I'm pretty sure it's a girl," the ultrasound technician said, explaining the fuzzy picture on the screen. Camryn was beside-herself excited, lying there gushing over it with her slime-covered tummy exposed, the tech moving the ultrasound transducer this way and that for a better view.

"Really? Sure it's not a boy?"

"I'd bet my next paycheck on it," the tech affirmed.

Shit. I mean, I was happy having a healthy child, but I didn't want a house overrun with girls. A daughter might not "get" me. A girl might think me too rough and too reckless. Guys generally accepted me as I was and didn't care.

Later, over a celebratory dinner, I told Camryn since she got the girl she wanted I get the name I wanted. "We're naming her Harley."

Camryn threw up all over that idea, which I found unfair. After haggling about the fairness of it all and letting it simmer for a few weeks, we settled on Sydney. Not too girlish, not too boyish.

On Mother's Day, Camryn was in a funk. I chalked it up to her being large with child; she possibly could have popped any day.

"Why didn't you get me flowers?" she asked, nearly on the verge of tears like she was about to have a breakdown, interrupting my show on ESPN.

I clicked the pause button, confused by the question. "For what?" I asked.

"Mother's Day," she said, exasperation in her voice, again. She rubbed that huge tummy of hers.

"You're not a mother," I said with a nagging feeling that I had missed something. Then in an attempt to make amends for my apparent unseen error—thorns perpetually in my side—I said, "I'll take you out to eat if you want."

I flipped the channel, looking for something better. Camryn muttered something about me making her dinner at home, which sounded like a pain in my ass, so I told her to pick the restaurant and I'd take her. She'd pick this time. Couldn't turn down a deal like that.

* * *

Camryn woke me in the middle of the night. "I think I'm having a contraction," she said.

"You think," I said, wondering why she didn't *know*. I'd gone to those childbirth classes with her, and it seemed clear to me that you'd know, so I rolled over falling back asleep and didn't worry about it.

I thought I heard her say, "I'm going to call the doctor," and then the next thing I heard was Camryn in the tub, apparently trying to relax.

I looked at her confused, "Let me know when we need to go then."

She finished getting dressed. "We should go soon," she said, still not looking very urgent.

Being the dutiful husband I thought myself to be, I warmed up the truck while she got last minute things together. When I came back in the house, she was doubled over the desk chair in pain. Finally, the Kodak moment real men could understand.

"Wait, let me get some pictures," I said, wanting to catalog the event.

"Let's just go," she said, not appreciating my efforts.

"It'll take just a minute," I assured her as I fiddled with the lens, positioned the camera in front of my face and then decided it'd work better with the lens cap off. Click, click, click. Camryn's face turned red, apparently from . . . what? It took a moment to register—agony.

When reality set in, I rushed, camera still in hand, to help Camryn to the truck. By then her face turned white again, and she looked all better so I snapped a few more shots of her sitting in the front seat—on our way!

Camryn started writhing in pain again during the short trip to the hospital, causing me to miss the turn. "I don't want to do this," she said, almost in tears.

I wondered if she was afraid, but how could she not want to do this when it's all she's been talking about for nine months?

"You don't have much choice at this point."

Camryn sat there in silent discomfort with her head on the glass. I thought welcoming a baby was supposed to be a joyous event. She looked anything but joyful, and that bummed me out. Great—another major life event getting started on the wrong foot. #StoryOfMyLife. Only we didn't have hashtags back then.

I helped Camryn in to the reception desk where Camryn explained her symptoms to the nurse in perfectly coherent sentences. She suddenly turned a fantastic shade of red and set her head down on the counter into the crook of her elbow.

"I'll get you a wheelchair," the nurse said, revving into high gear. They assigned Camryn a bed, told her to change into a gown, checked "down below," and declared it wouldn't be long. We also got into a messy business of breaking water and having Camryn do laps around the hallway, but not before it seemed like she'd had an accident all over the floor in the process. I felt sorry for her, but having no clue what to do, I pushed her to speed the thing along.

"The nurse said to keep walking, so let's do one more lap," I said as Camryn was heading back to bed, still interested in doing this the natural way.

"Oh my god," Camryn kept saying, so the nurse ran for the doctor, and he suited and gloved up just in time while I held one leg out of the way, helping to make an easy exit for my daughter. When the nurse told me to hold her leg high, I did as I was told, nearly lifting Camryn off the bed since more is always better in my book.

Camryn looked like a deranged animal, something you should shoot out of its misery. She couldn't answer any questions and could hardly breathe. Her lips turned blue. "Have a cow, man" popped into my head. But then I remembered seeing cow births with someone's arm in to the elbow, and this wasn't that way.

"It can't be that bad," I said, searching for some words of comfort, which I think backfired. Camryn shot me an if-looks-could-kill slay. But then a slimy bloody head emerged with slight matted hair on top followed by the shoulders and then the rest of her, slippery like a rainbow trout. I'm surprised the doctor didn't have scaling gloves on so the baby wouldn't fall.

The nurses bundled Sydney up and then handed her to Camryn so we could get a good look at her. For Camryn, it was love at first sight, all that pain and worry quickly forgotten. I wished she looked at me that way.

*   *   *

Camryn was a great mom.

"She got up three times last night," Camryn said, feeling exasperated as a new mother.

I was amazed and relieved she could hear the baby because I couldn't. "I didn't hear anything," I said.

"If it was up to you, she'd starve."

"Good thing it's not up to me then," I said, meaning it. But Camryn seemed to take it all wrong. She was also pissed off because I'd also asked her to do some ironing since she was home all day with the baby. I figured she'd have free time, but she assured me — and not so nicely — that there was no free time as a new mother.

I went back to leafing through a magazine full of house plans, eyeing something I liked better than the house we had. Whenever I brought it up, Camryn came back with affordability issues, squashing my dreams. Sometimes she could be a real downer.

"Why do I always have to be the finance police?" she asked, getting worked up, again.

"No one asked you to," I said. Because I didn't. The finance shit would work itself out. So instead of dreaming together with my wife, I had taken matters into my own hands and found a nice chunk of land on a nearby island to build on. "It'll appreciate in value," I told her. "It'll be an investment." We closed on that land before Sydney hatched, but now that Camryn was headed back to work, it seemed like a good time to make plans to build.

"There's no way we can afford two childcares and a higher house payment if we have another kid," she said. Then she went into detailed explanation about timing and budget alternatives and other uninteresting details.

I wanted a new house. I decided right then and there I was too old for more kids anyway, so even though we'd decided to wait until Sydney was a year old to make firm decisions on our family, I told Camryn that one was enough. Problem solved. End of discussion.

Camryn didn't seem too happy with the arrangement but eventually suggested a vasectomy so she wouldn't have to stay on the pill. While I didn't like the idea of sharp objects anywhere near my nuts, it made sense. No accidents.

* * *

"XB wants us to move," I told Camryn just after having the nut job. The very next week my boss had told me about the relocation offer. I shared the exciting news right away.

"Wha—" Camryn said mid-bounce as she played horsey, Sydney riding on her knees.

"Colorado Springs. Excellent opportunity for me. More Top Secret stuff."

Camryn set Sydney down on a blanket to crawl around with David, who hovered way too close by for safety. Sydney'd come up with a fistful of fur more than once, but that dang cat never bit, which amazed me. Camryn didn't say anything at first, instead burying her eye sockets into her palms. Resting? Thinking? I didn't know. Then when she came up for air, it appeared she'd been crying. "I don't want to go," she said. She said it again three months later when the movers had come and our footsteps echoed as we walked through the house one last time, making sure nothing got left behind.

* * *

"Maybe I won't have to work here," Camryn said, looking through real estate listings on the Internet. "Stay home with Sydney."

"My mom always worked," I said.

"But we could get something affordable. Something that fit one income."

She showed me the houses she had in mind.

"I don't like 'em. No view."

"View homes are so much more," she said, policing my finances again.

175

I started to get irritated. "I'm not getting a house I don't like!"

She shut up after that, not bringing her ideas up again, so I figured it wasn't important to her in the first place. Camryn started her job two weeks later, and we moved into a nice upper middle class home, mountains in full view. I loved it.

Shortly after settling in, Camryn sent "We've moved" notices to all our friends and family — it turns out, Natalie and Raine included.

"What'd you send them a notice for?" I asked, Raine's name still a bad taste in my mouth. Natalie had written Camryn back, catching her up on their news.

"Natalie's still my friend, Glenn."

"So what are they up to?" I felt compelled to ask even though I didn't care, another brain-jerk reaction.

"Not much. No kids yet. I think they're having problems in that department."

I thought the world would be a better place without the spawn of Raine, but since procreation was a touchy issue in our household, I decided to change the subject, bringing up some home improvements I had in mind.

"We'll have to see about adding on. Maybe a screened in porch with a hot tub. And a pool," I said, dreaming aloud.

Camryn tensed up, taking me way too seriously. "Can't you ever be happy with what you have?"

It pissed me off that she never thought I was happy. I was, but I liked to dream and who wouldn't want more if they could have it?

"What about what I want?" she asked.

"You never want anything."

"Not true. I just don't go around talking about everything I want when I know I can't have it."

"What can't you have?" I asked, knowing I'd give her anything.

"Another kid. I want another baby," Camryn said, in tears this time.

Except that. Maybe.

"Well, it's a little late now, don't you think?"

"How was I supposed to know things would change?" she asked, drying her eyes.

I felt bad for her. It seemed like she wanted this impossible thing more than anything. And she never wanted anything.

"Maybe you could have it undone?" she sheepishly suggested. "A vasectomy reversal."

The things I do for my wife, I thought. "We can look into it," I said even though I was happy with one kid. She'd owe me for being subjected to the knife again. "We're naming it Harley."

"Wait a minute." Camryn went into a spiel about naming rights in exchange for my invaded nuts not being a fair deal, but I disagreed. Then she tried blaming our predicament on me in the first place, which I didn't get either, but I entertained her charade because she thought outside the box. I loved that about her.

*   *   *

The microsurgeon's office smelled funny, kinda like old folks home mixed with dental office. Once I saw another guy reading *Aerospace Daily*, I calmed down, struck up a conversation. "You like airplanes?"

"I work on this one," the guy said, referring to the cover story.

Then I was all ears because that airplane was highly classified. I thought, I'd love to get a piece of that action. The whole reason we were in the office escaped my mind. "You work at XB?" I asked.

"Yeah, California."

"They hiring out there?" I asked, always keeping my options open. I would have died to work on that plane.

Finally, when the nurse called us back, I gave him my card in exchange for his. I looked at his card as I was terrible with names, and had promptly forgotten his the moment he introduced himself. Stan. His name was Stan.

"I'll put in a good word for you," Stan said.

I rose, offered my hand. "Nice meeting you."

Camryn had collected Sydney off the floor, removing her from the toys at hand, but Sydney soon found a new one, a stuffed sperm, inside the doc's office, which kept her amused while he kept asking personal questions that Camryn answered. Dates and mundane details didn't stick with me. She took care of that stuff, which I appreciated, so I let her do most of the talking.

After the doc assured us of a good prognosis for the vas reversal, I said, "Cut me up, get it over with."

The next month I found myself in la la land on the operating table, which was a bigger deal than getting cut in the first place. This sucker took over an hour, maybe two, but since I was out of it, I didn't care. Camryn had to do the waiting, Sydney in tow.

Still, a good six months later, I seemed to be shooting blanks. Camryn researched the heck out of fertility on the Internet, giving me this and that supplement, even putting me in boxers so not to overheat the jewels. I had a sperm count done, and even though there weren't as many as there could have been, there were some limping across the slide, doc assuring us his job was successfully done.

Then later still, during the months when we were still trying to pump out a kid, Stan contacted me about a job on that super-secret program I had been lusting after. I decided to bring it up to Camryn when she was in a good mood, so as she lay on the bed, pillow under her ass, encouraging sperm to find their way, I said, "Remember that guy from Dr. Millhouse's office, Stan from XB? He wants me to come and work in California."

I explained that all my hopes and dreams rode on this opportunity and, after all, she did owe me. Still. I'd even back off naming rights for this one, but I wouldn't play that card unless forced.

"California?" she said right as David hopped on the bed, snuggling next to her. She kissed the damn thing between the ears. I even thought about offering to get her another cat if I had to, I wanted it so bad. "We haven't even been here two years!" she said. She reached out for David then closed her eyes while stroking him in some sort of meditative trance.

*   *   *

Camryn found a job, also at XB, right away and we settled into this fancy house with granite countertops and a pool out back. Gotta love it. She didn't give me

179

any flak this time as long as she had extra rooms for another kid and her own office. Since bigger is better, I said "fine" even though no children were imminent, and it looked like the whole vasectomy reversal thing was a bust.

XB California was all Stan had promised and more, but not without its challenges, as always. "I can't believe those guys at work," I told Camryn. "They're not following blueprint. Someone's gonna die."

"You?" she teased, a little too happily.

"We need more people. We're understaffed, and management isn't watching anybody," I said, clearing my throat. I lifted a beer bottle to my lips, took a quick drink while still talking. "It's been up to me. I've had to do everything, rushing here, rushing there, keeping everything straight. And safe. At least I don't get bored."

"Sounds stressful," Camryn said and then muttered something that sounded like "sounds like home," but my brain ignored that.

"We're getting a new guy. Transfer in, but I don't want him." The scratch in my throat wouldn't go away, so I took another swig. "I told management he wasn't qualified. Be more trouble than he's worth, but they won't listen. They said he's had a rough go and instead of dealing with him in a RIF, they're putting him to pasture here."

"So he's not performing, they won't lay him off because they feel sorry for him or something, and you get him because he's a warm body and you're shorthanded," Camryn said, capturing the corporate essence. "What's his name?"

Aerospace was close-knit. Everyone knew everyone or at least knew someone who knew someone.

"I don't remember. Bab something. Babcock I think. First name starts with an R, rhymes with pain, I think." I shook my head. "Probably for pain in the ass." I didn't amuse easily, but I amused myself with these clever associations.

"Huh," Camryn said, looking like those gears were grinding away in her head again. "Babcock was Natalie's married name."

"Oh, god. Please don't let it be him," I said. I couldn't think of anything worse being added to the shit pile, but a bigger piece of shit. "He doesn't still work for XB does he?"

"I don't know," Camryn said. She went off onto another tangent like she often did. "Last I heard, Natalie had cancer. Wasn't doing so hot. Ovarian cancer, I think."

Speaking of stuff like ovaries made Camryn revisit our just-one-child issues. "Maybe we should have you tested again," she said. "Maybe the reversal didn't work."

It had been two years or more. It shouldn't take two years to get pregnant if all systems are go. Knowing Camryn, she'd run all the trap lines and run the problem to ground. Even though it'd probably result in more torture for me, I loved that about her, how she left no stone unturned, sniffing shit out like a bloodhound. "Fine," I said.

"They need a fresh sample." Camryn referred to me making love to a specimen cup, which Camryn already had in a bag, ready and willing. "Fresh within an hour."

I made the deposit, an activity which turned out to be a great stress reliever after the Raine Babcock scare, but I left the timely delivery up to Camryn. I'd willingly participate up to a point but dropping off bodily fluids was not on my list.

*   *   *

Camryn reported the test results. No squigglies. Dr. Millhouse had botched the job, screwing me out of a few thousand dollars, just like an expensive hooker, but not nearly as much fun. That was one thought I kept in my own head, controlling the verbal diarrhea that usually polluted everyone around me. Camryn wouldn't like it if she knew such thoughts went through my mind. She'd think I'd have unsavory ways if I could, but I wouldn't because deep down, I wasn't an unsavory kind of guy. I didn't want to have to explain it because it was nearly unexplainable. Over the years I'd discovered that spelling out my contradictory thoughts and actions was an exercise in frustrating futility for all. "If you think A, why'd you do B?" they'd say. Like if I said I hated a messy room, Mom would ask why I didn't keep mine clean. I had no idea. That's just how I rolled.

"I found a specialist," Camryn said. "Highly recommended in re-do reversals." She went on to explain his credentials and all the particulars of the procedure, setting me at ease. Well, ease enough for our fucked-up circumstances. She seemed so excited about the prospects, like making sure Sydney was not an only child meant the world to her. I'd give her the world if I could, so I agreed, doing my best.

182

Turns out the surgery was scheduled for two days after 9/11, adding to my jitters, but Doc Gordon didn't say a word about the world crumbling around us, instead giving me his full attention. Camryn waited in her own personal waiting room fully equipped with comfy sofa, drinks, snacks, magazines and a television. She watched rehash after rehash of the twin towers coming down while Gordon reattached my plumbing.

After an agonizingly long wait for recovery, a week or so, we tried making a kid again, which turned out to be bad timing and not a botched job this go around. Doc Gordon checked another sample, this time revealing a microscope slide full of motile sperm. A huge difference from Millhouse's microscope slide, which pissed me off all over again, having been had. But Camryn had the whole monthly cycle thing down to a science, and now, with guns loaded, we tried, tried again.

CHAPTER 16 – GLENN

Camryn was in a mood. We both worked long days, and I even had bowling league, but I didn't whine about how tired I was. I did something about it and took a nap. She bitched about her schedule, about taking Sydney to daycare, me buying cigars, and even had the nerve to complain about me taking an open beer in the car, yet would have complained if I'd left it half drunk and wasted at home. Damned if I do; damned if I don't.

Since there was no pleasing her, I didn't try.

If she was so freaking tired, I hadn't a clue why she wanted another kid, but at that point we'd spent a Harley's worth trying to get her what she wanted. We weren't quitters.

"I'll make Sydney's lunch," I offered, after Camryn seemed to have an exceptionally bad day. She hadn't eaten much at dinner, merely scooted the food around on her plate. She hardly even put up a fight when I'd scolded Sydney for eating her beans first and not her hot dog when I'd specifically said otherwise. Normally, Camryn corrected every damn thing I said, so I knew something was wrong.

I started looking in the fridge for peanut butter, but couldn't find any so had to ask.

"In the cupboard to the left above the sink," Camryn answered, sounding annoyed.

How the hell would I know where the peanut butter was? I never used it.

When I couldn't find the peanut butter, I asked again. Camryn walked over, moved a boxed cake mix then pulled it out. Silence. She went back to the recliner.

"What else should I fix her?" I asked.

"Peel some carrots," Camryn droned.

"Where's the peeler?" I never peeled anything other than a banana. I had no clue where the peeler was and short of some damn GPS coordinates, I wasn't going to find it.

Camryn got back up, clearly not appreciating my help, and found the peeler in the dirty dishes.

"Would you wash that for me?" I asked her.

"What?" She gave me a snide look to go along with the snide in her voice.

"Earlier you said you were going to do the dishes . . . so, would you wash that?" I asked, practicing that psychobabble crap we'd learned, explaining back what I'd heard her say. I explained, "You know, 'Say what you do, do what you say' kinda thing?" I hadn't intended to come across as an asshole, but that screwed up look on her face made me feel like I was one. She put down the unwashed vegetable peeler and walked away.

"Are you mad?" I asked, not understanding her cantankerous mood.

"Will you leave me alone, please?"

I felt horrible and helpless and couldn't understand what was eating at her. She'd already put Sydney to bed. I was getting Sydney's lunch. All she had left to do was wash dishes. It wasn't a big deal, yet somehow I felt like it was my fault. I finished making Sydney's lunch, setting it all aside in the fridge then went looking for Camryn. I opened the bathroom door and found her soaking in a hot, bubble-filled tub. She looked fine, laying there all naked, but when she saw me standing there, she pulled the bubbles close, trying to cover herself. I had no idea why she did that. Nothing I hadn't seen before.

"Nice titties," I said, paying her a compliment. But she didn't take it that way at all, instead interpreting my adoration as cheap gawking. I felt insulted. "You could at least say thank you. Can't I even admire my wife?" I finally yelled. She pissed me off. Helping after dinner wasn't enough, complimenting her body wasn't enough. Was *I* enough? By that time, I was furious. Annoyed. Hurt. Camryn was in tears, still naked, and I wanted to punch something. But inside I knew I was a gentleman, and gentlemen didn't punch things. "See you in bed," I said, storming out of the room, which to me was the ultimate insult—leaving someone alone, but she deserved it.

When she did come to bed, wearing pajamas head to toe, she didn't even give me a goodnight kiss, like she wanted to stay mad forever and that pissed me off too. "You're not making me feel any better," I told her. That did the trick, so I thought. She reached over and kissed me on the cheek, and I thought we were good; all was forgiven. I ran my hand up her leg to her crotch, gave a little squeeze. Rather than turning on the heat, she actually winced, but I pressed on and asked, "Was that romantic?" Camryn thought my type of romance was crude.

"No," she said, knocking me down all the notches I had left.

I slapped her on the ass. "Let me know when you want some."

* * *

We spent Christmas in Seattle that year which was close enough to Canada for Camryn and her best friend, Megan, to arrange a visit. She'd kept up with her for over fifteen years from way back when they were exchange students in Australia.

"You two have a good visit," I said, keeping Sydney with me. I'd take her slug hunting or seagull watching while those two were away talking girl talk.

When the girls came back, Camryn seemed relieved of her funk, like it was almost gone. I silently thanked Megan for that, realizing that even though I wanted to be Camryn's everything, I couldn't take the place of a girlfriend. I chalked up Camryn's funkiness to another month with no bun in the oven, even though her distance wasn't conducive to trying very hard to make it happen.

Megan graciously offered to watch Sydney for us while we went for all-you-can-eat crab, one of Camryn's favorites despite the smoky atmosphere of the dive-bar restaurant. You know it had to be good if Camryn put up with that. We chitchatted a few, me trying to steer Camryn into talking about our future, which I had unease about. Did she love me? Then she dove into my favorite subject: my work.

"They're counting on you," she said. "It's an airplane you're working on, isn't it?"

"Camryn . . ." I warned. She was always trying to be sneaky and pry out top secrets.

"I was just wondering," she said, covering up, poorly.

So I turned the tables on her. "You pregnant yet?"

"Will you please stop asking?" she said, annoyance in her voice.

We hashed out her relatively sudden reluctance, she seeming to debate with herself in her head rather than sharing her thoughts with me. Finally she said, "Yes, I want a baby."

I reached for her hand, which brought a slight smile to her face. Her smile brightened further when the waitress arrived bearing crab legs and clam chowder. Comfort food, I was sure.

* * *

We had a come-to-Jesus meeting at work. That meant we had a bigger problem than usual with the airplane, and shit had to be fixed *now* even though it was a momentous issue. While stressful, these were my favorite kinds. Exciting. I kinda got off on it; it gave me a high and made me feel alive. All the experts were called in, including me, which made me feel good. I wasn't necessarily an expert, but a facilitator, sometimes called a shit-disturber, and the shy management would have me do their dirty work. I was the heavy, which really helped the ol' ego. The couple dozen of us worked together like essential parts of a body, each of us vital in our roles.

"Conroy," my boss said. "Get with supply. We need these materials stat." He handed me a list. I had a reputation for being able to speed along the procurement chain. I don't know why. I was just friendly with the key people, and they did me favors. It helps to get to know people. Sometimes people said I was shootin' the shit during work hours, but I wasn't; I was networking. Then other people would give me crap about being the boss' favorite and not getting in trouble for socializing during work hours. I worked on the fringes, pushing the line, but not going over enough to get reprimanded. It worked for me. "And I need these authorizations signed too. Pronto. All the way up to the General. Get on that too." The General and I talked golf, even playing a few rounds together during late lunches, and my boss knew it but pretended not to.

"Yes, sir," I said, grabbing my moment to shine. An organization is only as strong as its weakest link. It wasn't going to be me. And when I saw the weak link, I jumped in to help, almost like a reflex. Some people got their undies all in a bunch when I got into *their business*, but management liked my rebuffing the "it's not my job" mentality, especially when there was a crisis at hand.

"Relax," I said to Camryn after telling her about spending thirty minutes swapping beer-making techniques with the floor foreman on company time. Stuff like that made her nervous, but I told her I wasn't going to live in a box, being a corporate drone. "Trust me," I said. "My boss does."

* * *

Camryn called me at work, something she rarely did, wanting me to meet her at home before she picked up Sydney.

"I was thinking about happy hour, why?" I said, focusing on drinks with the guys.

Then she got coy. "You'll see."

189

I did as I was told. She greeted me at the door, grabbed my butt in a warm squeeze and then led me to the bedroom. Three weeks later she called me again, wanting to meet at our favorite gyro place for lunch.

"I'm pregnant!" she announced.

I felt like a proud dad all over again. Siring a child was virile—made me feel like a man. I liked the feeling, when the stars aligned and my life as a responsible, respected man all came together. It was a feeling I strived to live up to, yet more often fell short despite my best efforts. When that happened, I felt like a mouse. And to make up for it, I scratched and clawed and puffed myself up into the biggest goddamned mouse I could possibly become. Trouble was, most people regarded mice as pests.

* * *

The stresses at work paled to the stresses at home. At work I yelled "jump" and my deer-in-the-headlights peeps yelled "how high." At home when I yelled, all I got was tears which made me feel even worse. I wanted results, not tears, not to make anyone feel bad.

Camryn's father died. She ended up with a high-risk pregnancy and had to take it easy, and I had to work more than ever. "Dammit, Camryn," I said after work when she reminded me to clean the cat box. All I wanted to do was rest, taming the squirrels that seemed to constantly chatter and run around in my head. "Does it have to be done now? I swear, the second you have that kid, you're back on cat box duty." I meant it. Cat box duty was for the birds. "Tell Sydney to do it."

"She's four," Camryn said, like being four was an excuse for not pulling your weight.

"I shoveled snow at four." I snatched the pooper scooper from under the sink.

"Why do you always have to give me a hard time whenever I ask you to do something?" she said.

In my mind it sounded like she was picking a fight. Then the squirrels jumped in, the shit-headed ones, and I said, "Like you never ask me to do anything."

"What the hell does that have to do with anything?" Camryn asked, scratching her head, trying to figure out what I'd just said. I wasn't sure what I'd just said either, but I didn't let on that my head was swiss cheese and full of holes, the stuff mice were made of. Apparently Camryn gave up trying to follow my train of thought and finished, "At least I'm not rude."

"Listen to you. Sure as hell sounds rude to me."

Camryn collapsed in a heap of tears, and I wondered what I'd said.

*　　*　　*

Elizabeth Conroy arrived in the nick of time. Camryn decided to forego au natural this time, instead opting for total absence of pain via epidural. Her legs fell to the side like they were dead weight. She couldn't move them at all.

"I think you should get the doctor," Camryn said while I was eating popcorn.

She pulled that women's-intuition bit on me, but instead of going along with it, I had to ask. "Why?"

At that point, Camryn may have punched me if I'd have been within punching distance. I wanted to know and my God-given, incessant curiosity had to ask. I never outgrew the "why, why, why's" of most people's early childhoods. Some people called it a lack of faith on my part. Those were the nice ones. I called it getting to the bottom of things.

"I can't even feel my legs, but I *feel* something," she said, which didn't make much sense, but given the circumstances, I did as she asked.

The doc came in, checked Camryn. "Wow, you're ready," she said hurrying to prepare for an imminent delivery. If I'd have waited any longer, we would have dealt with that baby's arrival alone.

*   *   *

Here's the thing about babies: they cry. They scream. They shit. Normally Camryn dealt with all that, and I loved that about her, but I couldn't escape one hundred percent of the time. Give me the annoying lowlifes at work any day (ahem, Raine), but I couldn't handle an inconsolable infant. They made me frantic and helpless like there was nothing I could do to make it better. I wasn't in control with them, and I fucking hated that.

"Can you help me here?" Camryn asked out of nowhere. I'd been sitting on the couch, minding my own business, but Camryn acted like I was a slug for not immediately springing into action. She stood there next to Elizabeth. The air was fart-laced, but I didn't understand her sudden freak-out at first. Camryn stopped the swing-o-matic. Then I got a glimpse of the poo oozing out of Elizabeth's diaper. Up her front, by her legs. Camryn even said up her back.

"I don't do diapers," I said, hoping to get out of it. "I'm no good at that."

"Just help me!"

I did get up, but I didn't know what to do, so I stood there. Camryn barked orders, telling me to change the seat covering, put it in the washer, help her get Elizabeth undressed and about five other things. My brain shut down after the first two. Probably the fumes.

I walked into the bathroom after Camryn had finished cleaning her up. Elizabeth said, "Ma" and Camryn pounced all over that, saying she said, "Mommy," which she clearly did not. Annoyed with me again, Camryn sent me away with more baby-tainted laundry. When I came back, I stood outside the door, listening to this heart-to-heart Camryn was having with Elizabeth. Turns out I'd just missed Elizabeth's first roll-over. I missed a lot of things.

Watching quietly, I saw Camryn's tender way and how she oozed "mom" with no effort. She looked like an angel sent here to watch over her family. I stepped into the room. "You're such a good mom."

Camryn jumped, having been immersed in her time with Elizabeth and not knowing I was there.

"I wish I could be half the mom you are," I said, knowing in the recesses of my mind that I could have phrased that better. I kissed her head before I could stick my foot completely in my mouth.

CHAPTER 17 – GLENN

My girls meant the world to me, all three of them. I had a lot of stuff. I was blessed with all the creature comforts I could possibly want and I knew that. Some said I took it for granted. I didn't. It just looked that way to the untrained eye and most people were untrained, including my wife. No one understood me and that was a fact of my life. I didn't fault her, because she's the one who tried the hardest to understand the real me.

"I do appreciate what I have," I told her.

Camryn had her face in her hands, refusing to look at me.

"But I'm always going to dream. I don't have anything left," I said, almost pleading, "if I'm not striving for something."

"I. Can't. Keep. Up. With. You," she said, literally down on her knees and in tears on the bathroom floor. She'd been giving me everything she had for fifteen years, and the well had run dry. "You want and want and want, and I can't deliver. It's never enough. I'm never enough. My. Best. Isn't. Good enough for *you*." Her sobs were gut-wrenching and primal. I realized my being myself ripped her to the core.

"But this is me. I need this. I gotta dream and once I achieve one dream, I've gotta move on to the next," I tried to explain. "You are more than enough. If I lost everything, but still had you three girls, I'd have more than I'd ever dreamed of." I was no help in helping her understand. She was on her own whether I liked it or not. We all have our journeys, and this one, with me in the sidecar, was hers. A bumpy road that I was powerless to smooth. I couldn't change my nature any more than she could change hers. And her nature seemed to match the nature of most people, the norm, so to speak; and I lived at the tail end, always feeling abnormal. Yet her keeping on keeping on was abnormal too—most people wouldn't put up with me—perhaps we weren't so different from each other after all. At least, that's what I told myself.

Once upon a time, I had a best friend who I thought was on the same wavelength as me. He was the only one who understood me besides my late grandmother, but he intentionally cut his journey short on his twentieth birthday. I don't know why. And when I helped lower his casket into the earth, I asked him quite loudly, "WHY?" My fists hit his coffin, and my throat nearly seized up. My pinky finger caught the edge, slicing a deep bloody gash almost to the bone. Tears came to my eyes, not from the flesh wound, but from the wound in my soul and I cried out again, "WHY?" And then I collapsed into the grass coffinside, wanting to return to dust too, but all that seeped in was blood from my hand and tears from my face.

I'm not a religious person, but I went to church when I was young and this passage, I think it was from Easter, flashed in my mind, "My God, why hast thou forsaken me?" I didn't know if that was an appropriate thought, but it seemed fitting at the time. I felt alone. And forsaken. Forsaken many times, but that time was the hardest.

Seeing Camryn—the only living person who remotely understood me—melt there on the floor was like having Simon die all over again. I didn't want to lose her too.

When it rains, it pisses bucketfuls. Not only was I worried about losing Camryn, but a few days later, I found myself speeding to the hospital. The trip that normally took an hour at the speed limit took forty minutes. When emergency vehicles rushed to an emergency they sped, so I did too. This was an emergency: my littlest girl had been admitted.

Camryn had called me off the golf course in a cryptic panic, throwing out words like "fever" and "lungs" and "barely breathing." She didn't answer half of my questions about when, where, and how. She said, "Just be there!" and hung up the phone. I felt lost and helpless and curiously, energized, like rushing to my critically ill little girl's bedside was something to live for.

I learned she had pneumonia shortly after I walked into her room after first passing through hospital security and asking directions three times. Elizabeth lay there sleeping, looking like a computer component with stuff wired into her to keep the system going. "She'll be okay, won't she?" I asked Camryn. She held Sydney on her lap, trying to comfort both kids, and now me all at the same time.

"Yes. She has to be."

We sat in silence for the longest time, fighting back tears. Camryn would look at me, and then I would look at her. Then we'd both look away at the floor or at Elizabeth's still body.

"I heard from an old friend," Camryn said, struggling to hold in the tears. "He wondered how I was." She reached for a tissue, dabbed her eyes and then fell silent again. I didn't know who she was talking about and didn't particularly care. Some guy she'd dated ages ago, I think. It's good to stay in touch with friends. God knows I was the worst at it and hardly ever did, so if she wanted to keep up a friendship, more power to her.

"Talk to him if you want."

She looked at me surprised, hesitant.

"Go ahead," I said. I trusted her. I had nothing to fear except for my daughter's life at the moment. We both went back to staring at barely breathing Elizabeth. Camryn set aside a notebook she'd been scribbling in and then reached for Elizabeth's little hand and held it like it was the most cherished thing she had, being very careful that it didn't slip away.

I took Sydney home with me while Camryn stayed the night in Elizabeth's room at the hospital. When I returned the next day, Elizabeth was up, even toddling down the hall with an oxygen tank in tow heading to the playroom to play with toys, thankfully out of the woods and on the mend. I believed in grace again that day. We kicked pneumonia's ass.

*   *   *

Not long after the Elizabeth pneumonia incident, Camryn's mother showed up announcing the death of Camryn's gay uncle, Francis. "It was pneumonia," she said, slowly nodding her head up and down conspiratorially even though there was nothing to conspire over. Then she started in with a butt load of religious talk that sent Camryn into shut-down mode.

Camryn's mother was one of those people who had rigid beliefs about how God worked and wasn't open to any other views. If she had been an extremist Muslim, she'd be the first one I'd check for a suicide vest in a crowded marketplace. But suicide vests weren't her Christian style, so instead she killed everyone off slow and painfully with biting, controlling and judgmental words.

"It's too bad Francis is going to hell," she said, which threw Camryn into a tailspin.

"He is not! He couldn't help being gay any more than you could help being born with brown eyes," Camryn told her. Then Camryn muttered under her breath, "Unless you took a massive dump because you're so full of shit your eyes are brown." She turned back to her mother and almost yelled, "It's how he was born. It's how God made him. You said yourself that God doesn't make mistakes. That He loves everybody."

Camryn looked like she wanted to ship her mom right back on the plane she'd come in on. We hadn't even gotten to Baggage Claim before Camryn said, "You're such a hypocrite." Then she shut up and made me listen to her mother all the way home, and I'd had an urge to punch her myself since she didn't listen to anyone who thought any differently than she did.

I put Evelyn's baggage in the guest room and then searched for Camryn who was hiding in our bedroom. "I should have treated Francis better," she said, confusing me, because Camryn was nice to everyone except maybe her mom, but she deserved it. "In some ways he reminded me of myself, but he scared me. He was so different, so off-the-scale smart, like he was retarded, if that makes any sense."

It made no sense whatsoever.

"He was protarded." Camryn chuckled briefly at her newly minted word. "He was so intelligent and forthright that he was a social reject."

I started to respond, but a hitch deep in my throat made me cough, probably coughing over Camryn's off-the-wall comment. I continued to cough all through Camryn's explanation about the things she had admired about her uncle and how she felt she had failed him as a human being. But I was more concerned about her saying they were alike; he was a social reject, and I saw her being one too.

I rubbed at my throat, having coughed it raw. "You need to be careful so you don't alienate yourself from other people like he did," I told her, with her best interests at heart.

Instead of receiving my best of intentions, Camryn looked at me again like I'd grown that third head with horns, maybe a fourth. Times like these I knew we were not connecting. Perhaps I was a protard too.

Before Camryn stalked off to the kitchen where her mother was getting a drink, she said, "You feel okay?" She felt my forehead, ultrasensitive to things like coughing and pneumonia. "You should get that cough checked out." I nodded agreement even though I despised all things doctors. Camryn had had enough with Elizabeth's pneumonia scare and then Uncle Francis actually dying of it.

When Camryn sat down at the kitchen table, Evelyn started right back in as if nothing had happened.

"Camryn, you do know that God created the heavens and the earth, don't you?"

Talk about a protard. She had no idea when to quit. She had blinders on the size of two full moons. I at least had enough sense to steer clear, and let them have at it. It wasn't even common sense, but an inborn self-preservation instinct; you don't go anywhere near a mother-daughter catfight.

CHAPTER 18 - GLENN

Sometimes I fleetingly thought I shouldn't have married Camryn; she was more interesting before the wedding, back when she desperately wanted me, and I was too scared to settle down. This is why I was scared: once the thrill of the chase was gone, I got bored. When I got bored, I pestered Camryn. The more I pestered, the less she wanted to do with me. There's a thing about vicious circles. Mostly, they're invisible and you get sucked in before you even see it coming. Somewhere deep inside I knew I'd get bored in marriage, when most people were expected to display responsible stability. Yet I still went through with it— kind of like screwing myself, but not in a good way.

"I thought you wouldn't mind," I said when explaining to Camryn that I'd already put a down payment on a new Harley.

Talk about getting the cold shoulder. And it wasn't any better when I insisted the two of us go to Sturgis for a couple of weeks without the kids. If she wasn't going to make time for us, then I'd make time for us.

But somewhere between ordering the Harley and going on our road trip to Sturgis, and I was tired of hearing, "I'm tired. I'm busy. I'm stressed," I again, took matters into my own hands.

Camryn wasn't due home for at least an hour, but I heard noises coming from down the hall. "Hurry and go potty," Camryn said to Sydney.

I had been relaxing, stark naked on the bed, some young hottie naked alongside me on the laptop. I could use my imagination when I had to. But even though I wasn't cheating or doing anything wrong, a startled and somewhat guilty jolt ejected me from the bed and into the walk-in closet to quickly put some clothes on. Camryn walked into the bedroom, saw the laptop on the bed, and said nothing about it, but her flush-red face and lifeless stare backed me into the corner and beat the shit out of my conscience.

"We've got to go. We'll be late," she said referring to getting Sydney to the dentist.

Several months before, I'd promised her I'd stop, but a porn addiction is like a drug habit, sometimes not kicked without an intervention. Her glaring, shit-kicking intervention was all I needed, all while getting caught with my pants down.

I'm not sure how she did it, but Camryn gave me a goodbye peck on the cheek. "See you later," she said. I wouldn't have blamed her if she never saw me later. I had broken a promise, and it wasn't the first one. She'd forgiven me for this, that, and the other more times than I could count. More times than anyone would ever expect her to, and I loved that about her.

*   *   *

I knew I was back in the doghouse basement, maybe even the doghouse dungeon with the key thrown away. Sometimes my spontaneous quick thinking got me out of trouble as well as in it: I sent Camryn a bouquet of red roses at work. She emailed a thank-you note back, along with an X and an O. Maybe she hadn't thrown away the key, but I had been shaken up enough that I knew the basement door was still closed. She was being as decent as she possibly could. She didn't keep shit going like some people.

*   *   *

Raine had unfortunately been in my organization at XB for some time, me tolerating his whiny ass daily. Camryn had been so excited when they first came to town, until she found out why they'd come. Natalie had a rare cancer, and California was the only place with top-notch physicians, experimental treatments — her only hope — *and* employment for Raine.

"I didn't want to come here any more than you wanted me," Raine said, clearly knowing I despised him. "I really didn't have much choice — come here or let my wife die. What kind of effing choice is that?"

"I get that," I said, "but we've still got a job to do. There's lives on the line here too. I'm counting on you to be here, doing *your* job." Raine had come in late for the third time that week. Each time, I got heat for it because he worked for me.

"You know what you are, Glenn? You're the second cancer in my life. I won't be sad when you're gone."

"Can't you control your own people, Conroy?" Fitzgibbons said, butting into our conversation. Fitz had been moved into Stockwell's position during the last re-org, a reorganization that made my life hell.

Raine's lip twisted into a nasty smirk. I wanted to it slap right off his face to next Tuesday. Thing was, Fitz didn't like anyone. Just because he was being an ass to me didn't mean he'd do Raine any favors. Fitz, displaying his best supervisor behavior, held his thumb and forefinger to his head in the "loser" position, aimed at me. "We've got a schedule to keep, loser."

He could go fuck himself as far as I cared, just like everyone else who'd ever called me a loser. I probably worked harder than all of them, all sitting around on their high horses' asses. As it was, I worked sixty-hour work weeks for the last seventy-six weeks and had started smoking again, just to de-stress. I hadn't had a vacation in longer than that. Every time I put in for one, Fitzgibbons pitched a fit and denied it, saying I was too valuable to the team. I was pretty sure he'd just miss having someone to piss and moan at because he sure never told anyone how supposedly valuable I was. Instead, I only heard him bitching about my work holding up the show. But if I didn't follow company policy, which sometimes involved extra time, it could be life threatening to aircraft, mission, or anyone in close proximity. What he never mentioned was that I got my work done twice as fast as everyone else did. But I knew when Raine worked alone, Fitz bypassed him altogether because Raine was incompetent, and Fitz only cared about schedule and lining his pockets with bonus money for on-time performance.

I never told Camryn about the smoking thing. Then I'd have one more nag down my throat. "Fitzgibbons smokes like a fiend," I'd say to Camryn after unwinding with the guys and a few drinks at the bar after work. It was true. I never bothered to mention that I smoked too. Fitz was good for something—a smokescreen for me. Yet, he was the enemy I kept closer than friends. I wouldn't trust him with my life.

I had five hot-ticket items to address immediately, or we'd hold up an airplane delivery. "Dammit Raine.

You show up on time, or I'll find someone else who will." I beat my hand into the table. The Plexiglas topper cracked and I pretended like my hand didn't hurt like a son-of-a-bitch.

"Is that a threat?" Raine said, throwing around harassment-free-workplace buzz words, trying to lay a trap for me to hang myself in.

Two could play that game. "It's a promise," I said, giving him my best eat-shit-and-die smile. I threw in my own buzz words, "integrity," "promise," "excellence," stuff like that. Around XB it was more about talking the talk than actually walking it.

Everyone ran on a short fuse when things depended on precision clockwork, and when people didn't precisely show up or perform, the deadline didn't change. Management kept the pressure on; something in the middle was sure to blow. Raine pissed me off so much, I had trouble feeling sorry for him and his soon-to-be widowerhood.

"I told you," Raine said, "I had to take Nat in for treatment." I'd like to think he cared enough about Natalie to do something like that, but my experience with Raine left plenty of room to think otherwise.

"Don't give me that bullshit, Raine. You know Camryn would take her. She's offered enough times."

Raine pushed my buttons on purpose. I knew he did. He's the one who kept shit going, accusing me of discrimination and harassment, taking me to the boss and HR, wasting everyone's time; because they knew he was a whiner, and they also knew the production line would fail without me. After all, it was they who took advantage of my workaholic tendencies, and they who were too cheap to hire another person who actually knew what he was doing. Raine had 'em scared and over a barrel; they couldn't fire him when his dying wife needed the insurance. It smelled of lawsuit and bad PR. A company like XB reasoned it was cheaper to keep this sort of dead weight, and let it stink up the place rather than cut it loose.

Again, two could play that game. I went to Fitzgibbons. "I need a vacation. Like now."

"Ship 064 delivers in three weeks, I can't let you go."

"I'm going to Sturgis. Bike rally's over in three weeks." I filled out my timecard, gave myself the two weeks' vacation I'd lose if I didn't use it and walked out the door.

Getting Camryn's buy-in on the Sturgis vacation was just as hard as getting Fitz's. She was coming with me, on my new motorcycle, leaving the kids behind, and we were gonna have fun whether she liked it or not.

The wind blew past at about ten miles over the speed limit, my normal cruising speed. Harley's motor purred between my legs. Camryn hung on tight. All was sweet until a driver cut me off. I sped up, passing everyone else on the road, intent on teaching him a lesson. Camryn clung to me in a death grip while I gave the jerk some universal sign language. He veered toward us, like he was going to run us off the road. I sped up even faster, showing him. At the next rest stop, Camryn got off the bike, removed her helmet and then threw up into the grass. She yelled into my face. "Do you have a death wish? Because I don't. This is bullshit."

A red Mustang that had been on the road along with us pulled into the next parking spot. "Nice ride," I said, admiring his wheels.

"That was some crazy driving back there," the guy said.

"Yeah, that asshole was way out of line," I said.

"No dude. I'm surprised she's getting back on that bike with you." He pointed to Camryn.

Huh? Camryn stared at the man, keeping all her thoughts inside. She didn't agree. She didn't deny. She looked at me; then her eyes, dull and vacant, looked at the ground. The shell of Camryn climbed back on the bike with me, holding on, but not really there. I wondered what was wrong. I got her a Starbucks to smooth things over, but even it didn't snap her out of her trance.

The rest of our trip wasn't much better. I got a kick out of the Sturgis crowd and side shows, but Camryn did a bad job of pretending to enjoy herself. The closest she got to having a good time was when we headed out to Mt. Rushmore at sunrise, but the cell phone rang, ruining that too.

"Hello," I said, picking up the call from Fitz. He outlined an urgent problem with the upcoming aircraft delivery. "I'm on vacation, man. What'd you call me for? Take it up with Raine. That's why you hired him." I almost hung up, I was so mad. I couldn't relax at work, couldn't relax on vacation, and now had my sucky vacation turned into a sucky working vacation. Camryn stood there, studying my face, trying to piece together what the call was all about.

"I can't call Raine," Fitz said. "Natalie passed away this morning. At home. In her own bed."

A few things flew through my head at once. I knew Camryn and Natalie were friends, and I'd have to break the sad news. Fitz wanted something. I'd help him out, but I'm sure he wouldn't give me a thank you. And Raine would either snap out of it and stop making excuses, or he'd become my worst nightmare.

"What'cha need?" I asked Fitz. Whenever there was a crisis at work, I was Superman, couldn't help the transition. Fitz gave me the low down, and I spent the next thirty minutes giving him instructions on resolving the issues. Camryn lay in the grass watching the clouds go by the whole time. "Glad to help. Bye Fitz," I said. I *was* glad to help. At the same time it still pissed me off he had no one else to call and had to interrupt my vacation.

Camryn sat up, still short on words, waiting for me to spill.

"Natalie died this morning," I said.

Still, silence from Camryn. She wiped at her eyes, until finally she said, "Poor Raine."

"Poor Raine? Shouldn't it be poor Natalie?"

"Natalie's at peace now. No longer suffering. Raine's the tormented one. He just lost the love of his life."

I kinda liked the idea of Raine being tormented, yet I could see where it would be sad to be him. It was sad to be him even before he was alone. I fought the urge to feel sorry for him. Then I was a little miffed at Camryn for feeling sorry for him. If she only knew how he tormented *me*, she wouldn't do that. Something about two wrongs not making a right scampered through my brain. But feelings aren't right or wrong, they're just feelings.

When we finally arrived home, the girls ran up to Camryn as if she was the only one they missed and sandwiched her in a big hug. It felt like no one appreciated me at home either.

CHAPTER 19 – GLENN

I thought I'd earn some brownie points by taking Camryn to lunch. "Hurry up, let's grab pizza."

"Just a sec, I'm listening to Oprah," Camryn said. She pecked away at her keyboard, radio going in the background.

"Oprah's stupid."

Camryn's lightning-fast fingers came to a halt. She looked up at me, which is what I wanted—her attention. "She is not."

I ignored her comment. More important matters were at play: my stomach was growling. "Hurry up, I'm hungry."

"You sound like a starved beast," Camryn said. To which I responded by bending my elbows and wrists at odd angles while twitching my torso, pretending to morph into that Jekyll-Hyde character Camryn said I was.

She rolled her eyes. "Pizza's gonna be the death of you."

"Yeah, unless you kill me first." I'm sure it had crossed her mind.

"I know I've made mistakes," I said to Camryn while we waited for our pepperoni and mushroom, double meat. She'd had a hard time thawing her cold shoulder from the whole Sturgis "fiasco"—her words, not mine. "I need you to wipe the slate clean."

She nodded in her best unconvincing I'll-do-my-best nod. In the recesses of my soul, I knew I was asking her to be superhuman, but I did have hope and faith, and that's the only thing that separated me from Simon. God rest his soul.

"We missed Natalie's funeral," Camryn said, changing the subject right about the same time the pizza arrived. "I wish we'd spent more time together. Life's too short. I miss her." Camryn picked off half her pepperoni, throwing it onto my plate since I couldn't see it going to waste. She blotted her piece of pizza with a napkin, soaking up the grease.

"That's flavor," I said and then went back to her Natalie funeral comment. "Yeah, I heard Natalie's mother flew over for the service. Raine apparently hugged her a little too tight for it to have been mutual grief. And from what I hear, they shared way more than a consoling kiss." I raised my eyebrows in suspicion. "Since when do mourning kisses involve tongue?"

Camryn gave me a disgusted, vomity face. "Seriously?"

"That's the talk."

"Natalie's mother always did have a thing for him, even before the wedding," Camryn said, lessening her surprise.

I felt bad that I was the reason Camryn hadn't seen Natalie much, especially there at the end. Hate twists people up, and I hated Raine; by default, Natalie and Camryn's friendship died a slow death too.

"You should go visit Megan," I said, thinking that might make Camryn feel better.

"I'll think about it," she said. I knew she wouldn't, always making excuses about money, time, kids, even me. She said safe stuff like "I'll think about it," in her words, "to avoid an argument," but how could she know if I'd argue or not? Sometimes I called her on it, but sometimes I didn't, making it two of us who didn't know. I knew I was unpredictable like that, but who likes predictable? Spontaneity is supposed to be a good thing, and that's what I told Camryn, and myself. Camryn, trying to be funny — I think — said, "Tell that to my ulcers."

*   *   *

"Dammit, Conroy!" Fitz slammed a folder down onto my desk, leaned his broiling face into my bubble.

I pushed my chair back in an effort to save my nose from his stench. "What this time?" I threw my pencil onto my desk, folded my hands in my lap and gave him my I'm-annoyed-and-disgusted-with-you-and-the-world face.

"None of these are done." Fitz flicked the folder of work orders that Raine should have completed the night before. "We've got a schedule to meet!"

I rolled my eyes at his mantra and mocked him with a snotty voice in my head, *we've got a schedule to meet*, and then the voice in my head stuck out its tongue.

Fitz invaded my bubble again, getting into my face. "*You* have a schedule to meet." He stepped back, adjusted his pants by hiking them up, and puffed out his chest in his usual annoying way. "Control your people, Conroy."

"You're late," I said as Raine walked in and hung his coat over the back of his chair.

He plopped his sorry ass down. "Fuck you."

"Don't you 'fuck me'," I said, hearing how awful it sounded the same moment it rolled off my tongue.

"You wish." Raine switched on his computer then started to surf.

More pressing matters at hand, I said, "Where were you last night?"

"Normally I'd tell you it was none of your business, but since Fitz thinks you're the boss of me . . . . I was getting Natalie's mother settled in. She's staying with me for a while, helping sort through Natalie's stuff."

"Yeah, right. That's not what I hear. That's probably not all you're doing. You're probably doing her too. You sicko." It was another insert-foot moment where I blurted out my first thought. Again, I regretted it.

The annoying *we've got a schedule to keep* assaulted my thoughts, so I planned to lay into Raine about punctuality and commitments and responsibility and shit like that, but Raine had other ideas. This time *he* was in my space instead of Fitz breathing down my neck. Raine's wild, crazed look took me aback for a moment, his visage considerably worse than usual.

Just then he took a flask from his pocket, emptied it into his mouth. He whiskey-breathed all over my face. "You're. Going. To. Pay."

His breath reeked. I coughed into my hand and kept coughing as I reached for our shared phone to call security, but he ripped it out of my hands and out of the wall, taking it with him, cord trailing behind. My heart raced like it'd explode any second. My cell phone was in the car, not allowed into our secure area. I emailed security.

There's been an incident.

Before security could arrive, Raine reappeared, pistol in hand.

213

CHAPTER 20 – CAMRYN

It's always a bad sign when the phone rings late at night when you're not expecting a call. I hadn't spoken of this before either, because I'd had enough trauma in my life to process, but there comes a time when it all has to come out.

"Hello," I answered.

"Camryn," Glenn said, his breathing labored, "I'm gonna be late. I don't know if I'll be home all night."

"What?" I asked, a sixth sense jamming my pulse rate into high gear. My heart pounded in my ears.

"Raine tried to kill me."

"What?" I asked again, sure I hadn't heard right, and it was another of Glenn's exaggerations.

"He came to work with a gun. The first shot missed me. The second try either jammed or the idiot forgot to load it," Glenn said, still breathing hard. "He fled the scene."

"Oh my god," I said. My heart pounded harder. I held my stomach in a futile attempt to keep my nervous indigestion at bay. This wasn't good. At all. For any of us. Once married to a victim, you're a victim too. Same for the kids.

"Security's got me in an undisclosed location. They won't let me go until Raine's in custody."

"What?" I said, losing my vocabulary, my brain garbled by the sudden stress.

"Security's coming to the house. Wake the girls up. Pack everyone two weeks' worth of clothes. Grab mine too. Pack like you're going on vacation," Glenn instructed. "Lock the doors, and don't let anyone in unless they show an XB security badge or it's a cop."

"What?" I said again, hardly believing my ears. Hardly believing *my* world could change in an instant. That stuff happened to other people, not me. Then I realized that plenty in my world wasn't normal, but weird. Uninvited stuff happened to me all the time. "Damn," I said to myself, but Glenn heard.

"What?" His turn this time.

"I can't believe this is happening." The thought of having to wake the kids and hurry them out of the house because a would-be killer was on the loose pitted my stomach even worse. *Keep it together, Camryn. Don't lose it. Don't cry.*

"I gotta go," Glenn said. "The cops want to talk to me. I gotta go." I heard the anxiety in his voice. "Pack up. Love you. Bye." Click.

As shocked as I was, I wasn't. Another insidious contradiction that plagued our lives. I *knew* Glenn was too hard on people, from me and the kids to drivers sharing the road, to the guy behind the counter at Burger King to co-workers. It was a matter of time. Like he'd had an unsung death wish, daring someone to do it. I wasn't surprised he'd pushed another fragile soul to the limit, the way he carried on. Then I got mad. "Damn him!"

Funny thing was—in a not funny way—I wasn't mad at Raine. I didn't blame him. Maybe I should have, but I knew how Glenn could be. In this case, though, it really did take two to tango, and they were taking my entire family down too.

I grabbed four suitcases and hurriedly threw in Glenn's and my clothes, making sure to pack work clothes too. Three police cruisers showed up as well as XB security.

"Mrs. Conroy," the XB officer said, "you know why we're here." He stood there in my doorway, all business. He looked like a hard-boiled movie detective, full five-o'clock shadow and dressed in a trench coat, I'm sure, concealing a weapon. He looked like a man I could trust, sent to look after me and my family like a personal body guard. I nodded dumbly, knowing but not knowing what was going down.

"Let's talk," he said. I let the man in, Clive, he introduced himself as. Clive spoke something into his radio, giving instructions to the others to stand guard outside. "Raine Babcock is still at large," he said to me, sending chills up my spine. "We've searched his home, recovered the pistol, but have reason to believe this was premeditated, and he may have other weapons."

I rubbed my temples again then folded my hands in front of my mouth, sighing into them.

Clive continued, calm and still all business. "We need to keep you safe. We're not taking any chances. People like this, well, you never know. Sometimes they stop at nothing, go after the family too, anything to hurt the victim."

"I know Raine. We went to school together. I don't think he'd hurt me," I said, cursing Raine and Glenn in my mind for putting me in this position. It wasn't just attempted murder in the workplace; it was assault on our sense of security.

Clive jotted some notes. "The police will want to talk to you about that. Your history, motives, things like that."

"Where's Glenn?"

"Safe," is all he said.

Just then Sydney walked down the hall, rubbing her eyes, hugging her favorite blanket. She cautiously walked around the strange man and snuggled up next to me, resting her bed head on my arm. "Sweetie, we need to go away for a while," I said. "You need to pack up some clothes."

She looked at me not understanding, and I didn't blame her. How could I explain that there was an attempted murderer out there, possibly looking for her father, or worse, looking to hurt his family as a back-door to hurting him? It dawned on me he was pained from losing Natalie, and perhaps he wanted to inflict pain on Glenn too.

I didn't know what information and evidence the detectives did and didn't have, but I did know they were using an abundance of caution until everything was under control. Right then it seemed like everything was out of control.

"Go get your suitcase, and put some clothes in it. I'll be in to help you as soon as I'm done talking to this officer. He says we might be in danger and wants to keep us safe."

"What about Elizabeth?" Sydney asked.

"I'll pack her things up too," I answered, all the while wondering if she felt me trembling inside.

"What about David?"

I hadn't thought that far ahead. I didn't know where we were going or how long we'd be gone or who'd take care of the cat. "I'll work something out," I said, trying to reassure her. She looked at me with wide eyes like she knew I wasn't giving her the full scoop, but she went on her way, never taking her sights off Clive.

"You have two girls. Who's David?" Clive asked.

"Our cat."

Clive jotted another note. "We have a couple of options. Stockwell offered his vacation home in Mammoth you could stay at for a while."

"The kids have school," I interrupted.

"Or you can stay in a hotel. Does Mr. Babcock know what you drive?"

"I don't know," I answered. All these questions. All these things to think about. All because we'd been violated without even being *near* a crime scene. It was our own personal 9/11 aftermath with our own personal terrorist on a micro scale. A holy terror for our family only, instead of the entire nation, and only we knew the pain. Ours were the only jets grounded, the rest of the world oblivious. Everything was normal for everyone else. They'd get up tomorrow in their own beds. "No, a hotel," I said, breaking my mental drift. "We need to keep a routine for the kids."

Clive jotted more notes. "We've got a lot to go over, but first thing's first. You finish packing so we can get you out of here now. An officer will keep an eye on the house all night and we'll bring you back tomorrow. Just one of you, to get any last minute things. And we'll get your cat then too."

Two officers stood outside keeping watch, looking up the street one direction and down the other. Another patrolled the perimeter out back while Clive checked my phone, doors and windows. I threw together Elizabeth's things, woke her, made sure David had water and then loaded into Clive's unmarked company car. It looked like any other car, kind of ratty actually, except for a fleet number on the back bumper. I hadn't known XB had underground workings with unmarked cars and body guards and private detectives. They kept it all under wraps unless you needed it, and then it became your whole world, like a witness protection program just for you. Car 46 took us to an extended stay just three miles from home.

Glenn was with additional XB security in the hotel lobby when we arrived. He hugged me. "Are you okay?" he said. It was a stupid question but a canned line anyone would say when there are no other words. I looked at him with a sad pain in my eyes, knowing he'd done God knows what in our lives and now this. It was like trouble followed him around, yet he'd always managed to skate by, barely on the side of innocence.

Clive made the arrangements at the front desk, handing them his corporate credit card rather than Glenn's. He'd fill out the expense report on behalf of the company, not us. No one knew our names, Clive saw to it. "You'll be in a single tonight. Tomorrow they'll move you to a connecting-room suite, so you'll be more comfortable."

"Can David come here?" Sydney asked.

"No honey," Glenn said. "Cat's aren't allowed."

Sydney's face fell and so did mine, but Clive corrected Glenn's assumption. "I've put a pet deposit on both rooms."

This time my jaw fell, and it fell even further when I found out the company was paying four hundred dollars for my cat to stay in a hotel suite with us. But then when I added it all up, an extended hotel stay with a cat to keep us feeling at home and happy as possible was by far less costly than a front-page news headline of murderous bloodshed in the workplace. To XB it was a cost of doing business, employing fallible, fragile human beings.

"Mommy, look, there's a swimming pool," Sydney said, getting more excited about being away from home, especially when she found out there was a breakfast buffet each day with rotating fare. I'll admit, the evening manager's special, a decent meal every night, was a nice perk despite the assumed reason we were there: because we were hunted by a would-be killer.

When we settled in to bed that first night, an eerie silence filled our room. It was hotel-room silence. I heard cars and trucks periodically rushing past on the highway, the refrigerator hum from the fridge in the kitchenette, and an elevator ding. I lay wondering what the hell I was doing there. Glenn broke the pseudo-silence. "If anything ever happened to me, I wouldn't want you to be alone. I'd want you to find someone to be happy with."

I was glad for the darkness. Finally with the stress, his thoughtful sentiment, and my longing for happiness, my emotions let loose. I cried into my pillow, unable to hold it in any longer.

The first days were the worst even though XB gave us both a few paid days off to get our mental and physical shit together. Glenn and I talked over coffee at the hotel Starbucks.

"What Raine did was wrong," I said to Glenn, "but have you thought about how you could have handled things differently?"

"I wasn't the one who brought a gun to work." Glenn's feathers started to ruffle.

"I know you didn't," I said, trying to calm him down, "but did you think of what might have made him *want* to bring a gun to work?"

"Because he's an idiot," Glenn said. Typical. It was always everyone else's fault, Glenn contributing nothing to the situation.

Normally, I wouldn't be so honest with Glenn because his ears weren't receptive to truth and honesty about his shortcomings, but desperate times called for desperate measures. "You pushed him too far. You push me too far."

"You gonna pull a gun on me too?"

"No." Although I wasn't sure I'd have missed his companionship had Raine aimed better. "It's just that there's better ways to handle situations."

"Yeah, like not hire idiots in the first place."

Glenn was missing the point, as usual. "You could be nicer," I said.

"What do you expect me to do? I was doing my job."

"Do your job with tact. Ever see those guys who everyone respects? They're leaders. They get the job done without yelling and losing their cool. They're firm."

"Yeah, I want to be one of them."

"Then be one," I said, wondering why he hadn't already stepped up into those shoes.

After our coffee talk, security gave me little time to collect David and a few more things, escorting me to my home while they stood watch outside. Glenn sat with police and detectives answering questions and making arrangements. Security would keep an eye on the house while we were gone. Glenn would drive another unmarked company car. He was essentially ordered to park his vehicle on company grounds because Raine knew what he drove. I got to keep my car because he'd never seen mine. "Take the kids to school a different route each day," we were instructed. "Be aware of your surroundings."

Raine drove a blue Ford F150. We saw blue Ford F150s at every turn. Before that, I hadn't noticed one. "He's not getting back on company grounds," Clive told us. Normally XB waved each employee in with a flash of a company ID badge, the long line of cars trailing smoothly in. But when they stopped each car in a backed-up line, physically inspecting each ID front and back, my ulcers flared with an extra ache because "we" were the cause of the delay. I imagined the security officer checking my badge, making a mental note, *oh, you're the one.* But reality was, garden-variety officers were on the lookout for Raine and didn't know the particulars.

"We've left a letter at his house telling him he's on paid leave until further notice," Clive informed us about Raine.

"Paid leave," Glenn said, starting to fume. "After what he—"

"We don't want to agitate him further," Clive explained. Another cost of doing business. And then there were the lawyers and the PIs and the paperwork.

"We've filed a restraining order against him for you," Clive said. XB left no stone unturned, taking care of everything for us, leaving nothing to chance, protecting both us and themselves. Sometimes I wondered whose interests were more important, but from a business perspective and finding out even the company president knew Glenn's name, it was with mixed feelings I surmised this royal treatment was more about staying out of the papers than it was concern for us.

I'd bought peanut butter at the store the day before this all went down. I found myself at Walmart rebuying groceries, even sandwich bags, so I could pack the girls' lunches. "I have peanut butter at home," I told Glenn, and for once he looked at me with sympathy. We weren't allowed to return home for our own safety, not even for peanut butter. It didn't get more messed up than that. We weren't allowed to tell anyone where we were staying either, so instead of friends meeting us at the house as would be normal, we'd creatively find another place to meet. These weren't the only inconveniences. The post office lady must have thought we were living the high life, arranging vacation hold after vacation hold, because they wouldn't keep mail any longer than three weeks at a time. And never mind managing a Girl Scout cookie order of eighty-four cases out of a hotel room. All that got old after a while, living lie upon lie while they hunted Raine down. When authorities finally found him along with additional weapons, they pressed charges, only to let him out on bail because of legal technicalities. After the snafu, they locked him up again and set a court date. He'd sent Natalie's mother back to the United Kingdom while he'd been hiding. How thoughtful. Guess he didn't think she'd want to see her son-in-law-turned-lover in the slammer.

"When do we get to go back home?" Elizabeth had asked.

"I don't want to go home," Sydney said. "I like it here. They make my bed, and I get to go swimming!"

To be in ignorant bliss, I thought.

"We're here until they get our alarm system installed. We need to be out of their way, so they can do the work," I said, only partially lying. The alarm system was finished in one day. And when word inevitably got out at school that the kids were living out of a hotel, the alarm story is what they told their friends.

The detectives interviewed me too, and they weren't just the local variety, but FBI as well. "You said you knew Raine, went to school with him."

"Yeah, I was friends with his girlfriend-then-wife, Natalie. I was kinda friends with him too, but Glenn never liked him."

The detectives looked at me as if urging me on to talk more.

"I don't know. Personality clash or something." An incident from our college days flashed back into my mind. Raine had walked into the video store just as Glenn walked out. I had known there was tension between them, but I had no idea why. Raine was a good guy, and we were just friends back then. For real. I had missed having a casual no-strings-attached guy friend at the time, one I could talk to and not worry about subliminal undercurrents or expectations. It was nice to feel free to be myself around Raine, the way I felt around Reese in our early days.

"Why do you put up with that guy?" Raine had asked back then, referring to Glenn. The question had struck me as odd, and a blush had washed over my face. In too deep.

"I see how it is," Raine had said.

Detective Mark Savage jolted me back from my wandering thoughts. "You know we found the pistol at his home."

"Yes."

"Ballistics show this gun was used in an unsolved murder in Illinois."

"Seriously?" I said, thinking the Raine I was hearing about these days wasn't the Raine I knew in college at all. He must have really flipped off the deep end when Natalie passed.

"It was registered to a Dennis James Parker. Mr. Parker said he hasn't seen that gun in years, not since someone stole it from him in the early '90s. I've got the police report right here regarding the theft."

I looked over the report, noticing the date of early April 1991, right around spring break.

"Specifically, this gun was used in the 1991 murder of a' Ms. Stacy Jenkins of 913 Juliet Avenue, Cahokia, Illinois. Does that ring a bell for you?" Detective Savage asked, knowing full well it might. Again, my life felt like I was somehow the accused.

My face blanched. "My old neighbor?"

I couldn't imagine Raine blowing away my old neighbor. I remembered having heard commotion next door way back then, on a routine basis, and I remembered the last day police—and an ambulance— showed up, never returning again.

"I thought her ex did it," I gasped. My insides churned five ways from Sunday. Was nothing I thought about anyone true? The only thing I knew for sure was that Glenn was a reliably hard worker despite his sometimes misguided efforts, beyond that; it seemed as if my life was a mirage.

"He could have, but he's been on the run for years. We think he fled the country," Savage said.

"You never found him," I said, restating the obvious.

"Never."

"So Raine's a suspect."

"We questioned him. He fiercely denied having anything to do with Ms. Jenkins' murder. Said he'd found that gun in a rental car he'd picked up from a return when he worked at Enterprise."

The blood drained from my lips. I buried my face into my hands. How much more convoluted could this situation get? I felt like I'd been punched from all angles, the blows not letting up until I was an emotionally bloody pulp. While my stomach knotted itself into nauseous spasms, I began to cry, quiet drips at first, but then my body gave in to full blown sobs. I wasn't crying for Glenn's close call or Raine's false accusal or Stacy's death or the probability that her ex got away with murder. I was crying for the events that led up to this situation and the misfortune that I'd known more than I should and perhaps that I should have done more to prevent it. The perfect storm.

"Raine didn't commit the murder," I said. Once Glenn found out I'd said such a thing, I knew he'd go ballistic on me for defending Raine, who was in for attempted murder with the intent to kill. He'd call me a traitor.

"What makes you say that?" Savage asked, intently taking notes.

I told the agents all about the time Raine had come to my place during college and told me about a gun he'd found in an Enterprise rental car. "I told him to turn it in. I thought he would."

After the agents finished with me, they questioned Glenn, again. As I left and Glenn entered, he saw my swollen face and teary eyes and assumed I was upset about his brush with death. I went to the restroom to compose myself. Saying the situation sucked was like saying being brutally whipped would only feel like a pinprick. The face in the mirror looking back at me looked literally whiplashed, with welts beneath my eyes where whip tails made their sting. Instead of composure, I broke down even more, knowing the worst was yet to come. Then, after questioning Glenn, Detective Savage said it as he placed a firm hand on my shoulder, "We'll need you to testify in court."

Testify to what exactly, I wondered. Appearing in court as a witness for one crime was the last thing I wanted to do, let alone two. I wanted this to all go away, to go home and turn back time before any of this ever happened. I wanted to erase it from my mind.

But it wasn't going away. It only got worse.

CHAPTER 21 – CAMRYN

"Follow us," XB security said to Glenn as they walked into the court house. Two off-duty police officers trailed behind, escorting Glenn, flanking him on all sides. They again left nothing to chance even though Raine was already in custody. I followed behind them, under instruction, and for all I knew, undercover security was behind me as well. I felt always watched, as if I were the criminal, those taking care of me making sure I didn't cross any retaliatory lines or contact "the outside" without their blessing. Early on we were instructed not to call or email or otherwise try to contact Raine and to report any contact from him. There was none.

As we settled into the court room, I looked over at the defendant's seating. Raine looked nothing like he used to. He looked ill and ten years older with unkempt hair, a far cry from his conquer-the-world youth.

The judge swore everyone in, taking care of housekeeping before getting the show on the road, bringing forth charges and all the rest of it. Even though I knew this was part of getting on with our lives, it was something I didn't want to go through. My legs shook with nervous trepidation, and I couldn't stop them, hard as I tried.

Glenn took the stand, answered the obligatory questions, adding nothing else as he'd been instructed a hundred times by his lawyer. When the stakes were higher than high, he was able to follow instructions and stick to the script rather than let his motor mouth take over. At those times he was always on best behavior, interjecting "yes ma'ams" and "no, sirs" with precision. I hated the irony that shit had to hit the fan at high-speed full force before Glenn showed his cool. But I was also thankful he actually had cool to show.

As the evidence and eye-witnesses came forth, a few things came to light.

"Mr. Babcock, how do you plead?"

"Not guilty."

Not guilty? WTF? Of course he was guilty. There were eyewitnesses. Not guilty, my ass. He was playing legal games, trying to get off easy. I shook my head. Glenn, red in the face, looked like he was about to blow. Thankfully, he wasn't fisting his hands this time. It wouldn't look good.

"Mr. Babcock, where did you get this gun, this gun that we know was used in a 1991 Illinois murder?" the prosecuting attorney said, insinuating further guilt while holding up the weapon used against Glenn.

"Objection," someone shouted, yet Raine was still ordered to answer the question.

"I found it under the floor mat of an Enterprise rental car."

We all basically knew our lines, what would be asked, and what we should answer. Raine was sticking to his script.

"When?"

"1992. Right around the time Natalie and I got engaged."

"Where?" the prosecutor further drilled.

"Collinsville, Illinois."

"No further questions at this time," the prosecutor said after running a gamut of questions, including questions about *the* incident. Raine's coffin was all but nailed shut. No, he couldn't get the death penalty, but he could waste away in prison for the rest of his life, close enough to a death sentence.

Then it was my turn.

This time, Raine's lawyer was quizzing me, and after an initial line of questioning, he changed tacks, digging for the jury's sympathy. "The gun in question was used in an October 1991 murder," he said.

My nauseous stomach returned as his comment conjured up Stacy's next-door screams all over again in my mind. The thought of this gun having killed or almost killed two people I knew made me sick to the nth degree.

"Where do you think Mr. Babcock got the gun?" he asked.

I wondered what trial he thought he was on and who he thought he represented, but he had his reasons, and since he was Raine's lawyer, there was no one to object.

"From an Enterprise rental car return. Raine told me about it when he came to my house. I remember it was right after he and Natalie got engaged. He didn't kill Stacy," I blurted, even though, at this point, it was weird for me to help the guy out. I'd had no idea Raine's lawyer would even ask such a thing. The stress and the question threw me way off the plan to answer only the questions and offer nothing more.

Raine's lawyer seemed pleased with my response, as if I had played into his hands well. Glenn gave me an evil eye, and I knew I'd get an earful when we drove home. Raine had a look of relief on his face that said even though he might be nailed on these immediate charges, thanks to me, he wouldn't be nailed on that unsolved murder. How I read all that in to his expression, I didn't know, but I knew he hadn't killed Stacy. He might have—no—*did* try to kill Glenn, but he didn't kill Stacy. And even though what he did was wrong, I wouldn't let him go down for what he *didn't* do. I couldn't betray him, or Natalie—God rest her soul—that way. It wasn't right.

"Whose side are you on anyway?" Glenn asked when the day's proceedings were over, and no one else was in earshot. His eyes were on fire, searing me with one pointed glance.

"Yours," I said. "The truth's."

"Coulda fooled me," he said.

"What do you expect me to do, lie?"

"You coulda nailed him to the wall. Instead you make him out to be someone who wouldn't hurt a fly."

It pissed me off that Glenn twisted the testimony into whatever served his purpose rather than what really went down. "I'm not on his side. What he did was wrong. What he did to *you* was wrong. What he was going to do to you was wrong. And now it's affecting the whole family. This whole thing has fucked up the whole family, okay? You happy now? You aren't the only victim here," I said, pouring out more than what needed to be poured, but emptying my hurt and frustration into a sticky heap. I'd worked myself up to the point I was yelling. "You pushed him, Glenn. Yeah, I'm mad at him, but I'm mad at you too." So much for showing whose side I was on, but it was the truth.

Instead of fighting me back, Glenn seemed to ruminate on what I'd just said. "You aren't the first person who said I pushed him too hard."

Fine, so he won't listen when it's just me, but when others say the same thing, he might listen? Whose side was *he* on?

"I'm sorry I've put you guys through this," Glenn finally said, leaving me to wonder if this time "sorry" was for real.

CHAPTER 22 – GLENN

When I saw Camryn after she'd packed up our stuff and the girls, that first night at the hotel, the night Raine tried to do me in; I saw the picture of composure. I loved that about her. Over the years, she nagged me about dirty socks on the floor and stuff like that, but when the big shit hit the fan, she was the epitome of accepting the things she couldn't change.

The next few weeks weren't easy on any of us, driving separately to work, taking different routes, making sure nothing was routine, but in the end, and even with Camryn's testimony I didn't like, Raine got life in prison with the possibility of parole for attempted murder with intent to kill—me. I'd been on people's lists before, but being on a hit list was a new one. I'd have rather there been no possibility for parole, but the only way that would have happened is if I'd actually died.

I felt bad for dragging Camryn and the girls through that mud. Some said I was a hard driver. I didn't foresee potential bad consequences coming along with driving hard even though Camryn seemed to think I should have known. I thought I was doing my job.

Shortly after that, on Easter of all days, Camryn and I had a figurative knock-down-drag-out. I'd never hit her with my fists, but according to her, my words hurt just as bad or worse. I was raised old-school, that sticks and stones will break my bones, but words .... I believed it. Made sense to me. Because she couldn't say anything right that day, I let her know it. I mean, it goes both ways. If I had my own attitude adjusting to do, so did she, starting with answering a question directly and cutting the double-speak.

According to Camryn, an appropriate answer to "What do you have for lunch this week?" is a list of crappy leftovers or frozen dinners when really I wanted sliced ham for sandwiches, and she knew it. That discussion took the better of two hours and a stint in the doghouse the rest of the day. Maybe things were getting to me. I don't know. Seemed like the thing to do at the time.

When she did warm up enough to speak to me again, we had it out once more, a different way this time. "Look," she said, like she was resolved about something, "I'm only happy with our life together twenty to thirty percent of the time." She sat there, looking down at her knees as if she were wondering what to say next. Usually she cried when we've had talks like these, but she seemed to have numbed. "I've thought about slitting my wrists in the shower," she said leaving me wondering why she'd say such a thing, "thinking it'd be superb to be washed down the drain and disappear. Then I think of you and the kids and wonder what'd happen to you three if I washed away." She looked at me, waiting for something—I don't know what. "It'd be irresponsible," she finally said. "What percentage are you happy with me?"

"About seventy percent. You're not perfect, but neither am I."

Her calibration of things was off. She only remembered when I yelled at her, which was only once a week. Maybe twice. Maybe once a day—I might have gotten that mixed up—but still, it was only for an hour, and then the other twenty-three hours were good. That's less than five percent of the time. I decided she's a nut, so I ignored her comments whining about how things should be better. I overlooked these flaws in calculation she had. I'm not sure too many other husbands would.

* * *

I hadn't been feeling well for some time, but I never let Camryn know. After she'd unloaded that her idea of superb was being washed down a drain, I chose not to burden her with my few aches and pains. In retrospect, she still was burdened because my growing discomfort and anxiety spilled out in other ways she had to field.

"Those guys at work are idiots, and I told them so," I said to her, venting between swigs of my favorite brew. The cold bottle felt good in my hand, and I then pressed it to my head to relieve my building headache. I took another gulp and started to choke a little bit, coughing to clear it away. I honestly just wanted to lie down. I tuned out her protests about my language and the lecture that I'm sure followed—something about treating others with respect, and hadn't I learned my lesson after Raine? I couldn't wash myself down the drain either; instead, I fell asleep on the couch.

Aurora Australis was the code name for the latest project giving me headaches. The project would have been fine if the management hadn't sucked. Phase Two of the effort was being carried out in Alaska. Stockwell sent me up to make sure the aircraft delivery came off without a hitch, and keep his ass out of hot water.

"We have to deliver an airplane on Thursday, and I have to be there," I told Camryn. Truth was, I didn't have to be there until Friday, but after a couple of doctor appointments I'd gone to under the guise of playing golf, my doctor wanted more extensive tests. I'd put it off for months, hoping the dull pressure in my chest would go away. It didn't. I thought I'd get used to it, a normal ache from growing older. I didn't. Thursday, instead of leaving for Alaska, I spent most of the day at Cedars Sinai in Los Angeles getting scanned and enduring other tests. I knew they'd been throwing around the "C" word. No so much "if" these days, but more like "how bad." My flight was early enough the next morning, XB put me up in an airport hotel anyway, so I didn't have to travel at O-dark thirty. I had plenty of time to think things over the night before I left, including packing it all in and building my dream home while I still had time.

When I hit the tarmac in Alaska, my company cell phone was loaded with messages, none of them good. I found things worse in the hangar, fuel leaking everywhere that no one seemed concerned about. Their primary concern was delivery, delivery, delivery. While my concern was safety, safety, safety. To hell with their delivery bonuses. It felt as if I was swimming upstream, fighting everyone at every turn.

"Don't worry about it," Ron said.

"I god damn will worry about it," I yelled. "I'm not signing off on it." I made them defuel the plane and reseal the tanks. Ron's gaze felt like knives in my back.

Then Kemp came around, the pilot scheduled to take delivery. "Not going so well?" he asked me.

"We'll get you taken care of," I said, masking any trace of the behind-the-scenes bullshit.

"I'm countin' on ya," Kemp said. I'd done a good job covering up because there was nothing but good nature in his voice. He made me feel like at least *he* was on my side.

When the repair was made and I asked for the inspection records, QA balked. Come to find out they didn't inspect to procedure and instead pushed the work through, still deadline-focused. I shook my head. These morons weren't helping the building pressure in my chest. They made it worse. I made a mental note to quit my job ASAP, confirming my plan to myself.

I crawled under the plane, making my own inspections, only to find it still leaked. To the untrained or unwilling-to-see eye, it looked like nothing to worry about, and that's what QA told me again. But I held firm, pissing them off for a second time.

"Open that panel," I ordered.

"You're crazy," Ron yelled back, clearly watching his bonus slip away.

I was disgusted with the lot of them, not even considering whose lives were at stake, not even their own. If the plane blew up, people could be dead, or at least out of a job. We were here to prove advanced technology, not have it blow up in our faces and then have funding pulled. The desk where Kemp sat caught my eye, photographs of his family. I already knew he was indeed counting on me, and I wasn't about to let him or myself down.

"This plane is grounded," I said.

"You can't do that!" Ron protested.

"Watch me." I placed a key phone call or two. Immediately, the phones rang off the hook. Even the CEO was in the loop, which was worse than the company president knowing my name for almost getting blown away. At least the president was able to keep *that* under wraps from HQ, but not this.

I pushed past Ron, went straight to a wrench-turner who actually did some work. "Open that panel," I said. Seeing that Ron was no longer in charge, he complied. And when he did, fuel poured out when the area should have been dry. This was one of those times I took the Camryn-major-shit-hitting-the-fan route and held a stoic silence. Everyone knew they'd been had. No need to yell and point out the obvious.

I sat back down at my desk, resting a moment until the onslaught of inspectors, investigators, and brass showed up. The catch in my throat caused me to cough. I sat back, concentrating on breathing.

"Thank you," a quiet voice said.

I turned around. Kemp. I opened my mouth to reply, but nothing came out, and I turned away. I certainly didn't want this pilot to see a grown engineer cry. I pinched at the space between my eyes, pushing the tears back inside and then turned back around.

"Where'd you go to school?" Kemp asked, respecting the man-code of pressing past the hurt and diverting to something other than feelings.

"Parks College. You heard of it?"

"Yeah, actually I have," he said, surprising the heck out of me. And then he surprised me again, more vigorously this time, "My mother was the dean there, back in the '90s."

I racked my brain, trying to think of any dean named Kemp. "The name's not familiar."

"She remarried after my dad died. Overdose," he confided, almost breaking the man-code. "He didn't always make the best decisions, and that one cost him. Her name's Shaunda Brewster."

"Dr. Brewster's your mom?" I asked, almost disbelieving. What were the odds?

"You knew her?"

"She saved my life," I said and then blatantly defied the man-code myself, telling him about my troubles in school.

He nodded, like he understood me more than I understood myself. "And you saved mine."

"I told her I wouldn't let her down." My voice cracked, and then I lost it, crying real man-tears, this time not bothering to hide.

*   *   *

We missed delivery. A critical award fee vaporized the moment I grounded the plane. All kinds of management heat crawled down my neck with blame, demanding my resignation. What'd they think? An exploded airplane and a few deaths or injuries would have been worth technical delivery and technically being eligible for the award? Short-sighted idiots. I was done. But they didn't need to know that.

"I won't resign," I said. I did love the airplanes. Didn't love the bullshit.

"We'll make it worth your while," Vance said, one of the upper-middle managers whose job it was to brown nose. The rest of the lot stared at me, nodding in agreement.

"Worth my while," I tipped back in my chair, held my fingers together up to my mouth, management-teepee style as if I were thinking.

"A nice severance package," Vance said.

I leaned in, indicating he should explain. At the end of the kick-ass severance explanation, I paused a good while, wearing my poker face, making sure not to act too eager to take the money and run. Since I'd made up my mind back in California to leave anyway, I'd consider this my send-off and parting gifts.

*   *   *

Camryn seemed in an unusually good mood when I arrived home, buoyed by brisk sales of a book she'd written, some sappy love story that people ate up. I hated the thought of bringing her down with my news.

"So how was the trip?" she asked. And I told her, leaving no detail untouched. She listened, hinged upon my every word. I loved that about her, listening when I needed an ear. Other times she blew me off, and I was annoyed she didn't indulge me, but when things mattered, she was always right there. A coughing fit struck during the middle of my sad tale, and she brought me some water. The look in her eyes was of concern, but she didn't ask any annoying questions like "You okay?" when it was obvious I wasn't. This wasn't simply a tickle-in-the-throat cough, and it wasn't a cold or flu cough. It was sinister, and I knew it even before the test results came back. I intended to put off telling Camryn as long as possible, have her treat me as normal as long as possible.

So I told Camryn I quit and wanted to build on Whidbey right away, and as usual, she needed time to think. Even though I relished spontaneity and chided Camryn for her lack thereof, deep inside I understood plans were good for something: to keep us out of trouble. Camryn was a good planner, and I loved that about her.

*   *   *

Even though I struggled with reading my entire life—another thing that made me feel stupid and acutely abnormal—I picked up Camryn's novel, giving it a go. Seemed like every other word I had to look up in the dictionary, but I went through the effort to show Camryn I really was interested in her and her work since so often she thought I didn't care. I didn't have much time left to show her how proud I was of her.

"Why do you keep looking things up in the dictionary?" Camryn asked.

My palms began to sweat. There were plenty of hard conversations I didn't shy away from having, but this wasn't one of them. I tried deflecting, but her intuition pressed on.

"Is that why I've never seen you read a book? Because you can't—?"

My ears turned off. My defenses went up. "I'm not an idiot." I cleared my throat. It was as if the cancer was reminding me to come clean. I softened, giving in, realizing fighting the truth was no longer of any use. "I've never tested much above second-grade reading. Essentially, I can't read books." As soon as I fessed up, the lead cloak I'd been lugging around my entire life lifted. I had nothing left to hide—except the cancer.

Camryn's face turned pale, as if this revelation explained a plethora of questions, yet she fired question after question back at me, wondering why I'd kept this hidden. When I told her I'd been embarrassed, she said, "Why aren't you embarrassed now?"

As I started to answer, Big C interrupted. Another violent coughing fit struck. Since I couldn't speak, I motioned for Camryn to bring me a tissue. When I spit out what I had coughed up, there was blood. Camryn rushed to get my shoes, placing them at my feet. "You need to see a doctor," she insisted.

I shook my head. "I've already been."

Camryn looked perplexed. I hated breaking it to her this way. Our house was nearly done, just a few finishing touches to polish it off. She and the girls would have a nice home without me.

"I haven't felt right for six months," I said. "I'm dying, Camryn."

"Dying of what?" she blurted out. "You insisted we move. You said you wanted to retire up here, be buried up here." Then she fell silent as her quick, ranting words registered in her mind.

I fessed up to my golf-game lies, explaining my whereabouts at the oncologist's office instead. "I have lung cancer. Stage four." I had plenty of time to cry about this in my sleep, about my life cut short, but when I gave the news to Camryn, I sucked it up, just like my dad had taught me, showing no pain.

Camryn had Oprahfied me enough that I knew grief had stages. Camryn seemed to be staging anger when she said, "You told me that cough was walking pneumonia, nothing to worry about. You haven't had treatment! Why didn't you tell me? Why do you want to die?"

"I don't want to die. I want to live." I explained that chemo and the side effects, given my slim chances, were no way to live. "I'm going to live until I can't live anymore, and then one day, I'll wake up dead."

Camryn, still in the anger stage, pleaded, "Why didn't you ask me?" Tears streamed down her face, which the Oprahfication also told me could be anger or sadness, especially coming from a woman.

"I've burdened you enough," I said, which seemed to be just the right thing to say because Camryn calmed to just sniffles. The cough took me over again. It hurt. The corners of my eyes moistened with tear droplets of pain, but I kept it at that, staying strong for her. And when that round of coughing passed, I patted my legs, inviting a much needed talking-over. "Come sit on my lap."

At the end of our back-and-forth, Camryn seemed to have blown through the grief stages, at least in that moment, and said, "We have to tell the girls." She closed her eyes and swallowed hard, probably practicing staying strong for them. "They need to know."

CHAPTER 23 - GLENN

I finished Camryn's novel before it was too late, a goal I had set for myself. It was the only novel I'd ever read, and I'm glad I did, but art imitates life, and it was a nasty look in the mirror. "Your book gave me nightmares," I said.

"Oh? It wasn't meant to be nightmare inducing. It was meant to be thought provoking."

"Well it was both. I liked it, but I didn't. You did a good job."

Camryn looked, considering me for a moment. It was as if we both knew what we were talking about even though we didn't talk about it. A first for us. "You want some hot cocoa?" she asked.

"Yes, please." I almost never drank cocoa, but now it seemed comforting. I took a sip. It soothed my throat. "Is that what it was like to live with me? In your book?" I asked, referring to the character I knew was based on me. I didn't like him very much.

Camryn tried to shush me and not talk about it, but I had my own unfinished business and little time left on earth to resolve it. "Yeah, pretty much."

"And that other guy. Was he real, or did you make that up?"

Camryn tried to tell me it was a work of fiction, skirting the question and coming the closest to lying that she was capable of. "You read it. You know it's not all real."

"Did you love him more than me?" I asked. I knew I loved her just as much or more than the other guy in the book did, but did a lousy job of showing it, even though I tried. I really tried. She took a long time to answer. I'm sure the question put her between a rock and a hard place, but she'd been used to being there, unfortunately.

"No," she said. Camryn picked up her steaming mug of cocoa and took a sip. "Here's the difference—" She wrapped her fingers around her cup, keeping them warm while raising her eyes to the ceiling in contemplation. "—He made loving him easy."

Her words were like a knife through my heart. The truth hurts. "I know I haven't been easy to live with, but I'm glad you did." The high road she chose wasn't the easy road, but she chose it anyway. I loved that about her.

"I'm glad I did too," she said, for reasons I could only guess at. Knowing her, it was for some lofty goal like "know thyself." If that was the case, glad I could help, because you never really know what you're made of until you're put to the test. Maybe ours *was* a match made in heaven; God matched us up to help each other grow, not for smooth sailing.

*   *   *

Camryn sat next to my hospital bed. There was nothing left for doctors to do but make my last days as comfortable as possible, which was a joke because there was nothing comfortable about dying of lung cancer. Maybe they'd drug me up, somewhat relieving the physical pain, but not having control of my faculties—

or at least the faculties *I* normally had control of—was uncomfortable too.

"I'm so lucky to have you three girls," I said to Camryn. Her expression said she didn't believe me, but it was true. I appreciated every moment Camryn shared with me as if they were sacred. I felt myself tearing up, thinking what a miracle she'd been for me, and I told her while I still had the chance. "You're the one who got me through all these years," I said with weakened voice. Speaking made my throat feel like a barren desert. Even the simplest things became difficult—breathing. "Would you get me a drink?"

Camryn still appeared unaware of how much I appreciated her, unconvinced, but she did what she always does: helps anyways. She wiped a tear from her eye, holding the tumbler with flex straw out to me with her free hand. Before I could sip, a searing coughing fit broke loose, reducing me to tears. I wanted it to be over. My unfinished business was finished, and I could only hope Camryn knew the depth of my love and all that I loved about her.

I wasn't quite all there after that. I faintly heard Camryn offer me a drink, but my lips couldn't hold the straw. My body coughed and strained and hurt. Gasping for breath I said, "It hurts, please make it stop." Even though I intended to leave on a positive note, the pains in my chest, burning in my throat, incessant coughing and cold sweat and shivers demanded to be shared. I yelled at Camryn one last time, "Find the doctor! Go!" And that pained me too because all I wanted to leave her with was love.

I was still coughing when Camryn returned with the nurse, this time coughing harder. The pain felt fresh, as if I wasn't on meds. I coughed up blood and a mass. I hadn't lived most of my life with dignity, and following suit, I wouldn't die with it either. Camryn reached for my hand, tears streaming down her cheeks. She bent down near my face. My mouth filled with blood; I couldn't talk, but I looked into her eyes and saw her soul. Tears leaked from the corners of my eyes. She placed a kiss on my forehead then whispered, "I love you."

Sweet angel music to my ears.

Which matched the angel music I heard on the other side.

EPILOGUE

Heaven was different than I imagined. Instead of pearly gates and streets paved with gold, there were airplanes everywhere, spit-shined and housed in brand spanking new hangars. The sky was the limit, because my imperfect body no longer held me back. In retrospect, that body felt like an enormous ball and chain, something to drag around, making me strong. Now I was at rest, in peace.

Upon arrival, I realized I'd been participating in "Advanced Life School," which is like Navy SEAL training for the soul. Brutal. An angel explained the whole thing, refreshed my memory so to speak. Come to find out, I'd signed up for the gig, along with Camryn and some others, all playing our parts on that grand world stage, just like Shakespeare said.

I could have been diagnosed and helped with ADHD back on Earth, but that wasn't the game plan this time. It almost happened back when I conveniently ignored it during those college days, dismissing the psychologist who had brought it up. Then there was another time when Camryn was listening to the radio. An Oprah rerun about adult ADHD was about to come on, but I insisted Camryn turn it off, demanding we go out for pizza, NOW! She would have figured it out, put two and two together. I agonized over the "could have beens" and "if onlys." I could have been helped, if only . . . . I could have been a better husband. I could have been a better student. I could have been a better son, father, brother, employee . . . person. Medication would have improved things, although it's not perfect, certainly no cure. But it's better than no treatment and better than struggling through with nothing like I did.

I thought about when Camryn called me a Jekyll-Hyde. There weren't just two in our marriage, but a tag-along third named Adult ADHD. If I'd only have known, I could have kicked his ass out long ago. It did take two to tango, and whenever the soul-suffocating tango was going on, it was between one of us and him. Damn him.

Yet, everything has purpose. While I would never choose that same path again, knowing now what I didn't know then, there were some good things. My kids turned out great, and that certainly wasn't an accident. The fact that I saved Kemp, and even my marriage were pluses. It wasn't easy by any means, but Camryn passed her own ALS course with my help. She needed those "special" challenges that I brought. I was like a polishing stone for her diamond in the rough, the catalyst the unique seed inside of her needed to sprout. Knowing this made me feel like the struggles were worth it. Mine was indeed, a life well lived.

Next incarnation, I'll do even better.

END NOTE

In *I Loved That About Her,* Glenn suffers from undiagnosed ADHD, which wreaks havoc on his life. If only he'd have known . . .

Attention Deficit/Hyperactivity Disorder originates in childhood, yet, the symptoms of childhood ADHD can morph into seemingly different disorders with age (i.e. addictions, lost jobs, impulsivity, anger management issues, insatiability, etc.) An estimated 67% - 90% of childhood ADHD cases persist throughout adulthood, ultimately affecting at least 4% - 5% of the adult population (conservatively 11 million adults in the United States alone, yet some experts estimate as high as 30 million). Eighty-nine percent of adult sufferers are undiagnosed and untreated. Most of those who have ADHD do not go to college, and many end up in jail. Glenn beat the odds.

ADHD can manifest itself in the boy who used to be the class clown who then becomes a disorganized adult, telling jokes and making fun of himself to cover up forgetfulness. Or it can be the character, Glenn, who is irritable and angry, blaming others for misunderstandings, physically unable to look inward at his own hurtful actions due to a neuro-biological disorder. Both men and women can be affected and not all display Glenn's characteristics; some can be very socially reclusive and passive. ADHD has many manifestations and "faces."

If this strikes a chord for you, see Gina Pera's book, *Is It You, Me or Adult A.D.D.? Stopping the Roller Coaster When Someone You Love Has Attention Deficit Disorder.* It is a wonderful non-fiction eye-opener and tear jerker, validating the experiences of those whose lives have been affected by undiagnosed ADHD, educating about the many myths around and manifestations of Adult ADHD, and explaining what steps can be taken next to help everyone involved.

ABOUT THE AUTHOR

I have been writing since my elementary school days. I even made a lame attempt in high school to write a novel but didn't have enough life experience behind me to make that project work. Then life and my "real" job (in finance of all things – not as far removed from creative writing as you might think) demanded all my time until about nine years ago when I made the time to start *Love, Carry My Bags* in spite of my busy schedule.

Today I am a stay-at-home mom and am able to pursue my true life purpose: make a difference through my written words.

Currently I reside in Utah, but grew up in Northern Illinois and have lived in a variety of other locations. I live with my husband, two kids, Shiba Inu, and cat. When I'm not writing, dinking with my website, connecting with my readers, or doing the mom thing, I'm cleaning up after the unruly pets. In my free time I like to read, usually while on a treadmill, bake, take walks and enjoy nature. Oh, and go to Starbucks.

http://www.creverett.com/
http://www.facebook.com/creverettbooks
https://www.twitter.com/authorcreverett

If you have read and and enjoyed, *I Loved That About Her*, please consider leaving a review.

More

C.R. Everett!

Please see the next page

for a preview of

Love, Carry My Bags

C.R. Everett's debut,

companion to

I Loved That About Her.

Hear the full story from Camryn's point of view.

Camryn Johnson's world is turned upside down when long lost love, Reese Dahlgren, re-enters her life at a pivotal point in her already challenging marriage. She faces an excruciating predicament: choose between a broken home for her daughter or a broken life for herself.

AVAILABLE AT ONLINE RETAILERS NEAR YOU

CHAPTER 1 (AN EXCERPT FROM *LOVE, CARRY MY BAGS*)

"What we really are matters more than what other people think of us."
— Jawaharlal Nehru

Thirty-one years ago, Dead Creek ran through my back yard. A stench from neighboring Sauget, Illinois stung my nose, but I didn't mind. Neither did the towering cottonwood trees which lined Falling Springs Road. Unaffected by toxic runoff, they thrived. The saplings, on the other hand, struggled.

I drove by pollution-spewing refineries and chemical plants on my way to Parks College. A dream come true. Moving into my own apartment was the dream, not earning my degree. College was a given, a milestone. I could be anything I wanted to be even though I had no idea what that was. I didn't care if I ended up being a housewife. An education was an essential element in my quest for self-actualization.

My modest two-bedroom apartment overlooked the campus. The linoleum in the kitchen looked clean at first glance, but filth, ground in from prior tenants, remained. Two crammed carloads of stuff furnished my abode. I squeezed in the essentials—a twin mattress, clothes, television, pots and pans which I had been given for Christmas, a small dresser, a radio and a travel iron. Milk crates served as shelving, tables, baskets, and general storage, the finishing touch.

My parents could have paid for my schooling, but didn't. Folks from Midwest America didn't hand things to their children on silver platters. Since I graduated from *the* Harvard High School in Harvard, IL ("Milk Capital of the World"), I was a subset of those Midwestern American children and received things on plastic McDonald's trays instead. The money I saved from part-time jobs wouldn't last long. Until I found a roommate, alleviating costs, I enjoyed my own place, watching what I wanted on my four-inch black-and-white TV when I wanted, and fixing whatever my heart desired in the kitchen, without worrying about anyone else. Free at last. Camryn Johnson had arrived.

Parks' cozy tree-covered campus sat a few miles southeast of the St. Louis arch. Rich history infused the red brick World War II era buildings. Cadet specters roamed the halls and populated the adjacent grass landing strip, taking off, one by one on their training missions. Parks is the only Jesuit aviation college in the world, its heritage probably held over from the Crusades, something that surely warmed Mother's heart. At least she didn't criticize my choice for higher education, which was the closest I'd get to praise.

Females represented just ten percent of the one thousand member, aviation-loving student body. Most course offerings centered around male-dominated aerospace engineering or private pilot curriculums. The men on campus felt shortchanged, and the women had a school to fish in.

I enjoyed travel; so not knowing my career goal in life, I chose the Bachelor of Science TTT program.

Travel, Transportation, and Tourism—which had a disproportionate number of girls—was essentially a travel-focused business degree and would surely take me somewhere.

Some people accused me of selecting this particular venue of education for the male population factor, an adjunct circumstance, the last thing on my mind. In love with Reese, my high school sweetheart, I focused on commencing a life together with him even though I had not seen him in quite some time—nine months and two days, to be exact.

CHAPTER 2

Paper, my canvass
Words, my paint
My heart, my brush
Writer, I am
— E.B. Whitmore

"The Bible says children should honor their mother and father," Mother reminded me. She called the Bible 'Life's Instruction Book.' Most confusing damn instruction book I'd ever set eyes on. And it didn't explain what to do when your parents were divorced and had divergent belief systems. The Bible also said something about a servant being unable to serve two masters.

"Father's not in on this."

Didn't matter. Mother's interpretation of the Bible came straight from the mouth of God, of course, and only her ears were finely tuned enough to receive the correct message.

Whiskers nosed my hand, a silent show of solidarity.

"Things will not go well with you . . ." Mother continued the same lecture every time I resisted altar calls, repenting, mandatory daily devotions of her choosing, or refused to raise my hands during marathon praise-and-worship jam fests before fire-and-brimstone sermons. And when religious dogma didn't work, she threatened, "If you don't confess that Jesus Christ is Lord, and witness, singing his name,

'Wonderful, Counselor, Prince of Peace, The Almighty,' accept him as your own and proclaim, 'My God reigns over *all* the heavens and *all* the earth...' I'll take Whiskers away."

Whiskers — my new puppy and closest friend up until moving to Harvard — was safe. We'd been truly saved. No more anxious nights home alone. No more being afraid someone would break into the house and hurt me. No more having my room purged of stuffed owls and frogs, toy witches and friendly pretend monsters because they were 'evil.'

Mother's jump from mainstream Protestantism to a cultish alternative was a hard horse pill to swallow. Healing after the divorce she insisted upon, she found solace in her new flavor of church, attending evening 'singles club.' My mother was in long-term recovery from a self-inflicted wound: a nervous breakdown due to years of suppressing her own wants and desires while constantly trying to please others. By the time I came around in her later childbearing years, Mother had had her fill of taking care of others and turned to taking care of herself, in any way she felt necessary, full-time.

'Welcome to Harvard — Home of Milk Day.' The sign at the city limits became a fixture in my brain. Smaller placards hung below the leading attraction including: Rotary Club, Kiwanis, Lions, Shriners, Moose Club.... Creosote-preserved telephone poles framed them all. Every weekend we passed by the town welcome. Then, after a snail's-pace drive through the block-long main business district, we passed the town's mascot — Harmilda the Holstein — a plastic cow. Her moniker came from "HARvard MILk DAys," the annual town festival held the first weekend in June. Harmilda, often the victim of rival high school pranks, suffered TP-ing and various other desecrations, even kidnapping, but she was safe at home this year, posing for pictures, the center of attention.

*　*　*

"MOOve it, MOOve it, MOOve it," Sarah bellowed to bed-racing team #7. Reese, running along with four other pajama-clad team members, sped down the whitewashed 'Milky Way,' main drag, Ayer Street, wheels a smokin'. The ears on Sarah's spotted bovine costume flapped with every cheer. I stood, dressed as a Holstein, along the parade route with my two new best friends. My very first Milk Day.

"Go Kurt!" Kate yelled from the sidelines, twirling her black-and-white tail with the RPMs of a full-throttle propeller. Bed #7 zoomed past the old Harvard Café to the first obstacle challenge. I clapped my hooves together, caught up in the rush of excitement. Kurt, riding coxswain, hopped off the brass bed and began stuffing his pillow into a pillowcase. The other four racers furiously installed the fitted sheet, a precision pit crew. Pillow in hand, Kurt remounted the bed with a confidence that belied his FFA-nerd reputation. They whizzed by Harvard State Bank, beating team #2's four-poster to the next event where mugs of warm milk awaited their chug-a-lug.

"Drink it, drink it, drink it," Sarah yelled to her brother, hurrying him along. Kurt gave her the thumbs up, appreciating support from his sister, who often joined others in nerd-bashing him. "He's just so geeky," she had said to me. "I mean, who kisses cows?" Then she shivered, grossed out and repulsed.

Reese wiped milk from his chin onto his pajama sleeve as they scurried beyond Sternberg's Department Store toward the finish line in a sensational contest witnessed by thousands.

Kate, along with the rest of Harvard's populace, celebrated milk. Her en*moo*siasm got the best of her as she pumped the udder of her cow suit rhythmically with fist and thumb, expressing real milk over the crowd. Eric, drunk on something other than life, opened his mouth as a target. Distracted by team #7 overtaking team #3's trundle bed for the win, Kate ignored him until he said, "Can I suck you dry?" She slapped him; even Kate had her limits. Sarah looked on, wishing Eric had asked her instead. She had been unable to squelch the waxing and waning crush she'd had on him since their shared kiss in a seventh-grade game of Truth or Dare. Sarah began mooing a celebratory chorus of "We are the Champions." Kate and I joined in her silliness, rushing toward the rest of our herd as we all celebrated sweet victory at the finish line. From then on, we became known as The Three *Moo*sketeers, a label that stuck our entire senior year.

A coronated Milk Queen presided over the subsequent milk-drinking contest — which Reese won — before the carnival rides, games, farm tours, cattle show, and hot air balloons got under way.

"Congratulations buddy," Kurt said to Reese and then became tongue-tied before he could say anymore. Another relatively new girl, Ashley, daughter of the Brown's (the only black family in town) walked by and caught his eye, rendering him speechless.

"Thanks, couldn't have done it without moo," Reese answered, raising his empty glass while an otherwise innocuous-looking man glared at Kurt.

"That guy looks like Eric," I whispered to Sarah while the man continued to glare. "Is that his father?"

"No, his grandfather," she whispered back.

I sensed a creepiness. "Come on, we're late," I said, herding my friends to the Youth Fellowship (YF) fundraising booth.

Kurt, Sarah, Reese, and I sold hot dogs for an hour before Kurt had to conduct farm tours at home. "Come along," he said to me. "You're a Milk Day virgin."

I blushed at the v-word.

"Our cows are famous," Sarah pointed out, waving a Milk Day flyer in front of my face.

"Just the beginning of better things to come," Kurt said proudly.

He showed me the pasture, stanchions, and hay. We came to the calf pens where he began cooing at the calves like the babies they were. He began humming along to the Michael Jackson tune playing throughout the barn, humming to the calves, an everyday occurrence according to Sarah.

"They are so cute!" I said, thinking they were kissable, but not about to admit that to Sarah, who tagged along even though she'd seen it hundreds of times. Still, she patted one's head. Kurt pet Ear Tag #47 under the chin. The calf nuzzled his hand then sucked in two fingers, looking for breakfast.

"Kurt, he's eating your hand," I said, in case he didn't notice.

"She," Kurt corrected. "She's my 4-H project. It's fine. You try." Kurt pulled my hand over to #47's cute

261

little nose. The calf let a crying moo, looking for mom. Her squared-off teeth left my fingers alone, but heavy suction and cow slobber ensued.

"I'm a cow pacifier," I said, enjoying the sensation, forming a bond, but most of all, happy I had new friends.

Since my parents' divorce, I had commuted back and forth for five arduous years. Mom's house during the week. Dad's house on the weekend. Mom's house. Dad's house. Mom's house. Dad's house. Always shuffled. Never settled. Finally, in my last year of high school, my wish came true. I resided permanently with Dad.

We addressed our parents as Mother and Father, unlike the vast majority of the population—the first example of many abnormalities, nothing to do with being stuffy or formal. And it had nothing to do with Father being a member of the clergy even though some kids thought otherwise, showing no mercy. But not my new friends.

"Number forty-seven's my second calf," Kurt explained. "My first one died and I had to start over for 4-H. Her name was Billie Jean." Kurt looked almost moved to tears. "I've been afraid to name this one."

"Died?" I asked.

"We found her dead in the pasture with her throat slit, KKK painted on her side," Sarah said.

"We couldn't figure out what the KKK would have against cows." Kurt kicked some hay, clearly re-living some frustration.

I remembered a freakish story my dad had told me shortly after he moved into the parsonage. "My dad said that Pastor Green, the pastor before us, had stopped by asking if he could get into the attic because he had left something up there. So my dad let him in, but the guy didn't find anything."

"What'd he leave?" Sarah interrupted. I held up my index finger, asking her to wait.

"My dad thought that was weird, so he told the church secretaries about it, and they started laughing."

Kurt and Sarah glanced at each other, wondering what this had to do with anything.

"Because they had cleaned out the attic before my dad moved in and they found a KKK uniform."

Kurt and Sarah looked at each other in shocked disbelief. My stomach felt ill, more so than when I had heard the story the first time. I looked into #47's innocent face and tried not to think of the time in eighth grade when we dissected a cow's eye. Kurt pierced the silence that hung sickeningly in the air.

"Pastor Green was a Klansman!" Kurt kicked a bale harder, causing #47 to startle. I pet her soothingly on her head, between her eyes.

Sarah shuddered at the small-town dirty little secret, revealed. "Good thing he's dead," she said.

"They should have pulled the plug on him sooner," Kurt said, referring to the state Pastor Green was in after the still unsolved hit-and-run that ultimately did him in.

We sat quietly together, each wondering how else our world wasn't what we thought it was and then stuffed those thoughts deeply away and moved on.

"We're going to New York this summer with YF," Sarah said. "Wanna come?" Kurt nodded, his eyes seconding her invitation, waiting for my answer.

I pulled my fingers from the calf's mouth, wondered where to wipe the slobber then chose Kurt's pants.

"What, and leave number forty-seven behind?" I teased, ruffling her ears.

* * *

A tourist bus took us to the main New York City sights: the Empire State Building, the Statue of Liberty, the United Nations complex, even the Bowery. Our tour guide took the microphone. "Where is everyone from today?" she asked.

Various people raised their hands and shouted out their origins. One man, seated way in the back, said with an accent, "Australia!" Aussie pride permeated the word. My ears perked up like a dog hearing an impossible-to-resist rabbit.

The bus driver turned the corner then stopped in front of a streetside shopping district. "Chinatown," he announced. We disembarked, entered a tourist shop. I wandered through the aisles and displays listening for Australian accents, seeking out the people from Down Under, almost hunting them down. Memories of the 1983 Newport, Rhode Island America's Cup yacht race and winged keel euphoria burning through my veins added to my adrenaline rush. I noticed a lady with a Union Jack- and Southern Cross-emblazoned shopping bag.

"You must be the couple from Australia," I said to them, almost like they were movie stars and I was starstruck.

"Yes. And where are you from?" the man inquired, genuinely seeming interested.

"Illinois. I'm here with a youth group."

"I see." He looked down the aisle at Sarah and Kurt, who were trying on Chinese masks, scaring tourist children.

"I've always wanted to go to Australia. I'm hoping to be an exchange student there some day."

"I hope you do," the Australian man said, his words filled with encouragement. "What's your name?"

"Camryn."

"I hope you do, Camryn. And when you do, look us up, won't you?"

"Sure," I said, but not really sure. Perfect strangers from Australia on a bus in New York were inviting me over?

We again boarded the bus. The tour guide droned on with New York City facts she must have repeated a thousand times. I hardly listened. I bubbled over with excitement about my new Australian friends. At the end of the excursion, the Australian woman handed me a slip of paper.

Randall and Judy Underwood
5654 James Street
Green Valley, NSW 2168

"Keep in touch," Judy said. And she meant it.

*   *   *

The New York trip strengthened my bond with my YF friends, yet, YF's religious aspect stunk, in my teenage opinion. For appearances sake, if nothing else, the minister's family participated in church events. It

265

was the law. Or it seemed that way to me. The law required attending church every Sunday, choir practice, youth group, special services, fundraisers, etc. with little or no reprieve. Sometimes I'd feign illness just to get out of it. Our dad even missed the birth of his first child in order to conduct Sunday services. Years in retrospect, he regretted spending more time with the church family rather than the *family* family. Father never explicitly said we had to attend church for appearances sake. Implicit expectation dictated that we attend. The guilt motor purred loudly. Our parents exempted my older siblings from church attendance when they had jobs and needed to work, but they grew up and moved out. No longer applicable. Mother later on surmised that letting them off the hook, work or not, was a regrettable and maybe even an unforgivable sin. They would be damned to hell for sure. When I landed a part-time job, Father let me 'sin' too.

Thrust upon me, youth group opened doors, creating lifelong friendships and one even longer than that. At school, between fourth and fifth hour, Sarah and I regularly exchanged notes—had been since school started five months ago. We updated each other with hot, breaking news, coordinated our social calendars, and expressed our deepest profound thoughts. Sarah handed me a note written on index cards.

Cammie,

I'm supposed to be doing my assignment on the solar system, so I have to look studious. I used a big word, aren't you impressed? Oh wow! The guys just walked by from gym class. My hormones are raging. Are you going to the dance this weekend? At least to see who is or isn't there? I want a boyfriend *badly*. I'm depressed. Write me a story, okay? I need something good to read—to cheer me up. I shall wipe away my tears on Uranus. See, I am doing my homework.

What am I going to do next year with you gone? Exchange student, what are you thinking?

—Distressed Sarah

* * *

"Mail call." My stepmother, Josephine, deposited the three Australia travel brochures I had mailed away for on my desk, right on top of the two I collected from the travel agency at the mall the day before. Last week the mailman delivered four brochures, the ones from my Australian tourism "800 number" inquiries. My mouth started salivating as I flipped through the pages. Kangaroos. Koalas. Opera House. Great Barrier Reef. Emu. Crocodiles. Coober Pedy. Opals. Tasmania and its Devils. I wanted it all, needed it for some inexplicable reason. I plastered an Opera House centerfold on my wall, right next to the kangaroo and above the koalas.

"Camryn, phone," Jo yelled from downstairs.

"Got it, Jo," I yelled back. "Hello." I picked up the phone in my room. The phone in my room that made me feel delightfully spoiled, a phone never taken for granted.

"Kate and I wondered if you wanted to hang out. Pizza, a movie, and stuff," Sarah explained while crunching potato chips in my ear.

"Sure." Sock drawer inventory could wait.

"We'll pick you up in a few."

Sarah's car was older, a gas hog, but hers nonetheless, and it gave our clique of 'the averages' a sense of freedom. Often, Sarah made the rounds picking us up for school in the mornings. The Three *Moos*keteers stuck together. None of us was super popular. We weren't total outcasts or in the wild drug-and-alcohol crowd either.

The horn honked outside. "I'm going to Sarah's," I yelled up the stairs. "Whiskers's coming with me." The parental units trusted me, no need to ask permission. I never overtly got into trouble or caused them to worry. I kept them informed. They let me be.

"Whiskers wanted to come along," I said as I slid into the back seat. "She likes playing sheep dog with your cows." Whiskers nudged the back of Sarah's head.

"Hi, Whiskers," Sarah said. She threw the heap into reverse. "I thought we'd stop by Crud's." Disgruntled, Sarah had renamed Eric, Crud. Her discontent nearly turned her into a stalker, but gave us daily entertainment. Earlier in the year, Eric and Kate sort of dated, but Kate was cool about it — no anxious waiting for phone calls, no knotted-up knickers.

"He's there. He's there. He's there!" Sarah screamed, flooring it before Crud saw us, a normal occurrence. We usually drove around town, making the rounds, spying on the interesting boys' homes — they, unaware. Often, we spoke in code referring to Crud's hangout — *Eric Bancroft's Farm Implement* — as 'The Place' so no one else understood. Eric claimed he owned the business even though he was really a Jr.

I looked back. "John's truck's there too."

Kate screamed. Her flavor of the month and Crud were friends.

"I'll ask John why Crud's been so mean lately," she said.

"Yeah, and find out what they're doing this weekend," Sarah said, happy to get answers. "And find out if he really likes me or what." She looked strung out between the glorious prospect of spending time with Crud and the hurt of being jerked around.

We group dated often, but when those one-on-ones came around, we demanded a full report. The interrogation began. "So Kate, how did it go with John last night?" Sarah quizzed.

"Fine." Kate fancied secrecy over spilling juicy details. She smirked. We all directed our ears her way, straining for information tidbits. "We talked." She smirked again. It was hard to tell if Kate was withholding vital information or just leading us to believe there was more to tell.

By this time, we had already arrived at Reese's house and picked him up to join us. He sat in the back seat. Whiskers' wet, black nose bumped Reese's elbow, and then she licked his arm.

"She likes you," I said. He scratched behind her ears. Satisfied, she took the window seat, forcing me closer to Reese. He casually listened to us press Kate for details, laughing. He was quiet, blending into the discussion, posing none of the usual opposite-sex threat. Sarah rounded the last corner sharply, causing me to on-purpose squish Reese against the door. "Oops," I said, smiling. Whiskers pressed her paws into my arm, getting in on the action. She reached her head across mine, showering Reese with doggie kisses, me smushed in between.

"Come smell our dairy air," Sarah announced as we pulled into her driveway. She then snorted in laughter, which tickled the rest of us too. Whiskers bounded out of the car as soon as it stopped, heading straight to the calf pens, sniffing smells that were new to her every time.

"Honey, we're home," Sarah called, continuing to be funny.

Kurt pulled pizzas out of the oven as we walked in. "Hey," Reese said.

"Hey," Kurt replied, their traditional exchange.

Sarah started up *Porky's* as we all helped ourselves and settled around the TV. Her parents were gone, unable to disapprove our R-rated video. "Mmmmm. Pizza." Kurt did his best caveman imitation.

"Mmmmm. Pizza," Reese echoed, a male bonding thing. Kate shot me a look, red-faced, as the guys on the movie were mentioning the desires of their nether regions. I pretended not to notice the uncomfortableness of the polar sexes even though there was a butterfly loose in my stomach. I stretched out on the couch and used Reese's lap as a footrest, my eyes focused on the movie. He looked at me, unbothered.

"The party has arrived!" Victor barged in, making his presence known. He surveyed the room and its occupants then took a seat furthest from me. I squirmed inside. He'd given me a homecoming carnation, asked me to dance at a social, and had planted other seeds of interest. Victor, Kate's cousin and friend of John and Crud, occasionally joined our assemblage. The last time, he had tickled me and carried me across the street to his car. I was smitten and began stalker mode in spite of the fact that right after deer season opened, he showed up at school with his fresh bow-and-arrow kill draped over his car. He thought it cool, drinking its blood, just like in the movie *Red Dawn*.

At Christmas time, I had painstakingly created a handmade felt Christmas card for Victor, complete with a thin brown teddy bear stuffed with emotional viscera. I implanted a red felt heart and sewed him up. Under cover of darkness, my accomplice, Sarah, and I conducted a covert operation to deliver the card, which was concealed in a gift box.

"Wait here," I had said, hopping out of the passenger seat. With heart pounding, I ran to his parked jeep. Thankfully, it was unlocked, so I placed the package on the front seat, closed the door and ran, breathless. Shaking with nervous fright and elation, I jumped back into the car. Sarah sped off.

"What did I do? What did I do?" I was screaming, laughing, relieved, and ready to be sick all at the same time.

"You're crazy," Sarah said, hysterical with laughter.

We calmed down over chocolate ice cream.

Later, when Sarah did her routine surveillance, she observed Victor take the box over to Crud's place, throw the teddy bear on the ground, and stomp it in the muddy snow. He stomped my heart.

Here he was, and I, embarrassed, hurt, and bewildered. How could he possibly have led me on like that? And then throw it all in my face? I was clueless. Reese knew all about these happenings as he heard Sarah's report first hand. He disappeared into the background when we girl talked, but sometimes we asked him for advice—from a male perspective. Usually the answer we got was "I don't know," and a little snicker.

Remembering all this, I felt vulnerable being stretched out on the couch, and adjusted myself. I turned around the other direction, so instead of my feet resting on Reese's lap, my elbows were, my hands propping up my head. I looked up at Reese with a ho-hum guise and continued watching the movie. Reese seemed anxious, but didn't throw me off or ask me to move. He scanned my backside. I was oblivious.

I never considered myself much to look at, but wanted to be. At 110 pounds and just over five and a half feet tall, I believed I had a big butt. I certainly had no chest, and zits were a constant battle. It wasn't the disfiguring kind of acne, but the generally distracting and annoying kind. I tried everything to solve the problem—routine zit popping, hydrogen peroxide, milk of magnesia facials, rubbing alcohol, salicylic acid, etc. Nothing worked. It was an inherited genetic defect. My whole body was a genetic defect as far as I was concerned. My eyes turned two shades of brown—another abnormality to live with. As a baby, I had one blue eye and one brown, just like some dogs. I spent a good share of time trying to restore my darkening blonde hair to its previous light blonde state. And I purged, and starved, but not in a major way. I mean, I was never institutionalized or anything. Mother even told me I was just average looking. Not that being average was a bad thing, but a real mother should tell her children they are pretty even if she just means on the inside.

When the movie was over, our gathering disbanded.

"What did you do New Year's Eve?" Sarah asked as she drove us home.

"Worked," Kate droned. "Waitressing is so much fun," she said, stuffing her finger down her throat in a mock gag.

"I was out of town," Sarah said, screwing up her nose in revulsion, "with my parents."

"I didn't do much," Reese said matter-of-factly. "I sat home watching TV by myself."

"So did I," I said, slightly stunned with coincidence. "You should have come over!" I sighed. Hanging-out time, wasted.

Neither of us was much into the drinking and party scene. Our group of friends, for the most part, accepted this perceived quirk. Sarah and Kurt were finding their identities, searching in wine bottles now and then. Victor, Crud, and John tried to be *bad* with beer. Kate imbibed socially on occasion.

"Come to the basketball game on Tuesday," Kate suggested. "We can be Reese and Kurt's athletic supporters."

Reese blushed. Reese was the only one who actually played, Kurt relegated to water boy after tripping over his own feet one too many times during a game.

"I wouldn't miss it," I said, ramming Reese even though we hadn't turned a corner.

"Go Hornets!" Kate yelled. "Woo hoo! I'll meet you after the game. I have to play in pep band."

"Hornets are great. Goin' down state," Sarah chanted. We all chimed in. It was easy to get caught up in the enthusiasm, the team undefeated, state championship tournament in sight.

www.ingramcontent.com/pod-product-compliance
Lightning Source LLC
Chambersburg PA
CBHW050014180626
46810CB00002B/413